The Que Club

"A fine coming-of-age tale . . . Shelby is delightful."
—*Midwest Book Review*

"A thoroughly enjoyable story . . . vibrant and out-of-the-ordinary characters keep the plot moving . . . Readers will be inspired by their antics and wish to befriend the Queen Geeks."
—*Kliatt*

"Give the nerd in you a chance to get up and shout."
—*Girls' Life Magazine*

"[A] fantastic read . . . a definite page-turner . . . A coming-of-age story that not only sparks the mind but also strikes a spot in your heart. *The Queen Geek Social Club* is a novel that should be on everyone's must-read list."
—TeensReadToo.com

"*The Queen Geek Social Club* is the perfect book for any girl who never fit the cookie-cutter image of Barbie."
—LibraryThing.com

Berkley JAM titles by Laura Preble

PROM QUEEN GEEKS
QUEEN GEEKS IN LOVE
THE QUEEN GEEK SOCIAL CLUB

PROM QUEEN GEEKS

Laura Preble

BERKLEY JAM, NEW YORK

THE BERKLEY PUBLISHING GROUP
Published by the Penguin Group
Penguin Group (USA) Inc.
375 Hudson Street, New York, New York 10014, USA
Penguin Group (Canada), 90 Eglinton Avenue East, Suite 700, Toronto, Ontario M4P 2Y3, Canada
(a division of Pearson Penguin Canada Inc.)
Penguin Books Ltd., 80 Strand, London WC2R 0RL, England
Penguin Group Ireland, 25 St. Stephen's Green, Dublin 2, Ireland (a division of Penguin Books Ltd.)
Penguin Group (Australia), 250 Camberwell Road, Camberwell, Victoria 3124, Australia
(a division of Pearson Australia Group Pty. Ltd.)
Penguin Books India Pvt. Ltd., 11 Community Centre, Panchsheel Park, New Delhi—110 017, India
Penguin Group (NZ), 67 Apollo Drive, Rosedale, North Shore 0632, New Zealand
(a division of Pearson New Zealand Ltd.)
Penguin Books (South Africa) (Pty.) Ltd., 24 Sturdee Avenue, Rosebank, Johannesburg 2196,
South Africa

Penguin Books Ltd., Registered Offices: 80 Strand, London WC2R 0RL, England

PROM QUEEN GEEKS

This book is an original publication of The Berkley Publishing Group.

PRINTING HISTORY
Berkley JAM trade paperback edition / September 2008

Berkley trade paperback ISBN: 978-0-425-22338-3

An application to register this book for cataloging has been submitted to the Library of Congress.

PRINTED IN THE UNITED STATES OF AMERICA

10 9 8 7 6 5 4 3 2 1

ACKNOWLEDGMENTS

Thanks to all my students at West Hills High School, and at Mar Vista High, Granger Junior, and all those teenagers who, over the years, have inspired me and made me crazy. (This includes my son Austin's very strange geek posse, all of whom seem to show up in my books although I'd never met them before this year.)

Thanks to all my new friends at Monarch School, Santana High, El Cajon Valley High, and to the mighty librarians Sue Arthur, Nancy Magee, and Steve Montgomery.

Thanks, as always, to my husband, jazz great Chris Klich; my sons, Austin and Noel; and my California mom, Helen Klich. (And to Father Richard, Mother Therese, and Opa . . . I miss you.) To my sisters Linda, Barb, and Ann, who always turn my books face out whenever they go to a bookstore. Also, to my great friends Becky, Becca, Kym, Stacey, and Glenn, who support me in my artistic endeavors and often watch my kids so I don't totally lose my mind.

Thanks to Laura Rennert and Jessica Wade for publishing and editing expertise.

Thanks to Julia Wouk at Booth Media, and Author Marketing Experts for helping me get the word out on the impending geek groundswell.

Thanks to Sam at Mysterious Galaxy Bookstore, a place you should definitely visit.

Thanks to all the readers who've e-mailed and told me that I got it right. And to all of you who have formed your own Queen Geek Social Clubs, I hope you take over the world one day.

PROM IS A FOUR-LETTER WORD

(or High Heels Aren't for Sissies)

The movie theater goes dark. Becca Gallagher, my best friend, and I munch on popcorn like rabid chipmunks. The music swells, all screechy, tense violins peppered with vocals by what sounds like tight-pantsed choirboys. The title fades in: *The Scent of Evil*. And then in the middle of a black screen: **Directed by Melvin Gallagher** boldly assaults our eyes.

"Boo!" Becca screeches. People, startled, turn to stare at her. "He's a moronic reprobate!"

"Nobody even knows what that means," I whisper to her. "Shut up or they'll throw us out."

"Well, that's what he is," she whispers back with malicious glee. The music, punctuated with thunder-loud cathedral bells, continues as Becca hisses in a more subdued way.

Melvin Gallagher, the guy who directed the movie, is Becca's dad. She doesn't like him. I've never met him, so I have no real opinion, other than the fact that I know he ditched Becca and her mom, and quarreled over who got custody of the Warhol prints, but not over who got custody of Becca.

Becca stands up and grabs my arm, pulling me out of my seat and toward the exit. "What are you doing?" I whisper as loudly as possible.

When we get outside the theater, she shovels a handful of popcorn into her mouth and tries to talk around it. "I don't want to see the movie, I just wanted to see his name and boo. Let's go see something good."

"Like what?" I snag some popcorn before she eats it all.

"I think there's actually a *good* horror movie where a bunch of unsuspecting teenagers go to the movies and wander around looking for something good to watch, then eventually they turn down the wrong corridor, and with only the butter from their popcorn to sustain them, they try to survive in a parallel universe."

"No more for you," I chuckle, grabbing the snack bucket.

We settle on a generic boy-gets-girl movie that has already started. Snuggly couples occupy all the seats in back, so we're forced to find a spot in the middle, much to the dismay of a few older ladies who shuffle impatiently like a bunch of hens whose nests have been disturbed when we sit in front of them. With Becca's platinum-colored, spiky hair and my dangerous, spylike auburn tresses, we frighten people, and besides, nobody wants to sit by us rude teenagers.

Becca munches loudly on the last dregs of the popcorn as I try to figure out what the story is about. An English girl is in love with some guy she works with, but he surprises her by announcing his engagement to someone else, and then the English girl quits her job, shaves her head, and becomes a monk. A monkess? I'm not sure what the proper term is. Anyway, she doesn't look very happy in her new scratchy robes. And I'm sure once your hair started growing out, it would itch like crazy.

"This movie sucks!" Becca hisses. "It's worse than my dad's movie, if that's possible!"

"We didn't even see your dad's movie." One of the hen ladies shushes us. I throw her an apologetic glance.

"I know this has to be worse. Come on." Abruptly, Becca stands up, sending a shower of napkins and popcorn kernels onto the floor. The hens cackle indignantly as I follow her into the lobby.

"I don't know why we bother buying movie tickets," I say. "We never seem to watch anything all the way through."

"I'm extremely picky." Becca struts into the lobby and approaches the snack counter. Oh no, I think. Not this again. Every time we go to the movies, it's the same thing. I should just stop going with her. I never learn. "Sir?" she says to a fat, pimply boy behind the concession stand. He wears an oversized button that says, "I Heart Anime," and he's anxiously poring over a graphic novel full of big-boobed cartoon girls.

"Large or small?" he asks, positioning his popcorn scoop strategically so he can serve us as quickly as possible and then go back to dreaming about his pen-and-ink girlfriends.

"No, we'd like a refund." Becca leans against the counter, bored. "Hurry, please. We have appointments."

Anime Boy doesn't know what to do. I suppose very few people ask for refunds from movies; I mean, once you've seen it, you can't really put it back or anything. He scurries away toward the almighty ticket booth and comes back with a manager in tow. "May I help you?" the manager asks, clearly communicating that he doesn't appreciate being called away from his important work.

"We'd like a refund." Becca stands taller, almost nose-to-nose with the manager. "The movie stinks."

"Could I see your tickets?" He holds his hand out, palm up, waiting.

"I don't have them anymore." Becca grins at him. "Sorry."

"Then no refund. Sorry." He turns to go, but Becca taps him on the shoulder.

"I really think you should reconsider." Anime Boy is staring at her as if she is a comic book girl come to life. "I'd hate to have to tell people that this movie theater takes advantage of innocent youth. I was in an R-rated movie, you know. Nobody even asked for my ID."

The manager's ears start to turn bright red, and his little brown mustache begins to twitch. "I suppose you want two free tickets?"

"That would be fine." Becca smiles her sweetest smile at him. Anime Boy tries not to laugh at the skewering of his boss.

"Well, I'm sure it would be, but it's not going to happen. Why don't you two run along before I call your parents?" He turns away, and I take a few steps back. I've known Becca long enough to know that when she's crossed, it's best to stay out of the way.

Just as the manager reaches his office door, Becca wolf whistles from the glass top of the snack counter, where she's standing like a semi-punk Statue of Liberty. Anime Boy, I notice, is getting a very nice view of her legs. "Attention! Attention!" she yells. Of course, people look. "I just want to let you know that the manager of this movie theater allowed both my friend and myself to see an R-rated movie, and when we saw the filthy content and language in the movie, we tried to get our money back, and he refused."

A small knot of people nearby murmurs. A couple of kids point at her and laugh. The manager turns, his lips pursed in a frozen expression of rage. Becca stands, arms crossed, on the snack counter. No one is buying anything.

Manager Mustache marches back. "Get down from there," he hisses at her even as he smiles at the gathering crowd. "I will call security."

"He's trying to have me arrested for standing up for my rights!" Becca screeches. "Are you going to stand by and let me be taken away in irons?"

"No!" Anime Boy shouts hoarsely, his voice cracking. He climbs awkwardly onto a stepstool, but can't quite make it up to the counter, so he lamely pumps his fist in the air. Manager Mustache drills him with a red-hot laser beam glare of disapproval, and he dismounts, coughing.

Manager Mustache makes the mistake of grabbing at Becca's leg. "Ouch!" she screams. "He's touching me!"

Now several parent types are approaching the scene, and Manager Mustache sees that he is outplayed. He puts on his best customer-is-always-right smile, and puts his hands up in the same gesture people use when trying to calm wild dogs. "Okay, let's all just take a breath," he says. "Could you please come down from there, young lady? I'm afraid you'll hurt yourself." A vein in his neck is throbbing like a Red Hot Chili Peppers bass line.

Becca reaches toward Anime Boy, who scrabbles to take her hand and help her onto the stepstool. Like a film star descending an elegant staircase, she gracefully lowers herself to the floor.

With everyone watching, Manager Mustache furiously yanks a form from his breast pocket, thunks it onto the glass counter, scribbles as if he'll wear a hole through the Milk Duds in the display case, and hands it to Becca. "Please accept my apologies, and do come back for another film as our guests." He turns on his heel, marches back to his office, and I suspect he will be dipping into his no-doubt extensive supply of pain relievers.

The crowd disperses, and Becca walks around the counter, waving nonchalantly at Anime Boy. He gazes at her in loving admiration.

As we walk out of the theater, she murmurs, "I really need something to do."

Last year, Becca and I started the Queen Geek Social Club at Green Pines, our high school. This happened mostly because

Becca, who is freakishly tall with a dragon tattoo on one leg, generally has trouble making really close friends, and she wanted to find others of her own kind. It worked out great, because we found each other and became best friends.

We met some other fantastic people too: Amber Fellerman, Elisa Crunch (please, no candy bar jokes), and our various boyfriends. For me, that meant Fletcher Berkowitz, a football player (I know, I know . . . but he's smart, too!). He and I had a rough patch earlier in the year, but somehow karaoke brought us back together, and we've been inseparable ever since.

Becca met a guy as tall as she is, someone I nicknamed Carl the Giant. He's into particle physics. The four of us (as well as Amber, Elisa, and their boys-of-the-moment) hang out, watch science fiction movies, eat pizza, and talk to Euphoria, my robot. A typical teenage lifestyle.

Except Becca has sort of an addiction. She craves global domination; she believes that everyone who's anyone should be a geek, and that it's only a matter of time before her geek army takes over the world. Because of this addiction, Becca sort of flips out if she doesn't have an impending mission. Last year, it was collecting Twinkies to send to skinny supermodels. Then it was hijacking a school dance. Then we stormed Comic-Con, started a website, and put on GeekFest, a huge celebration of the strangeness that is us. That last one helped pay for a juice bar on campus, so we sort of became local heroes.

But since that happened, Becca's been adrift. We haven't had a focus in Queen Geeks, and that's led to some problems. She's crankier than usual, she has no patience with her boyfriend, and she pulls random stunts like the showdown at the Cineplex.

Lingering over Pecan Turtle Madness sundaes at the ice-cream place (we eat a lot, too, when we're bored), she says, "That was kind of over-the-top, huh?"

I lick my spoon and nod. "Yes. Even for you."

"Well, at least we got free tickets," she says brightly, patting her purse.

"You almost gave that poor guy a stroke. But I bet you'll get free popcorn for the rest of your life. That snack jockey looked at you like you were a goddess."

"And why not?" She digs down into the layers of caramel, frowning, deep in thought. "But still, I think we need to get moving. We've just been sitting around . . . well . . . happy."

"Oh, yeah, we don't want that. Happy is bad."

"You know what I mean." Leaning her head in her hands, she gazes longingly through the sun-drenched windows. "I just want to create chaos. Is that so wrong?"

"Do you have something in mind?"

"Actually, I do." The door swings open, and our boyfriends, Fletcher and Carl, stroll in looking smug. Unfortunately, since Fletcher has walked into the store, a distracting buzziness begins around my belly button, and little crazy bees seem to hum inside my head. This has been a common occurrence lately; whenever he's within a few feet of me, some physical impulse takes over, effectively putting my mind into a headlock, literally. All I can think of is how much I want to knock him down and rub my face in his shirt. Instead, I just blush violently and preoccupy myself with arranging napkins on the table, hoping Becca won't notice.

Fletcher laughs maniacally and squeezes my shoulder. Whenever he touches me, my tummy starts doing little flips-flops, and the brain bees begin to hammer at my ears, asking to be let out. Today is no exception. I use a trick to help me focus: I concentrate on the least sexy thing I can think of, which usually turns out to be images of unattractive, wrinkly old people doing household chores in their underwear. "So, we found you!" he says dramatically, as if he's been searching the Amazon rain forest for years.

"I didn't know we were lost." Becca digs aggressively into the ice-cream dish. I don't think she's very pleased that we've been discovered just as she was about to hatch her next Big Plan.

Carl and Fletcher pull up chairs and scoot in next to us. "Did you think about what you want to do about prom?" Fletcher asks, getting straight to the point.

You see, two weeks ago, he asked me to go with him to the huge, overbloated excuse for spending your parents' money that is called the senior prom. I don't know why they call it "senior prom" because any junior or senior who can afford the ticket can go. Oh, and it's not a ticket. It's a prom *bid*. Like they're auctioning antiques or selling mail-order brides or something.

Since Fletcher asked me, I've been really wrangling with what I want to do. Of course, if I were going to go, I'd go with him; but the question is, do I want to go? Becca and I have been discussing it off and on since Fletcher asked, and Carl asked her pretty much right after, so we both have the same basic problem.

Becca twirls caramel on her spoon, staring at it as if it will give her some wisdom. "We're not totally sure we want to go."

Carl, whose huge frame makes him look like a wire sculpture bent uncomfortably onto the little café chair, has tipped back so far that the chair goes over, taking him with it. "Oops," he rumbles from the floor. "I'm okay."

Becca shakes her head and reaches down to help him up. "We need to get you a car seat for life," she says. "That's the third time this week you've fallen off a stationary object."

"The stool in science doesn't count. Melanie Flick kicked me." He dusts off his jeans, eyes the offending chair with determination, and sits cautiously.

"Back to prom," Becca continues as if nothing has happened. "It's too expensive. And it's just this big excuse for everybody to party and get a hotel room and waste a bunch of money on fancy dresses they'll never wear again."

"I, for one, will not buy a dress I'll never wear again," Fletcher says decisively as he eyes the menu board. "I will get a malt, though. Carl?"

"Sure."

"You just sit. I'll get it. I don't want any further injuries." Fletcher pulls out his wallet and saunters up to the counter to order.

"I just think it would be fun," Carl says, folding his arms to avoid knocking anything off the table. "I know it's expensive, but I can afford it. It's no big deal."

"It's a big deal to me," Becca murmurs.

I try to table discussion of the prom for the moment. I know the subject won't be dropped; Becca doesn't drop anything once it's entered her field of vision. "So you came all the way down here just to harass us?" I ask.

"And to buy malts." Fletcher sits back down, slurping like he's a vacuum cleaner.

"It's going to be kind of tough for me and Fletcher if you all won't go to the prom," Carl blurts out.

"Tough for you? Why?" I ask, knowing I won't like the answer. So much for tabling the discussion.

Fletcher squirms uncomfortably. I can tell that he wishes Carl hadn't brought this up again, but Carl doesn't really have the ability to keep things to himself. He also can't read people, especially girls. For someone who studies particle physics as a hobby, he can be kind of dense.

"I think Carl is talking in terms of the king/queen issue." Fletcher leans back in his chair and sighs. "Since I was on the football team, and Carl is a basketball freak, we're sort of natural picks for king. And then, if we get picked, we have to go. And if we go, we sort of have to have dates."

"So you're saying that if you get chosen to be the big prom king, you'll take someone else if Shelby won't go." Becca's blond hair spikes seem sharper than usual. Probably just my imagination. "You don't see that as a problem?"

"Let's not call it a problem," Fletcher says smoothly. "It's a challenge."

Now, just for the record, I never said I wouldn't go. In fact, part of me was looking forward to it. I'm a sophomore, and prom is one of those things that most sophomores don't get to do. I suppose it's sort of superficial, maybe even conformist, but the idea of getting dressed up and having a nice dinner and dancing with Fletcher seems appealing to me.

This is, of course, a huge change from last year, when I practically ran away at any hint of a serious relationship. Fletcher really tried to win me over, too; we had a romantic dinner, he called when he said he would, he even sang karaoke, but I messed it up. I guess I was scared. After a terrifying moment where I was forced to wear an Indian sari and sing in front of an audience, Fletcher sang, too, saving me from abject humiliation. We patched things up, and he gave me a beautiful silver bracelet inscribed with the title of our song, "Always Something There to Remind Me," and things worked out great. Why not celebrate? And nothing says "celebration" like a few sexy yards of copper satin and cheaply made crab cakes.

Obviously, Becca has other ideas on this. "Prom is like Valentine's Day. It's just something someone made up so they could make a lot of money selling dresses and tuxes and corsages and stuff."

"It's tradition!" Carl rumbles. "People have been going to proms since . . . since the fifties!"

Becca replies snidely, "People in the fifties also ate live goldfish and crammed themselves into telephone booths for fun. And don't *even* ask me to wear a poodle skirt. Not gonna happen."

Fletcher senses defeat and grabs Carl by the collar. "Let's go. I think they want to be left alone." To me, he says, "Anyway, could you just think about it?" Becca snorts as if that's the last thing she'll do. "I'll call you later," Fletcher says as the two scramble out the door.

"That went well." I sigh, scraping the last of the sticky sweetness from my dish.

"See, that's what I'm talking about." She throws her spoon onto the table. "They want us to go to this stupid prom because they want to look 'normal.' We could all have a much better time playing video games or watching a movie. Why would we want to spend a lot of money on something so obviously lame?" Then suddenly her eyes sparkle with something I've seen before: the signature of an off-the-wall idea that will bring me nothing but misery, pain, and probably a major time commitment. Jumping up from the table, she exclaims, "I have an idea!"

"I was afraid you'd say that," I mumble as I follow her out of the store to find my chauffeur, dear old dad.

Even though I turned sixteen in January, I can't drive yet. This is grossly unfair, but my dad insists that my frontal lobe is not developed enough for a stick shift. Instead, at my sixteenth birthday party (which was held at a bowling alley and featured a cake in the shape of an actual bowling ball), Dad gave me a little Hot Wheels Corvette, blue to match my eyes. He's such a sentimental guy. I wanted to kill him.

Becca's birthday is also in January, so she also turned sixteen, and she also cannot drive because her flaky mother, Thea, says her natal chart advises against it. That's astrology stuff. What I say is that if Thea's natal chart tells her she *should* drive, that's proof right there that the whole thing is a lot of crap.

Thea is possibly the worst driver on the planet. Oh, and for her birthday, Becca got a zebra-patterned Hot Wheels Jeep. Our parents thought that was hilarious and wanted us to race our cars to see which one was fastest. Psychos.

I suppose I should mention that my dad is a single parent, not by choice, but because my mom died several years ago. It's really weird when other kids complain about their mothers (especially Becca, although I totally see why she complains because her mom is nuts). I mean, there are days when I would give anything to have my mom back and to be able to talk to her about the stuff that goes on in my life, especially guy stuff. Dad just doesn't understand, plus he's got that overprotective father thing happening.

But another really disturbing thing is that I can't always remember what my mom looks like. I keep a picture of her in my room, and I try to look at it every day, but more and more, it almost seems like it's a picture of a person I don't even know, almost like a picture of somebody out of a catalogue. I hate myself for even having that thought; what kind of hideous person forgets their mother? I try not to think about it.

Thea and Dad are pretty good about transporting us to various places. Dad usually drops us off at the mall and then cruises through the electronics and computer stores, looking for cheap deals he can buy and turn into something superior; he's a true electronics and robotics genius. Today he's waiting in the parking lot, frowning over some technical manual. For him, that's light reading.

"Hey, Dad," I say as I yank open the door of the Volvo

wagon. He jumps a bit, obviously not expecting anyone to ruin the page-turning suspense of *Robotic Circuitry: New Frontiers*.

"Back already?" He runs a hand through his wild, salt-and-pepper hair, pushes his glasses up (he reads through them like a blind librarian, with the frames perched on the very tip of his nose), and he grabs his seat belt. "How was the movie?"

"We didn't watch anything." Becca straps herself in, but doesn't even tell my dad about her fantastic battle with the movie theater manager. That means she's definitely snagged some idea that has her totally occupied.

"I thought I saw Fletcher and Carl," he says as he maneuvers out of the parking lot.

"Yeah, they came by to harass us about going to prom." I look over at Becca to see what kind of reaction she has to that. It's probably only my imagination, but it seems to me that little tiny devil horns poke out amongst the blond spikes. She says nothing.

We get to my house without much conversation; she's clearly deep in the plotting stage of something. When Dad pulls into the driveway, she has her seat belt off and she's bolted out of the car before he even has it in park.

"Wow," Dad comments. "She's on fire about something."

Inside, I track her to my room, where she already has my robot, Euphoria, engaged in conversation. Euphoria is sort of my electronic nanny and sound system. My dad built her after my mom died a few years ago (I told you he was a genius). She helps around the house with chores, like doing dishes, vacuuming, and reprogramming our satellite dish when necessary. She's also intrigued by human behavior, so any time she can be in on one of our schemes, she's ecstatic.

"Shelby, quick! Close the door!" Becca commands. "Euphoria is going to help us."

"Help us do what?"

Euphoria, who bears a striking resemblance to the Rosie the Robot maid in *The Jetsons,* beeps excitedly, and says in her pseudo-Southern accent, "Becca was just telling me about her idea." She swivels on her wheels a bit and shakes her claws, looking for all the world like a mechanized Elvis. Well, if Elvis had worn an apron and had blinking electrode terminals. "I want to be part of your special night!"

"What special night?"

"Here's the beauty idea. Brace yourself." Becca puts her hands in front of her, as if to calm the excited masses, which don't exist at the moment. "Geek Prom."

"Okay."

"Shelby! Aren't you amazed? Isn't this like divine inspiration?"

"Well, if you'll explain what you're talking about, I'll let you know." My stomach sort of flips over; I've had this feeling before. I usually get it when Becca comes up with a crazy scheme that is going to put us in the spotlight and cause a lot of work, and possibly force us to wear weird costumes. I'm sure that doesn't sound likely, but trust me, it's happened several times since I've met her.

"Okay. Picture this." She drags me down to sit on the bed next to her.

"I can see it!" Euphoria bleeps enthusiastically.

"You can't see anything yet, Euphoria. She hasn't even started to describe it." I hate to rain on everybody's parade all the time, but I have to be the voice of reason. It's not a fun job, but somebody's got to do it.

They both ignore me. "The popular kids do their whole prom thing. They advertise some trite theme, sell their stupid bids, buy their overpriced poofy dresses, hire a crappy DJ, and rent their useless limos. Why do people go to this obviously substandard event? Why, Shelby?" She stares at me expectantly.

"Because . . . they want to?"

"No!" she screeches. "Because they have no other options!"

Euphoria pipes up, "Because they're all a bunch of lemurs!"

"I think you mean lemmings," I point out. Euphoria still has some trouble with slang and sayings and such.

"So." Becca stands, and starts to pace my room like a general mapping out a plan of attack. "We give them an option."

"Okay. And what is that option?"

"As I said"—she takes a deep breath—"Geek Prom."

"As I said, I have no idea what you're talking about."

"Geez, do I have to spell it out for you?"

"Apparently, yes."

Becca beams at me. "I don't have all the details worked out yet, obviously, but here's my vision: We find an alternative location, we advertise to the whole school, and we make our prom way cooler, and cheaper, than the other one. Then we'll lure the kids to ours instead of the big, fat expensive prom."

"And how would ours be different?"

She licks her lips. "I don't know yet. But it will be geek formal. We'll wear formal dresses and all, but with our tennies, and instead of corsages, we'll all carry . . . I don't know . . ."

"Laser tág equipment!" Euphoria squeaks.

I put my head in my hands. See? Weird costumes. I knew it.

2

BREAKFAST SERIAL

(or Pancakes and Panic)

Sunday morning, my phone rings. Euphoria, who also serves as an answering service, picks up the call. Unfortunately, she's plugged in in my room, so I hear the conversation whether I want to or not.

"Good morning, Chapelle residence. May I ask who's calling?" Her metallic Southern drawl grates on my consciousness. A pause. Then she says, "One moment. I'll connect you."

Then she scoots over to the bed, and tickles my neck with a feather duster. I slap at her as if I'm still asleep, moaning incoherently for effect. "It's Fletcher," she whispers. Her whispers don't exactly sound like whispers, either; her voice just gets raspier but not softer, so it's a cigarette-smoking garbage-disposal sort of sound.

"I don't want to talk. I am unconscious." I roll over and cover my head with my pillow. She won't leave me alone, though. The traitorous toaster grabs my pillow and throws it across the room. "Hey, what was that for?"

She says nothing, just hands me the receiver.

"Fine." I grab it. "Hello?"

"Good morning."

"Well, it's *morning*."

"Don't be cranky." He hums into the phone, which really bugs me.

"Did you call for some reason? I mean, other than to hum at me?"

Fletcher stops humming. "I want to talk to you about this prom thing."

"Awww," I groan. "Let me wake up first! Why do we have to talk about it right now, Fletcher?"

"Because Becca was at the copy shop at midnight running off hot pink fliers advertising something called Geek Prom. Do you know anything about that?" He sounds like one of those crime show guys interrogating a murderer. But the only thing killed here is my nice, peaceful morning.

I sit up, resigned to the fact that I'm not going to get to go back to sleep. "Fliers?"

"Yeah, fliers. John Bitner works at Copy Shack, and he saw Becca last night. He told Jeff, who told Naveen, who told Carl, who told me."

"And you guys say *we* gossip," I mutter. "Why is everybody all upset about fliers anyway?"

"What is Geek Prom?"

"Geez, you wanna wait till you can get me in a windowless

room with a naked lightbulb? Don't I get to consult my lawyer or something?"

He lightens up a bit. "I'm not interrogating you. I just want to know what's going on, and mostly I want to know if this is going to interfere with our going to the real prom."

Real prom. These words really bug me. "Why is the school-sponsored thing the only *real* prom?" I ask snottily. "What's wrong with a little healthy competition?" Okay, so now I'm defending something that a) I know very little about and b) I'm not even sure I actually support. Why am I doing this? Simple: I do not like being backed against a wall. And when I have to choose between my boyfriend and my best friend, that's a pretty uncomfortable wall.

He sighs. "Okay, maybe 'real prom' is the wrong thing to call it. But here's the thing: I think I'm going to have to go."

"You don't have to do anything you don't want to do." I swing my legs over the edge of the bed and feel for my slippers. "Besides, why would you *have* to go?"

"Well, you know, in case I get in the prom court or something," he says breezily. "And so, I'd have to go. And I'd need to have a date."

"I'm not even a junior," I say. "I couldn't even go."

"You could if you're my date."

"I don't want to spend my college money on a dumb dress. And I don't want you to spend all yours on tickets to an event with crappy food and crappy music and tinsel," I say.

"Couldn't we just do both? I mean, couldn't there be a geek prom *and* a re—I mean, traditional—prom, too? On different nights. Then we could both go to both events, thus solving our very sticky problem."

I can almost feel him smiling smugly over the phone. But then I think to myself: Do I really want to fight with him? I spent a lot of time thinking about this very question earlier in the year, and I came to the realization that I do, in fact, almost love him. I say almost because I am not willing to admit that I truly love any guy at this point in my life. But if I were going to love one, it would probably be him.

Which leaves me again with the problem. I am feeling pushed against that wall, but rather than run, maybe I should try to work out some compromise. Then we can all be happy, right? "Okay," I say to him. "I'll talk to Becca. Maybe we can have it on a different night."

He exhales as if he's inflated his argument balloon and I've popped it with a pin. "Could you repeat that?"

"I said, maybe I can talk to Becca about having Geek Prom on a different night."

"Wow." He clears his throat. "That's great. Okay, so keep me posted."

"So now that you've woken me up, I suppose you'd like to take me out to breakfast?"

"I'll be over in fifteen minutes." The receiver clicks.

Euphoria has, as usual, been listening in on the whole conversation, something I've repeatedly talked to her about. "Shelby," she says as she rolls back into the room, "you know that Becca won't change her mind, don't you?"

I rummage through my dresser drawer to find a clean T-shirt and jeans. "What do you mean?"

Euphoria snorts, not a pleasant sound. "I would think you'd know her better than I would. Do you think she's going to compromise on something like this?"

"Well, if I know her better than you do, why are you arguing with me?" The truth is, I do have a suspicion that she won't like the compromise idea. I am conveniently tucking that little doubt into my little doubt closet, the one at the very darkest, dustiest part of my mind, in the same place that I keep old television show plots and the memory of public humiliation.

"Pardon me for exposing the obvious." My robot sounds condescending. I don't think most people can actually say that, but I can.

"I'm sure Becca will listen to reason," I say. "And I'm going out to breakfast with Fletcher. He should be here soon, so can you tell Dad that I'm going out?"

"Why don't *you* tell him?" she snips.

"Because I'm getting ready," I say, running a brush quickly through my hair. Not bad, I think as I look in the mirror. For just rolling out of bed, especially not bad.

"I'll tell him. But mark my words, young lady. This will bring trouble." It's weird getting social advice from someone related to our Volvo. As I apply lipstick and a light coat of mascara, I say, "You sound like a nanny out of an English melodrama."

"Do you really think so?" she asks eagerly. "I've been watching some of the old nanny movies, and I'm trying to copy their speech patterns. I'm so happy you noticed!"

"There are nanny movies?" Who knew.

I'm barely ready by the time the doorbell rings. Slipping on my tennies (the ones with no laces . . . too difficult to tie on a weekend), I grab my purse and head for the door. But when I open it, it's not Fletcher. It's Becca. And she looks very upset.

She marches in with her mom, Thea, trailing behind her a few paces. Thea drives her around in an old Jeep, and lately has been spending a lot more time at my house, mostly because she and my dad started to kind of hit it off. I didn't even meet her until months after I met Becca; she's an artist and she holes up in their mansion, making mosaics out of broken dishes and stuff like that.

She has a nose ring, too, something that took some getting used to. There are not a lot of moms with nose rings. "Honey, I really don't know why you're so upset," she's saying as she closes the door.

"Really, Thea? You really don't know why I'm so upset?" She throws her purse into the corner and flops down on our couch. Thea touches my arm and nods in the direction of the hallway to my room. I follow her.

"Shelby, I think she and Carl had a fight." Thea glances over my shoulder to see if Becca's still on the couch, which she is. "He called this morning, and the next thing I know, I hear her screaming from her room. I ran up to see what was happening, but she'd already hung up. All she said was that he was a traitor. Do you know what happened? Did he cheat on her or something?"

A cold feeling wells up in my stomach. "No, I think I know what it is." Think, think. What to do? First, get rid of the mom. "Hey, Euphoria, could you tell Dad that Thea's here?" I grab her arm and lead her toward the kitchen. "Could you leave us alone for a minute?"

Becca's lips are pursed so tightly that they look like two white half-moons pushed together. Her hands are balled up in fists, and she's compulsively picking at the fringe on one of our throw pillows. She's already plucked off a couple of tassels. At this rate, our pillows will be bald by lunchtime.

"Hey," I say softly.

Tears start to spill down her cheeks. "Carl said he has to take me to the prom or else."

"Or else what?"

"Or else we're through, I guess." She reaches for a pillow and dabs at her eyes.

"Why would he do that?"

She bites her lower lip, denting one of the half-moons. "It's probably because I told him that he was a slow-witted moron with delusions of grandeur. And that we were having the Geek Prom on the same night as the real prom."

"Why does everyone call it the 'real' prom?" That's starting to really bug me. "Anyway, why did you call him all those names? Oh, and by the way, Fletcher is on his way over here to take me out to breakfast. You want to come?"

"Ha!" she gestures helplessly. "See? It's all about the guys now. Whatever they want, right?"

"Hey, to be fair, I didn't know you were coming over." I do

feel bad about leaving her in tears, but I'm hungry, too. And since I appeased Fletcher and made him feel better, I want to get the benefits of doing a good deed. I can feel like a real girl-friend. Except for this nagging feeling that I'm somehow be-traying Becca.

"Sure." She has stopped crying for the moment. "I'll find Thea and we'll just get out of here. Sorry I bothered you." She stands up, shoulders stiff with anger.

"It's not a bother." I put my hands on her shoulders and push her back down to the couch. "Listen, let's just do it on a differ-ent night from the other prom. Then we can have two. What's wrong with that idea?"

"You've been brainwashed!" she screeches, frustrated. "You've gone over to the dark side!"

"Please." I sit down next to her on the couch. "I'm just being practical. You're being stubborn. End of story."

"No, not end of story!" She punches a pillow in frustration. "Don't you see why this is so important? We have to have it on the same day because that's the point. We want to give people an alternative to the tuxedo-and-taffeta world of traditional prom." She grabs her purse and rummages, producing a pad of paper and a pen. "Tuxedo and taffeta," she mutters. "That's good. Gotta write that down."

"I understand what you're trying to do, but why can't their alternative just be on another night?"

"Look at you." She crosses a *T* viciously. "You're going to go to both, aren't you?"

"Well, I—"

"Yep. That's my point. There won't be an alternative, just an addition. The special prom for the special people. But we can all wink at each other and go to the 'real' prom to let everybody know we're still cool."

Since the timing in my life is nearly always awful, the doorbell rings. Fletcher opens the door. "Shelby! Let's go. I'm starving!"

Becca stares coldly at me, daring me to have French toast while she's in crisis. "Uh, just a minute," I call. He's already in the living room, and from the look on his face, I can tell that he has figured out that high drama is going to ruin our morning.

"Hi, Becca." He acts casual. Only a highly trained boy watcher like myself would know that he's really strategizing, trying to find a way to sway the situation to his advantage.

I guess Becca knows it, too. "Hi, Fletcher," she says with an edge. I feel like I should go put on my bulletproof hoodie.

"Would you like to join us for breakfast?" he asks formally.

"No, but thank you very much," she answers.

Silence fills the room, that awkward silence when everyone has too much to say and no one says anything. As the person caught in the middle, I guess it's my duty to break the ice. And there's definitely a glacier forming in my living room.

"So, I guess if you don't want to go with us, we'll just get going," I say as casually as possible. The glare I get from Becca lets me know that she does not approve of my decision.

Fletcher doesn't have a high tolerance for pretending, so he says, "Let's just stop this right now. What is your problem, Becca? Let's just get it out in the open."

"My *problem*, Fletcher, is that you and your friend are trying to sabotage our Geek Prom instead of helping and supporting us. If you guys really cared about us and what we do, you'd be the first in line to buy a plaid tux or something."

"Never mind the fact that I would never wear a plaid tux for *anyone*," Fletcher says, "but if you stop for a minute and try to think past what *you* want, you might see that there's a larger issue here."

This is just like earlier this year. For a while, the two of them were fighting because on one particular Saturday Fletcher wanted me to go to a party and Becca wanted me to work on a project with her. It was so bad that I actually ran away from both of them and locked myself in my room after school. They chased me down, of course, and then there was a big fight, and it was not pretty. I have to stop this train wreck.

"Look, the problem is that you don't support us—" Becca begins.

"No, the problem is you don't think there might be any other point of view than yours," Fletcher says, his voice getting louder.

As the volume increases, the gap between them decreases; in a minute they're nose to nose. "Why is it so terrible for me to want to go to a prom and be part of the regular school culture?" Fletcher asks.

I try to interject. "Well, maybe we could just—"

"What's so wrong about trying to be different, and not going along with all the robot people who run the school?" Becca matches his volume.

I try to butt in. "Hey, maybe we ought to—"

"You just don't think anyone else could be as cool as you!" Fletcher is yelling now.

"You just think you're too cool for everyone else!" Becca is yelling, too.

I meekly raise my hand and say, "Hey, I think—"

"Shut up!" They both yell at me.

I stare at them, stunned. "Shut up?" I ask.

They exchange glances, knowing that they both blew it, and that generally it's not a good idea to tell your best friend or your girlfriend to shut up. "Sorry." Becca smiles apologetically. "We just got carried away."

Fletcher nods uneasily. "Yeah. Sorry." He puts his arm around me; I know this will infuriate Becca, because it's that boyfriend-trumps-best-friend thing. It's like he's staking his claim to me since we have a sort of physical bond that Becca and I don't have. Not like we've really physically bonded, I mean in the literal sense. It's just that he can put his arm around me, and generally that's not something girlfriends do. Plus, it makes my toes melt. Anyway, I know it makes her mad.

"We're going to breakfast now," Fletcher says calmly, steering me toward the door.

"This is not the end of it!" Becca calls after us.

Over coffee and eggs, Fletcher drops another bomb on me. He waits until my mouth is full of toast to say, "They've asked me to be in charge of decorations for the prom."

"Oh, that's fantastic," I mumble through the crust and crumbs. "Why did they ask you? You're a guy."

He looks offended. "What, a guy can't be good at decorating? Only girls have the genetic coding for stringing crepe paper?"

"No, I'm not saying that. It's just kind of unusual, that's all. Who did you say asked you to be in charge of decorations?"

"I didn't say." He grabs his coffee mug and slurps a big gulp of avoidance.

"So . . ." I gesture, encouraging him to continue.

"So what?"

"So who asked you to be in charge of the decorations?"

He sighs heavily. "Okay. It was Samantha Singer. But don't jump to any conclusions!"

Samantha Singer. You've seen her, or someone just like her, because in every high school in the world, this rare creature exists. She is born with a golden tan, perfect white teeth, a shiny curtain of never-fuzzy hair, amazing muscle tone, and a closetful of clothes that never cling or ride up or gap. Usually, she excels at some nonsweaty sport like tennis or gymnastics. She has a flawless grade point average, and runs the student government. And her goal in life is simple: to conquer every aspect of high school life and to make every guy fall in love with her. That's Samantha Singer. She is our archenemy.

She also has a very large crush on Fletcher. Last year, when the Queen Geeks took over the spring dance, she nearly managed to steal him from me by roping him into being the "king" while she was the "queen" of the event. Luckily, Fletcher had better taste at that point. But who knows now? Samantha Singer is older and wiser, and has worked on her strategy for a year. I have no doubt that this is a way for her to get close to Fletcher. And I have no idea if this time he'll be able to resist her witchy charms.

But if time has taught me anything, it's that telling a guy *not* to do something is the best and surest way to push him into *doing* it. So, instead of freaking out and telling him to resign immediately from crepe paper duty, I act as if I couldn't care less. "Well, if she thinks you can do it, I'm sure you can. What's the theme this year?"

He's eyeing me as if I might jump across the table and stab him with a butter knife. "Uh . . . I think it's something to do with Mardi Gras."

"Oooh. Beads and feathers and oversized heads. Sounds like fun!"

We finish our breakfast in relative silence; he spends most of it staring at me, trying to figure out why I haven't snapped his head off for mentioning Samantha Singer.

Breakfast finished, Fletcher drives me back home, and as he steers the car onto my street, I check to see if Thea's Jeep is still in the driveway. With relief I see it is not. I get a momentary reprieve.

"Bye," I say, giving Fletcher a peck on the cheek. Even being that close to him causes my hormones to rev. He grabs my arm. "What?" I ask.

"Why are you being so nice about the decoration thing?"

I pretend to be surprised. "What do you mean?" I try batting my eyes at him, but I think it just looks like I have an eyelash stuck or something.

"You're planning something." His eyes narrow. "Are you going to sabotage the real prom?"

"Please stop calling it the 'real' prom!" I start to lose my composure, but then smile brilliantly. "Why would I do something like that?"

"Why?" He snorts. "Because Becca will tell you to do it!"

"Becca's not the boss of me." He thinks I just do whatever she says? That's not very flattering, I must say. "Besides, we all make our own choices. You make yours. I'll make mine."

"That sounds kind of threatening." His reddish eyebrows are scrunched over his green eyes like angry caterpillars waiting to pounce.

"Threatening?" I laugh, carefree. "How could I threaten you? You're a big jock prom king and I'm just a humble freak. You have all this decoration expertise, and I can't even draw a straight line. You—"

"Enough!" He revs the engine and peels out of the driveway.

As I watch the car jet angrily down my street, I realize that I've just signed up for another episode of teenage drama. Well, what else is there to do?

Becca refuses to answer her phone. I call like twenty times and she won't pick up. So instead, I call Amber. "Hello?" she yells into the phone. I can barely hear her over the pounding bass of some punk band.

"Can you turn that down? It's Shelby!" I yell.

The music cuts out. "Hello?"

"Geez, Amber, you're going to go deaf."

"Oh, hi, Shelby. What's up?"

"Has Becca talked to you about this prom thing?"

She pauses. I can hear her mind maneuvering, which means that Becca has, in fact, told her about the prom thing, and probably also about my going over to the dark side and supporting my boyfriend. "Well, she did mention it."

"Uh-huh. What did she say?"

"Oh, you know, I don't want to—"

"Come on. Just spit it out. I'm going to find out anyway."

Amber sighs heavily, as if I have asked her to reveal to me the sacred secret of the pain-free bikini wax or something. "She says you've been brainwashed by your sex hormones."

Sex hormones! What?! "Go on" is all I say through tightly clenched teeth.

"She says that you've betrayed the Queen Geeks because you're going to help Fletcher with the real prom." I hear her exhale, as if that took a lot of effort.

"Okay. That's kind of what I thought." I have to think of a way to open lines of communication so I can set things straight. "Listen, can you call her and let her know that I've got a plan? So she'll talk to me?"

"I guess." She doesn't sound too sure. "Do you? Have a plan?"

"I will. Thanks." I hang up and flop down on my bed, waiting for Amber's phone call to work its magic. As expected, my phone rings about ten minutes later.

"Traitors R Us. Can I help you?" I answer.

She laughs in spite of herself. "Funny. What's this great plan of yours?"

The truth is, I don't have a plan. All I know is that I am feeling torn again, yanked on one side by my loyalty to Fletcher and what he wants, and pulled on the other side by Becca and what she wants. I'm trying to play the whole thing on both sides, but I sort of doubt that's going to work for very long. At some point, I guess I'll have to choose, but for now, I'm going with avoidance.

"My great plan. Well, I'd love to tell you, but then I'd have to kill you."

"Right." A large, chasmlike pause fills up the space. "So, what is it?"

"Can I tell you tomorrow? At school?" That's it, buy some time. Queen of avoidance. Queen *Geek* of avoidance, I guess.

"Sure. But it better be good."

Yeah. This plan better be good. I wish I knew what it was.

3

PARENTAL MISGUIDANCE SUGGESTED

(or The Frisbee of Destiny)

Monday morning sucks. It sucks especially if you wake up in the dark with a lump of dread parked in the pit of your stomach. Nothing worse than a big old hairy lump of dread.

Euphoria, who is plugged into her charger in my room, bleeps to life, her green eye lights flashing. She pretends to yawn. "Why are you awake so early, Shelby?"

"What time is it?"

"It's five A.M. According to my perspiration and respiration readings, and the fact that you yelled something about penguins in your sleep, I'd say you were having a nightmare."

I don't remember anything about penguins, but the nightmare part doesn't surprise me. "I just have to have a plan and I don't have it yet."

Her lights flash in the dark, and I hear her processor whirring. "I don't understand. Sorry."

I swing my legs over the edge of the bed and grab my fuzzy robe. It's cold at five in the morning, even in the spring. "I have to have a plan to tell Becca. I'm supposed to be convincing her that I'm still one with the cause of the Queen Geeks."

"Why does she doubt that?"

I consider explaining it all to her, but decide against it because it's too complicated and I don't really understand it all myself. "Let's just say that we're all having a little territory problem."

"Oh." She activates the room light, bringing it up from dim to bright at just the perfect rate for my eyes to adjust. Bet Samantha Singer doesn't have a robot who can do that. Bet she doesn't have a robot at all.

"Becca thinks I've betrayed her." I decide to skip a shower, even though I have plenty of time, and I look through my closet for the loosest, most comfortable clothing that is still within the school dress code (no pajamas, no slippers, no fun).

"Why would she think that?" Euphoria picks up the clothes I discard and hangs them up as I throw new ones down on the floor. Again, I bet Samantha has a maid, but not one that works that fast.

"It's too complicated to explain." I decide on an outfit, slouch into it, and turn to Euphoria. "Essentially, they both want me to take their sides on this prom issue. But I can't be on both sides, so I'm stuck in the middle."

"Prom?" She follows me into the hallway, activating lights as we move toward the kitchen.

"It's a kind of dance. Can I have pancakes?"

"Well, it's a school day . . . but what the hick."

I can't help but laugh at her. "What the *hick*?"

"Isn't that the way to say it?" She pulls ingredients from the cupboard and fridge, then sighs a mighty robot sigh. "Slang gives me problems. I should probably stop trying."

I hug her shiny metallic shoulders. "Don't stop trying. It's fantastic."

Euphoria doesn't eat, but she likes to watch me while I do, and make sure that I don't eat too much. Although I'd love to drop the whole prom conversation, she won't let go of it. "So, why would they be fighting about this prom dance?" she asks as she sets a plate full of perfect golden yumminess in front of me.

"Becca wants to have this weird Geek Prom, and Fletcher is working on what he calls the 'real' prom, the one sponsored by the student government. The problem is, they want to have the events on the same night, sort of as a showdown." I drizzle amber syrup all over my plate, making a little Samantha Singer face that I can stab with my fork.

"And each one thinks the other is trying to steal you away." Euphoria grabs the syrup bottle and delicately tucks it back in the cupboard. She's always watching my sugar intake.

"Something like that. I have to come up with some great plan to tell Becca today, and I haven't thought of anything at all."

Euphoria's processors click and whir, a sign that she's trying desperately to solve this problem for me. When Dad built Euphoria, I think he unconsciously intended her to be a sort of stand-in for Mom, so he programmed her with this weird maternal instinct. Consequently, she likes to interfere and meddle with every situation, just like a real mom. The only plus is that she has a super logical mind.

After a minute or two, the whirring stops, and she says, "I have it!"

"What do you have, exactly?"

"The solution to your dilemma."

"I can't wait. What is it?"

"Well," she whispers confidentially, "you let them hold both events on the same night."

I wait, and nothing more follows. "That's it? That's your great plan? How does that help me?"

"There won't be any more fighting. They will both think they've won the argument, and you'll all get along perfectly. Until the night of the dance, of course."

"And then what happens?"

A couple of clicks and whirs, and she says, "Well, that's more of a problem. But you'd at least have a few weeks free of conflict!"

"I've got to talk to Dad. Is he up?"

"He came in quite late last night. I think he's still sleeping."

"Well, it's his own fault for staying up too late in the lab. I need a ride to school."

"He wasn't in the lab," she says softly as I walk down the hall toward Dad's bedroom. That doesn't register, of course, although I hear her say it. I'm too focused on getting my ride and solving what I think is my big problem.

"Dad?" The door creaks as I open it; his room is like a cave, totally dark, and he's huddled up under the covers in a big lump. I gently poke at his exposed arm.

"What?" He bolts upright as if I've tapped him with a Taser.

"Hey. Just wondered if I could get a ride to school? Please?" I try my best wheedling daughter whine, which usually works. "It's been raining."

He rubs his eyes and squints at the clock on the nightstand. "Isn't it Saturday?"

"I wish." I grab his arm and pull. "Let's go. I don't want to be late."

He grumbles, but he gets up, stumbling in the dark for his pants and shirt. "Why can't you walk again?" he mutters.

"It's raining. And I need your advice, actually."

He nearly falls over as he pulls on a sock. "You need *my* advice? About what?"

"I'll tell you in the car. You don't want me to be late for school, right?"

We pile into the old Volvo wagon, and since the skies are still gray and overcast, I'm especially glad I scammed a ride. "So, what's the big crisis?" he asks.

I tell him the whole Becca/Fletcher prom tale. I tell him about Euphoria's solution, which is to pretend I'm siding with both of them until the night of the prom, at which time I beg the earth to swallow me whole. He chews on the inside of his cheek, a thing he does when he's thinking really hard. Finally, he says, "I don't know."

"That's it?" I explode. "That's your great advice? They ought to kick you out of the Dad club."

He grunts. "Well, if you don't want to choose sides, you don't have a lot of choices. You can't persuade either of them to change their minds, so you're stuck. The only other option I see is to not be involved with either dance. And by the way, do you realize that in the larger scope of things, this isn't really a problem?"

He pulls up in front of the school, and in my self-absorbed cloud of anxiety, I am unable to comprehend how right he is about this not being a big deal. There are many, many things worse than my little problem, but I am unaware of that at the moment.

As he drives away, I slosh across the grassy campus in search of a dry spot. Since our whole school is bungalow-type buildings exposed to everything, a dry spot is kind of tough to find. I guess the people who built it figured it would never rain in Southern California, so we didn't really need any shelter.

I spot Becca and Amber huddled under the drama building overhang, so I trot over there. "Good morning, fellow drowned rats," I say. Immediately, my cheerful attitude is popped like an overinflated balloon by the look on Becca's face. "What happened?"

Amber sighs heavily and looks down at the ground. Becca has her arms crossed and looks like she's barely slept. Instead of answering me, they just stand there like tragic dolls. Elisa skitters into our space clutching a soda, and shakes her rain-soaked jacket like a wet dog.

"Thanks for that," I mumble, wiping the droplets off my own coat.

"So?" she asks, taking a long swig of caffeine and sugar. "Did you tell her yet?"

"Tell me what?" I look from one sad face to another, hoping for some hint about what's going on.

Becca puts her hands on my shoulders and looks me square in the eye. "Your dad is dating my mom."

It takes a second for this to register, kind of like when you see people in movies get into car crashes and everything goes in slow motion. I process the information, and I determine that this is all a joke.

"Ha!" I shake off her hands. "You had me for a minute. Good job."

"No, Shelby. I'm serious." Becca's hands drop listlessly to her sides. "He was over at our house last night. Our house is so big, I guess they figured I wouldn't notice, but God, what am I, stupid? It's insulting."

I am speechless, something quite unusual for me. Amber puts an arm around my shoulder.

"Why didn't you call me?" I hear myself squeak.

"Thea took my phone. She said I was 'abusing my privileges,' and then she basically banished me to my room for the rest of the evening. I wasn't even supposed to see your dad, but I managed to spy on them a little bit. I would've called you, but I didn't have access to any electronics. Not even my computer." The bitterness in her voice is unmistakable. Never tear a teenager away from all lines of communication. It's like taking the oxygen away from a scuba diver.

"Well, it's not like we didn't see it coming." I lean against the wall and feel an iron basketball in the pit of my stomach. "I mean, last year's Halloween party, the flirting, the questions . . . I'm not surprised at all. Just disgusted."

"Hey, it's not so bad," Elisa says. "If they got married, you guys would be, like, sisters. Wouldn't that be convenient?"

Becca and I stare at each other for a minute. I can't even think about that . . . what would it be like, if we were actually related? Oh, but then we get to the whole idea of my dad getting married again, and her mom being my stepmom . . . and I feel like I'm going to throw up. Even though it's not a total surprise, it's still like the vaccination shot you get as a little kid: You know it's going to hurt, but nothing prepares you for that nasty stab.

Luckily, the bell rings for first period. I've never been so happy in all my life to go to class.

We're reading *Hamlet* in English, but I am totally unable to concentrate. My mind is on the whole earth-shattering revelation that my best friend's mom is somehow involved with my dad. Involved . . . and what does that mean? Did they have dinner? Did they kiss? Oh, God. What if they have a baby together? I plunk my head down on my desk, unable to focus on Hamlet's petty problems.

My English teacher notices, of course, because they always notice if you're in a particularly bad mood and really don't want to do English. It's like they have radar or something. "Shelby, what do you think about Gertrude and Claudius?"

"They shouldn't be dating!" I blurt out. "Her mother is dead, for God's sake. Doesn't he have any respect?"

She looks confused. "Whose mother is dead?"

"Mine! I mean, Hamlet's!"

The class giggles. The teacher gives me a quizzical look and moves on. Not only is my own life in ruins, I've rewritten Shakespeare. I'm probably going to hell.

It's still raining at lunch, so we are forced to huddle under the overhangs again, sheltering our runny nachos from the drips of water. Becca seems to be in a better mood, although I'm still feeling like a wad of gum under someone's shoe. My dad's shoe, I guess.

"Let's look on the bright side," Becca says, scooping fake cheese onto a soggy chip. "At least we know the person our mom or dad is dating is actually not a serial killer or used car salesman."

Elisa arches her eyebrows. "Wow, that's some serious positive thinking." Rain drips down in sad little ropes.

Becca pulls her coat more tightly around her and brushes some droplets from her blond spikes. "I think I'd prefer to put my energy into Geek Prom instead of worrying about something I can't control, like my mother's love life. So, Shelby, speaking of love life, have you decided whether you're siding with the boyfriends or your real friends?"

"That's pretty unfair," I respond, trying to buy some time. "Boyfriends can be real friends, too."

"Not in this case," Elisa says, wagging her head. "Naveen is with us, though. He doesn't want to go to the real prom anyway, because he doesn't want to rent a tux." Naveen became Elisa's boyfriend earlier in the year when they met at a Halloween party and ended up making out in my laundry room. Seeing Raggedy Ann and an Indian pasha rolling around in the dryer lint no doubt caused me permanent psychological damage.

"Jon doesn't want to go either," Amber pipes up. "He's totally into our event. He wants to dress up like Rob Zombie." Jon, a black-clothed artist type, became Amber's sidekick after last year when he helped us create a website and then basically spurned Becca's puppy-dog advances in favor of Amber's darkly poetic charms. Now they share black clothing, and they both seem happy. Or depressed, I guess, since all they wear is black clothing.

"See?" Becca turns to me. "Everybody's on board except you. So what are you going to do?"

I remember the conversations I had with Euphoria and Dad; I stare blankly into space. I realize they're all waiting for an answer, and that words of some sort will need to be uttered. I just can't figure out what they are at the moment.

Luckily, I'm spared when a girl we don't know chases a Day-Glo pink Frisbee from the rain into our little overhang space, upsetting nacho cheese all over the drama building wall, and leaving Elisa with nothing more than greasy cardboard for lunch. "Hey!" Elisa yelps, checking for cheese burns.

"Oh, sorry," the girl says as if she's just noticed we are all standing in the line of Frisbee fire. "Really. Can I buy you some more of those nachos?" She says *naa-chos*, and has an Australian accent. She's almost as tall as Becca, with short-cropped brown hair, large hazel eyes, and mod-looking black rectangular glasses. "Seriously, I'll get you some more."

Elisa thaws a bit when replacement nachos are mentioned. "Never mind. Lunch is almost over anyway, and it's being kind to even call that lunch." She picks up the pink Frisbee and hands it to the Australian girl. "I'm Elisa."

"Hey. I'm Evie Brandt." She extends a hand. "I just got here two weeks ago. And I'm damn sick of playing Frisbee by myself, so do any of you by chance have a personality?"

"You sound like that *Crocodile Hunter* guy. Or his daughter," Elisa says.

Evie kind of stares at her. "That's probably because we're both from Australia. But for the record, they sound like me."

"Good point," Elisa says, nodding. We all kind of awkwardly stand there waiting for someone to speak. Evie gestures with the pink plastic disk and says, "Well, thanks again for understanding about the Frisbee. They have minds of their own." She turns to go, although it seems as if she wants to stay.

"So what brings you here from Down Under?" Becca asks. Evie turns back toward us, and smiles slightly, a crooked, gentle smile. It's that unspoken high school code: If a stranger intrudes on your conversation, you have to invite them to stay with some unimportant question, otherwise, they have to leave immediately in order not to appear desperate or stalker-ish.

"I'm here on an exchange program, actually," she says. "I've only been here for two weeks, and I'm ready to lose my mind. I'm staying with a family and this girl, their daughter . . ." She shudders in something like disgust. "She's a galah if I ever saw one."

"Galah?" Amber asks.

"Sorry." Evie shakes her head, as if to remind herself that we do not speak Australian, if there is such a thing. "Galah—stupid, foolish. It's a bird that does crazy stunts. And she certainly fits that description. Of course, I suppose I should shut up, because some of you might be friends with her, right? Same problem I have everywhere; I never know when to shut up."

"Who is it?" Elisa asks.

"I shouldn't say—"

"C'mon," Becca coaxes. "I'm sure that if she's so galah we're probably not friends with her. Who is it?"

Evie wants to tell us, you can just see it: She probably hasn't had anyone to talk to for two weeks. "All right," she says finally. "Her name is Briley. And what kind of name is that? Sounds like a kind of cigarette or something."

I wonder . . . "Hey, is this Briley somebody who looks like an overcooked Barbie doll?"

"Yep, that's her." Evie smiles, crosses her arms, and says, "So, if you're friends with her, sorry."

"She's my next-door neighbor," I say. "And she *is* a galah." I guess I never noticed Evie moving in next door, probably due to the glaring whiteness of Briley's perfectly bleached teeth. I really try to avoid looking over there to avoid retinal damage.

With the mention of Briley, we all relax. Clearly if Evie doesn't like Briley, she would like us. Briley is one of the perfect blond robots who populate our school, the girls who point and stare at us in the cafeteria, the ones who ask for help with their homework but then pretend they don't know you during sports assemblies. Last year, we tricked her into doing a promotional commercial for our club, and we made her look pretty stupid, which wasn't exactly nice, but she did volunteer.

Evie leans against the drama building between Elisa and Amber. "Well, it's nice that they hosted me and all, but she and I are as opposite as it's possible to be. All she seems to care about is manicures and makeovers, and I'm into computers. And, of course, Frisbee."

Becca perks up at the mention of technology. "You're good with computers?"

Evie squints at her through the rectangular glasses. "Absolutely. Why?"

"I have a great idea," Becca says, grinning maniacally. But just then the bell rings, and it's back to reality. "Evie, can you meet us after school? I have a really interesting proposition for you."

Evie smiles broadly. "Sure, if it means I'll be able to have a conversation that doesn't involve lipstick."

"I can almost promise you," Becca says, clapping an arm around Evie's shoulder as they walk toward the middle of campus.

"What do you think she has in mind?" Elisa asks as we follow them.

"That's a good question," I answer. "I really have no idea."

Amber falls into step beside us. "If it's something she just came up with off the top of her head, it usually means it's something really big, really difficult to pull off, and something that will involve a lot of work for us."

"Sounds exciting," Elisa says, nodding. "I was getting kind of bored, actually. We need something to spice up the end of the year."

As for me, I don't feel quite as excited as Elisa. In fact, a little cold fish of fear has started to swim around in my stomach; what possible use could Becca have for Evie Brandt, Australian computer geek? And then a thought hits me, a thought I had been shutting out thanks to Evie's pink Frisbee invasion: My dad is dating Becca's mom. Nothing can be as bad as that.

Becca is waiting outside the classroom when I finish my last class of the day. "Hey," she chirps.

We walk together, me trying to keep up with her monstrous strides. "You're happy."

"Sure. Why not?" She gazes off into the distance as if she's looking for something.

"And would this unexplained happiness have anything to do with an Australian computer geek?"

She grins. "Maybe."

"How about you let me in on whatever the big plan is." I grab her arm to slow her down. "And stick to the speed limit. I'm getting a leg cramp."

She turns, her eyes sparkling. "I got this brainstorm. We have to talk to Evie about it, of course, but get this: What if we invited people from all over the world to our Geek Prom?"

I stare at her blankly. "I don't think people from all over the world are going to want to travel to Southern California for cocktail weenies and punk music."

"We're not having punk. Anyway, of course they can't *physically* travel here."

I shake my head. "I'm officially confused."

"Webcam attendance. We'll have other people set up webcams in all these different places, link them to our event, have huge screens, and up-link all the people from all over the world so they are virtually attending our prom!"

Once again, Becca is obsessed with global domination. Same old story. It's not enough for her to have a few really good friends, or even a boyfriend; she wants the whole world to be her friend. It's like she has some need to prove that she's more popular than everyone else, even though she makes fun of people who need to be popular.

Evie, Elisa, and Amber are all waiting for us by the drama building. "Can we go to your house?" Becca whispers before we get to them.

"I guess," I mutter sullenly. It doesn't feel like I have much of a choice.

"Gorgeous day," Evie says, pointing toward the stubbly hills and sky. Luckily, the rain has stopped, leaving the sky powder-blue with a few puffy clouds, and the air unusually clean and clear for a Southern California afternoon. "I don't think I've ever seen that particular mountain before."

"Yeah, on the rare occasion that it rains, you can see all kinds of stuff that's usually hidden," I say cryptically. I'm not even sure what the comment means, but it sounds like it's meaningful.

"Hey," Becca calls out. "Shelby says we can go to her house to plot our scheme."

"What scheme is that, exactly?" Elisa asks as we walk toward the street.

"Becca wants to invite the whole world to Geek Prom," I say.

She shoots me a dirty look, as if she doesn't like my tone of voice. "Kind of," she says. "Evie inspired the idea, actually."

"I did?" Evie says, surprised. "How so?"

Becca explains the whole webcam idea, and everybody reacts in various ways: Elisa gets a high-tech gleam in her eye (no doubt figuring how her beloved Wembley, her Palm Pilot, will fit into the plot), Amber looks uncomfortable, and Evie grins like she's just been given a day pass to Apple headquarters.

"You'd better tell Evie about your robot," Elisa mentions casually as we walk to my house.

"Your robot?" Evie squeaks. "What, do you have one of those things that vacuums your carpet while you're away?"

"Sort of," I say. "She also cooks and makes bad puns."

Dad's not home when we get there. Big surprise. Becca and I exchange uncomfortable glances, and I know what we're both thinking: Are they together? It's really just too creepy to consider, so we both pretend that we're extra interested in our backpacks (me) and what's in the refrigerator (her).

Euphoria rolls in from the laundry room, beeping with glee.

She loves it when I have people over; I think Dad must have somehow programmed her with Southern hospitality, and if she can't feed a bunch of people, she's just not happy. "Well, hello there, girls!" she drawls in her pseudo-Georgia accent. "So good to see you all again. Can I make you a snack?"

As most people do the first time they come to my house, Evie stands staring, mouth open, at my silver nanny. Elisa walks by, tucks a hand gently under Evie's chin and closes her mouth for her. "You really have a robot," Evie says with awe.

"Yeah." I put my arm around Euphoria. "We go way back. This is Euphoria."

"Pleased to meet you," Euphoria says, politely extending a claw. Evie takes it gingerly, shakes it as if it might explode, and then wipes her hand on her jeans as if she expected to get metallic cooties.

"It's kind of a long story," I say in answer to Evie's silent question. "Dad made her."

"I am a self-servicing auto processor with an ancillary emotional chip," Euphoria offers. "That means I can tell when you're having a nervous breakdown or something."

"Not that we've ever really needed that particular skill," I note, just in case Evie thinks we're all nutcases, which we kind of are. But you don't want that to be your first introduction to a new friend, right?

"I just made cookies," Euphoria sings as she rolls merrily to the kitchen. "I'll bring out a plate to the living room. Milks all around?"

I lead the girls to my living room, and we all stake out our usual spots. Evie sort of waits until everyone is seated before she chooses, which just shows that she has good manners. She ends up sitting next to Becca on the wine-colored velvet love seat.

"So, Evie," Becca starts, clapping a hand on Evie's shoulder. "I feel like you were sent from the universe to be part of our destiny."

"I actually flew in on a 747."

"Right. But what I mean," Becca says, "is that we needed someone with your particular talents, and here you are, which means that the universe is definitely supporting our effort."

Amber, who has been mostly silent and brooding, pipes up. "Maybe the universe is simply setting us up for failure."

"You read too much Edgar Allan Poe," Elisa says, shaking her head. "Not everything ends in death, disaster, and molting black birds."

"I don't believe Poe ever mentions that the raven molts," Amber says frostily. She's kind of sensitive about her Poe obsession. "I just mean that I'm not sure this whole Geek Prom thing is the way to go. I think we should look at our reasons for doing it."

Becca shifts uncomfortably. "Well, I told you. I just want an alternative for people who don't want to sell a major organ to go to prom."

"But we're not even juniors or seniors," Amber continues, although she knows that Becca doesn't like this train of thought. "Why do we care what it costs? We can only go if we're invited by a junior or a senior anyway, so what's the big deal?" She looks up and meets Becca's steely gaze. Becca's gaze gets all steely whenever she's pissed or whenever somebody crosses her. It's looking extra steely today, probably because she doesn't like to hear criticism of her brilliant global domination plans.

"Well, what do the rest of you think?" she asks with a restrained tone of courtesy. I think she'd really like to simply rip Amber's head off, but since we haven't eaten cookies yet, she's willing to wait.

Elisa, the only one of us dating a non-junior or -senior (Naveen is our age), says, "Well, actually, I had sort of the same thought as Amber. Why are we doing this? Just to piss off someone?"

"Like who?" Becca asks, lips pursed.

"Your boyfriend, maybe?" Elisa doesn't usually pull any punches.

Evie raises her hand timidly. "Um . . . listen, I don't really know what's going on. Could you fill me in?"

Becca smiles, relaxes, actually laughs. "Oh, sure. Sorry. We want to have a Geek Prom, where everybody can come for practically no money, and where you don't have to wear uncomfortable shoes. We want to have it at the same time as the regular junior/senior prom at our school, which costs some outrageous amount of money and is supposed to be held at some fascist consumerist hotel. Plus, the food's just going to be those little pastries they buy at Wal-Mart, but they're charging one hundred dollars per couple for it."

Evie considers this for a moment, then says, "What's the boyfriend thing about?"

As the sort-of hostess here, I figure it's my turn to risk the wrath of Becca's ego by trying to explain her motives. "Becca and I are dating these two guys who are juniors. And our two dates feel they need to go to the 'real' prom because they're also super jocks and will probably be on the prom court. Becca wants to have our event on the same night as their event, sort of as a protest."

"But this is causing a problem with the boyfriends," Evie says, nodding.

"Except for mine," Amber says. "Jon doesn't care about adolescent rituals. Plus, he says wearing a tux is a symbol of the oppressive middle class."

Euphoria rolls in with the plate of cookies and five glasses of milk (something no human maid could ever juggle, I'm pretty sure, but she has a built-in drink tray), and Evie once again shakes her head in amazement at my fantastic luck. "Wow. I just never thought I'd see an actual robot serving me cookies."

"You ought to come for dinner," Euphoria brags. "These cookies are nothing compared to my eggplant Parmesan."

Becca's cell phone rings and she fishes it out of her backpack. "Hello?"

She says nothing for a few seconds, but by the look on her face, I can tell that something is going on. The voice on the other end of the cell gets louder and higher, and finally Becca says, "Are you sure? Why?" And then, after a minute of high-speed babbling from the other end, she says, "Okay. I'll wait for you."

"What was that?" Elisa asks as she snags another cookie.

Becca sighs; her good mood has deflated and even her little hair spikes look depressed.

"Geez, what happened? Who was that?" I ask.

"That was my mom." Becca stands and angrily zips up her backpack. "She's coming to pick me up."

"Why?"

"Because," she says, lips pursed tight, "my dad is apparently waiting for me to come home."

4

CRUSHED BY
A CRUSH

(or When Hormones Collide)

Thea arrives about twenty minutes after the phone call, and we hear a frantic honking from the driveway. Becca waves half-heartedly.

"Call me," I say as she closes the front door behind her.

"What was that about?" Amber asks, peering out the front window. "Becca's yelling at her mom."

"Her dad, Melvin, is here, I guess." I know what this means to her. Melvin and Thea were divorced almost two years ago, the summer before she came to Green Pines, and Becca's never forgiven him. She hasn't talked about him much, except to tell me that he's a movie person, and that he has a severe case of stupid. We did have to go to see his movie, so I guess she must care about him in some way. But then again, she did boo through the opening credits.

"They're divorced, huh?" Elisa asks. "That's tough. Wonder why he's here all of a sudden."

I wonder if it has anything to do with the fact that Thea is dating someone.

We all hang out for a while, but without Becca things sort of go flat. Amber calls her mom for a ride, and pretty soon everyone is gone, except for Evie, who simply has to walk next door. "I really don't want to go back over there," she says. "But I guess I'd better. They might worry about me."

"Why do you think they invited an exchange student anyway?" I ask. It seems out of character for Briley's family, since they pretty much only care about stuff like cars, clothes, and consumer electronics.

"All I can figure out is that they wanted Briley to date somebody with money and an accent. They seemed pretty disappointed when I got off the plane. They kept asking me if I was sure my name wasn't Evan."

"Sounds like them."

"Can I ask you something?" Evie asks as she pulls open the front door.

"Sure."

"How do you feel about this whole competition thing with the boys? Are you as keen on having a rebel prom as Becca is?"

I have to think for a minute. If I tell the truth, am I betraying my best friend? I decide not to think about that. "Actually, I wish she'd just drop the idea. It's not worth all the hassle and we could easily have it on another night if it's something that important. I think she's just being stubborn. But since she's my best friend, I'll stick with her and help her with it. When it comes down to it, friends are more important."

"It's hard to remember that if the guy's a good kisser, though, huh?" She laughs and waves as she crosses the lawn to Briley's house. "See you at school, Shelby. I'm glad I hit your friends with a Frisbee!"

"Me, too!"

As soon as she leaves, I race to the phone. I know I probably shouldn't call Becca right away, and in fact, she might not even be home yet, but I can't help myself. Her cell rings twice, and she picks up. "What?" she hisses.

"How's it going?"

"I just got home, so I don't know yet." I hear two people, a man and woman, talking loudly in the background. "I'm going to try to escape to my room and then I'll call you back."

Euphoria asks me to help her with dinner, and since I have nothing to do but wait, I agree. As we chop carrots and onions (well, she chops the onions, because they don't make her cry), I hear Dad's car pull into the driveway. I stop chopping.

"What's wrong?" she asks with concern.

"Nothing." I chop the carrots a bit more viciously. Poor little root vegetables.

"I can tell by your body temperature and pulse. Suddenly you started to go tense." She stops and pivots toward me, her green eye lights flashing. "Don't try to pull the woof over my eyes, young lady."

"Wool."

"Hmm?"

"It's 'don't try to pull the *wool* over my eyes.' " I continue to furiously hack at the carrots.

"Why would somebody do that?" She scrapes onion bits into a skillet. "Wool over your eyes. That's just silly."

The back door slides open, and I hear Dad wrestling with some plastic bags and stuff. When I peek around the corner, he's setting the bags down on the floor, whistling some ridiculously happy tune. It's enough to make me puke.

"Hi," I say. He jumps about a foot. "I live here, remember?"

"Sorry." He scoops the bags up hastily, as if there are things in there I'm not supposed to see.

"Where've you been?" I continue chopping, punishing the innocent vegetables for my dad's stupid behavior.

"Just had to go to the store." He grabs one white plastic grocery bag and tries to sneak out of the room with it.

"Hang on." I block his way, my arms folded. "What's in the bag?"

He turns bright red, then stutters a bit. "Nothing," he says finally.

"Well, if it's nothing, then let's see it." I put my hand out, waiting for the supposedly empty bag of nothing significant. He hesitates, pulls back, and looks over to Euphoria for moral support.

"Don't look at me," she bleeps. "You two need to work it out. I'm not programmed for drama."

I grab the bag. A little voice reminds me that if my dad did this to me, I'd be screaming about respect and stuff, but I just shove that little voice into a closet in the back of my mind, and I hope there are many dust bunnies to make it sneeze.

Inside the bag, there's nothing but a greeting card.

"This is your big secret?" I snort. "You really need to get out more. Greeting cards were legalized in 1989."

Dad laughs nervously and tries to snatch the card out of my hand. "I know, I know. It's silly. I just wanted it to be a surprise. So, if you could just give it back—" He grabs at the bag and card, but I'm quicker than he is, so I elude his grasp.

"What's the card for?" I slip it out of the cream-colored envelope. "Oooh. Fancy. It even has gold on the envelope. Is this because I did so well on my progress report—"

The words choke in my throat. I'm a total idiot. I just assumed the card was for me, but when I read the front, it says *To a Special Someone*, and there are stylized pink roses and irises in sort of an Asian design. Panic rises in my throat, but then I think, Hey, I'm special to my dad. Right?

"Shelby, don't open that." He has regained composure and now sounds more like a dad than a teenager caught smoking in the bathroom. "Please give it back to me. It's none of your business."

I open the card. Inside, there's a handwritten note: *The last few weeks have been wonderful. I feel alive again, and I have you to thank. Just wanted to let you know how much it's meant to me.* And then the card is signed: *Love, Rich.*

Now, even if my dad loved me more than anything, which I used to think he did, he'd never sign my card *Love, Rich*. Which means it's not for me. Which means there is "someone special" in his life, and it's not me. And I'm betting it's not Euphoria either.

"Shelby," he begins, but I drop the card and storm out of the room, flee down the hallway, and slam my bedroom door. I lock it from the inside. He's knocking gently, like he's afraid he might break the door down or make me go over the edge and turn into crazy-psycho-teenage daughter. Come to think of it, that's a strong possibility.

"Shelby, can I please come in so we can talk about this?"

"What is there to say, Dad?" I feel a ball of anger knotted in my stomach, and although I'm unreasonably pissed off, I'm also sad, so my traitorous tear ducts start flooding.

"I want to explain about the card." He taps again. "Please let me in."

I decide to open the door, if only so I can let him see the severe damage he's inflicting upon me, his only offspring. I twist the lock open, and flop back down on my bed, facedown. I hear the door swing open slowly, then feel the weight of my dad sitting on the edge of the bed, making the old mattress sag a bit.

"Honey," he says softly. "Thea's just a friend."

"Just a friend!" I snort into my pillow. "I don't think so. She's apparently 'someone special.' Right?"

"Can't friends be someone special?" He sighs heavily. "Look, I did try to keep you from seeing the card. You're nosy."

I sit up, furious. "Nosy? Nosy?! Don't you think I have a right to know who you're interested in? Doesn't it affect me, too? I mean, if you're actually dating my best friend's mom, don't you think that might have some slight impact on me? And what's that whole bit that you feel alive again for the first time? Have we just been living here in the emotional meat locker waiting for somebody to thaw us out?"

"No, it's not like that—"

"Then what is it like?" I wipe at the tear tracks tickling my cheeks, furious with the stupid tears for ruining what would probably have been a pretty impressive hissy fit.

Dad stares down at the floor and absently rubs the edge of the card that he's still clutching. "It's hard for you to understand, I know. You're my daughter. That kind of a relationship is wonderful, and I love you very much. But it's not the same as—"

"Oh, so it's all about sex, is it?"

"Aw, Shelby, please. You're making this much more difficult than it needs to be." He holds up the card. "It's just nice to be able to have someone my own age to be with. You're fantastic company, but it's different."

"What about Mom?" It kind of pops out, unexpected. "How could you date someone else? Mom was your wife. You promised to love her forever. You can't just throw that away because it's not convenient anymore!"

There is a huge silence between us suddenly. He stares down at the floor, purses his lips, and seems about to say something, but then just drops the card and stands up. "I'm sorry," he mumbles, then walks out of the room, leaving *To a Special Someone* lying on my carpet.

The phone rings, and I welcome the distraction. "Yeah?" I answer tonelessly.

"It's me." The sound of crinkling cookie wrappers sizzles over the phone line. "The hurricane has blown over for now. Melvin stormed out, slammed the door, and peeled off in his sports car. Very dramatic." I hear her munching.

"Yeah, we just had some drama over here, too." I kick at the card with my toe. "So, where do we go if there's drama everywhere?"

"Well, he's gone, so I guess you can come over here, but if your drama's with your dad, how can you get a ride? We really need to be able to drive."

"I'll e-mail the governor and see if he'll let me do it without the permit since I'm such an amazing kid."

"Good plan." Munch, munch. "What was your drama?"

I sigh. How do I tell her the awful news, that my dad has a big fat crush on her mom? I guess it's like a scabby scrape on the knee: Best to just rip off the Band-Aid and be done with it. "Dad bought your mom a card and it was for a 'Special Someone,' and I flipped out. He signed it 'Love, Rich.' I mean, what am I supposed to do with that?"

Becca is extremely quiet on the other end of the phone. Even the munching has stopped. "A card?" she says softly. "Oh my God. Maybe they're going to elope. Or maybe they're going to go adopt an Ethiopian baby. What *shall* we do?"

"That is so *not* funny." The thought of my dad adopting any more kids isn't even something I'd considered, even in my most paranoid moments, of which there are many. You can always count on Becca to troubleshoot more trouble than could possibly exist in the known universe.

She's braying her donkey honk laugh at me. "Listen to

yourself, Shelby. Ooooh. He got her a card! I mean, geez. That's *so* not even a thing."

"It is *too* a thing." Obviously, the only way out of this stupid loop is to change the subject. "So, what's up with Melvin?"

"Ah." I can hear her rip open another package of cookies. It's a two-pack Oreo kind of day. "From what I could hear, he's here to win Thea back."

"What?"

"Yep. Apparently, he's seen the error of his ways and realizes now that she's the one for him. I think it could have something to do with the fact that she's now somewhat interested in someone else, and he doesn't like to lose."

"Didn't he already lose her?" I ask. "I mean, they're divorced. And didn't he leave her?"

"I'm not clear on the whole sequence of dramas." Becca's mom is yelling in the background. "Hey, gotta go. I think Thea needs some moral support or something. Romantic first aid. Don't you think it's kind of screwed up and unnatural that we have to help our parents with dating issues?"

"Yes," I say as I click the phone off. "I think it's really screwed up."

I just sort of hang out in my room for the rest of the evening, studiously avoiding Dad. When we meet by accident in the kitchen, we ignore each other. An arctic wind blows from the refrigerator as I grab some cheese. Okay, well, that's a bit of an overstatement, but it does feel kind of frosty in there.

Euphoria, of course, notices the tension. As she's carefully stacking dishes in the cupboard (dishes my parents probably bought together!), she uses a free claw to pat me on the shoulder. "Shelby, what is going on?"

"Oh, did you notice the amazing lack of communication going on between me and Dad? Or was it the intense silence and the pretending we both live alone that tipped you off?"

"It was pretty much because your dad told me you weren't getting along." She turns and blinks her eye lights sadly. Don't ask me how she's able to communicate feelings without eyebrows. She has skills.

"Not getting along." I shove the cheese drawer shut, reach for a Pepsi, and pop the top with unnecessary roughness. Poor little Pepsi can, taking the brunt of my anger. "Yeah. Well, did he tell you that he's dating someone? That's he's dating Thea, my best friend's mom? Isn't that sort of sick? Kind of like dating your sister or something."

"It's actually nothing like dating your sister, since you don't have a sister," Euphoria points out. "And they're also not genetically related."

"It was more figurative than literal." I stomp to the kitchen counter and begin savaging my pieces of cheese, biting into them with fury.

"I'm not human," Euphoria says tentatively, "but I do know that your father loves you very much."

"Sure, right now," I spit at her. "But what about when it's no longer convenient? What about if he wants to just replace me with a cooler, less difficult daughter?"

Euphoria bleeps, and her bleep sounds puzzled. I don't blame her really; as I listen to myself blather, I can tell that I'm making pretty much no sense. But when your hormones kick in and you're feeling like the little bit of family you have is being threatened, I guess you say and do things that aren't quite sane.

"He's not trying to replace your mother, if that's what you think." Euphoria turns away from me and rolls toward the living room. "He still talks to her picture, you know."

"What?"

"He keeps a picture of her in his room, and he talks to her. I hear him sometimes when I'm cleaning. I don't mean to eavesdrop, but it's hard not to when you have supersonic hearing. I hope you don't think I'm rude."

I'm still stunned by the idea that my dad talks to my dead mom's picture. It's sort of sweet and kind of strange all at the same time. "So, he hasn't just forgotten her." It's more of a statement than a question.

"Of course not." Euphoria tries to snort with derisive laughter, but it comes out sounding like a blender choking on metal washers. "He's just kind of lonely, that's all. Humans can love more than one person, you know. It's not like there's a limited amount of love and once you spend it you run out." She sighs and rolls off. "Good night."

I slug down some of the soda and leave the can on the counter. As I shuffle down the hall to my room, I realize that I have been a real jerk to my dad. And another thing I realize: What Euphoria says is right. You can love more than one person at the same time, and in different ways. I love Fletcher (yikes! I said it!) and I love Becca (as a sister), but I don't have to choose between them, do I? There's enough of me to go around, right?

As I wash my face, I notice the dark rings under my eyes. Very attractive. I look a little like the Bride of Frankenstein with better fashion sense. "Stress will do that," I remind my reflection. The girl in the mirror shakes her head at me. She's right; I'm an idiot. As I shamble off to bed, I vow that tomorrow, I will be less stupid.

I wake up early on Tuesday morning, get dressed, eat breakfast, and head out the door before Dad even wakes up. I want to talk to him about the personal revelations of my own stupidity, but I think I'll wait until I've had some time to become one with my dumbness.

At school, Becca's already waiting for me at the drama building. "Morning," she says, chomping her way through a breakfast burrito.

I lean next to her against the cool stucco. "What are we going to do about our parents?"

"Hmmmf." All I hear is burrito babble. She gestures for me to wait a minute while she swallows the huge bite she just took. "First of all, we're not going to do anything. I really think this will all blow over. Let's think about it." She belches and throws the burrito wrapper into a trash can painted with little wide-eyed panthers, our school mascot. "Thea is artistic and flaky. Your dad is scientific and . . . well, kind of flaky. But other than flakiness, they have very little in common. Once they realize this, the whole thing will be over on its own, and we won't have had to do anything." She gives me a self-satisfied smile.

"What about Melvin?"

She dramatically flops over at the waist like a tragic, spike-haired rag doll. "Melvin!" she screams. "He is driving me crazy and he's only been here, like, a day."

"What did he do? What did he want?"

She straightens out, shakes off whatever anger she's feeling, and smiles broadly. "As I said, he's decided that he and Thea should get back together. Horrible idea. She told him it was ridiculous, and asked why he'd driven all the way down to San Diego without calling first. He said he'd had an epiphany and that it couldn't wait. He's full of it."

"So, that's not why you think he's here?"

She donkey honks again. "Please. Melvin have an honest motive? He's a moviemaker, for God's sake. His job is lying to people."

The curb at the front of the school is getting more and more crowded with kids, and out of the milling bunch Evie and Amber navigate toward us. "Morning," Evie says.

"Tell them!" Amber says excitedly. Since Amber's gone black goth, she very rarely gets excited about anything except dark poetry and depression medication, but today she's perky. Perky!

Evie beams at us. "Okay, you two," she says, her Australian accent getting a bit thicker with her excitement. "I've found a way to make sure that Geek Prom will be the event of the decade."

"Wow, a little ambitious, aren't we?" Becca arches an eyebrow. Ambition is usually her department. Maybe it feels weird for her to be out-ambitioned by an amateur.

Amber is practically jumping up and down, her creepy skull earrings bouncing happily off her earlobes. "Evie's been chatting with some friends in Australia, and they have an idea about how we can get people to actually hold Geek Proms at other locations in the world, patch in to our conferencing equipment, and then we'll have, like, five dances going on at once! They wouldn't just be attending our dance, they'd be having an extension of the event in their own locations, so we could attend theirs, too."

"Could I dance with someone from Bulgaria, hypothetically?" Becca asks. "It's always been a secret desire of mine."

"I don't really have a lot of Bulgarian connections, but we could try," Evie says, grinning. The bell rings, and amidst general chatter about virtual proms, we all head off to our first classes. I, however, am not as bubbly as I appear to be.

As excited chatter of my friends washes over me, I get a cold feeling in the pit of my stomach. If we make this event the event of the decade, there is no possible way to skip it, or move it, or make it go away. Now that Evie has introduced an even bigger plan than Becca's (is that possible?), there is literally no going back.

And, of course, this leaves me with a huge dilemma, an even bigger dilemma than I had before. If Fletcher won't budge on attending the "real" prom, and I can't avoid attending our big fat Geek Prom, how can I be in two places at once? Maybe if I could somehow bump into a wizard somewhere between first and second period . . .

Instead, I bump into Fletcher. Literally. Trying to make sense of a handout on literary terms, I slam right into him, sending my papers and backpack cascading to the dirt. Sadly, the only thing I can concentrate on is how he smells. That's right. The primal pheromones of our ancient ancestors rise up and all I can think about is how I want to burrow my face into his chest and inhale until I pass out.

He's bending over, picking up my stuff as I try not to allow my traitorous knees to buckle. "Hey," he says softly. "Must've been something really important there. You actually made physical contact with me."

My cheeks go red, and I feel the heat of the blush rising like I'm an organic thermometer. "It's good to see you," I stammer.

"Right." He grins and loops my backpack over one of my shoulders, patting it paternally. "I'm assuming we're still seeing each other, yes?"

"Yes." Mmmm. Boy smell. I want to roll around in it like a puppy in wildflowers.

"I haven't heard from you, though," he says as he puts an arm around me and walks me in the direction of my second-period class.

"I've been busy," I say thickly.

He doesn't answer, but all too soon we're at my class, and he lets go. "Well, can I see you after school?"

My nose and my tummy are conspiring with each other against my brain. The argument goes something like this: The nose says, "We have to smell him some more," while the tummy says, "He makes me feel all fuzzy and warm," and then the brain butts in, screaming, "You guys are all wimps! If you give in every

time you come within a foot of him, what chance do I have?"
And then the nose and tummy vote the brain down and tell it to
take a long, hot bath with a cup of herbal tea, and to just shut up
already.

"So?" he asks, unaware that I was just in a three-way conversation with several body parts.

"Sure." The brain is still screaming at me, but I ignore it. It's
kind of a bully, really. "But let's meet at the baseball field instead of at the Rock." Ah. The brain gets onboard and pitches
in something useful. Can't risk having Becca and Fletcher run
into each other at this point, can we? As Euphoria said, I should
just string this thing out for as long as I can, and maybe by the
time the dances roll around, I'll have a solution that will keep
me from being killed by anyone.

"Baseball field it is," he says, flashing me a freckly smile. He
bends down and gives me a quick peck on the neck that sets my
whole body to vibrating like an urgent cell phone call.

5

ATTACK OF THE TEENAGED LUST MONSTER

(or Three Shelbies and a Spiderweb)

I wade through the rushing river of teenaged bodies as I make my way to the field after school. It's an unpleasantly hot day, and even though I'm dressed in a cool cotton shirt and a short skirt, sweat trickles down my back.

Avoiding the other Queen Geeks is tough because I know they'll be looking for me. Geez, it sounds like I'm on the run from the law or something. Honestly, the whole conflict has made me feel like something of a criminal; I'm not a good liar, and knowing that I can't commit totally to either side has made me feel like I'm being dishonest with both.

Fletcher is leaning against the backstop, and little swirls of tan dust dance near him in the hot wind. "Hey," he says, walking forward to meet me at the pitcher's mound. He leans down and catches me in a long, sweet kiss, and I totally forget for a moment that it's hot, that there's weather, or that I have any problem whatsoever.

"So . . ." He smiles adoringly at me, his green eyes crinkling at the edges. "Want to hit the malt shop, Scooby-Doo?"

We link arms and start to walk toward the street. I lean into him, enjoying how our bodies fit together like puzzle pieces. "Too hot. Let's just go find a nice glacier to park under."

"Not a lot of glaciers in Southern California," he points out sensibly. "We could go to my house."

I've only been to Fletcher's house a few times, mostly on our way to somewhere else, never as an end destination, really. Today, the idea really spooks me. "Your house?" I squeak.

"It's cheaper than the mall." We've never walked to his house; he steers me toward a side street that I haven't traveled down before. "Nobody's home, anyway. We can hang out undisturbed."

All kinds of thoughts are fighting in my head, and the battlefield is crowded and getting bloodier by the second. In my mind I see Becca, hands on hips, glaring at me as if I've betrayed her. Then I see my dad shaking his head as if I'm really stupid to even think of going to a guy's house with him *when no one is home*. Then I see Euphoria working her claws up and down like the old robot on *Lost in Space*, yelling, "Danger, Shelby Chapelle!" My mental self confronts the three of them. "Danger? Absurd. Fletcher's about as dangerous as dryer lint."

"Hmmm?" Fletcher murmurs. "Did you say something about dryer lint?"

"Huh?" I hadn't realized that my psychotic mental images

had worked their way out through my mouth. "Dryer lint? That's silly."

We walk for maybe ten minutes, and then he stops in front of his nice, yellow one-story house with a well-trimmed yard and a big oak tree in front. "Not exactly Superman's Fortress of Solitude, but we can probably get at least an hour of peace before anybody else shows up."

Inside, my eyes adjust to the dimness: I have time to actually check out the rooms instead of just rushing through or waiting in the front hallway like I usually do. As usual, the place is neat, full of dark wood antique furniture, and the room smells of lemon wax. Parked near a sliding glass patio door, an ebony grand piano crouches like an oversized black lab waiting to fetch a ball. Although it's been there every time I've visited, I've never bothered to ask why. "Who plays piano?"

"I took lessons for about five years." Fletcher sits at the bench, pulls me down next to him and begins to caress the ivory keys, picking out a pretty tune. The warmth of his arm where we touch seems to leave a mark on me.

"Wow, you're pretty good." I marvel at the way his slender fingers glide over the cream-and-black field of piano keys, but he abruptly stops playing and closes the lid.

"I've never given you the official tour," he says. "I guess we've never really come over here without rushing off to somewhere else, huh? Now you can see everything more clearly."

What I see clearly is that Fletcher and I are alone, and that thought keeps pounding against my brain like one of those paddle balls on a rubber string. "How long will we be alone?"

I ask, sounding like Little Red Riding Hood confronting a hungry wolf. What is wrong with me? I think I must be the most paranoid person ever born. Fletcher, the kindest and most decent guy I've ever met, would never do anything but respect me. So why do I feel shaky about being alone in the house with him?

"I don't think anybody else is here at the moment." He checks the dining room and listens for a moment. "Nope. Mom's gone, Dad's at work, and my sister has practice. It's just us. Are you hungry?" He heads for the kitchen.

"Uh, sure." If we're eating, he can't really try anything, right? I imagine us dunking cookies and milk, and him lunging across the table at me, crumbling innocent Toll House yummies and spilling milk everywhere.

Fletcher is submerged in the refrigerator. "Diet Pepsi?"

"Sure." At least that won't really leave a sticky spot if we spill it, I figure. The paddle ball continues to thump incessantly in my brain.

He hands me a can of soda and pops one open for himself. "Chips?"

I nod. He pulls a crinkly bag of potato chips from a cupboard, pours a bunch into a green plastic bowl, and motions for me to follow him. Down a dimly lit hallway, he points to several doors. "That's Mom and Dad's room, the bathroom, Denise's room, my room—" Does he pause when he says "my room"? Is there some dramatic message I'm supposed to get from that?

"It's nice" is all I say after I take a swig from my can of Pepsi, and we head back to the living room.

He motions to the sofa, a green tapestried thing with over-stuffed cushions. I sit as far to one end as I can.

"Do I smell bad or something?" He sits next to me, and I feel even more nervous. Those images of my dad and Becca and Euphoria pop up again, all giving me disapproving looks. What am I thinking, being alone in this guy's house with him? They all shake their heads at me, and Euphoria holds up a photo of me, pregnant.

"Ah!" I scream and jump off the couch as if I sat on an electric eel. I spill the Pepsi all over my lap and on the nice silver carpet. I'm an exceptional houseguest, especially if you're looking for someone to begin demolition for a remodel or something.

"What happened?" Fletcher darts into the kitchen and comes back with two towels. He hands me one, and gets down on his hands and knees and starts dabbing at the carpet with the other. "You acted like somebody stuck you with a tack or something."

As I stare at his curly red hair and watch his muscular arms dabbing away at my soda stain, I realize suddenly why I am afraid of being alone with him. It's not because of him. It's because of me.

I lower myself to the floor and catch his hand as he dabs. He looks up, surprised. "What's up? Am I doing it wrong?"

I just put a finger to his lips, lean in, and kiss him. Blue electricity courses through my body, like someone just threw a switch and all of the nerves that had been asleep are suddenly awake. He mumbles feebly in protest, but I just keep lip-locking him, pull him to the floor, and—with a hand on each of his shoulders—I drag him down so he's lying flat on the floor and I'm sitting on top of him. We're not just kissing, we're practically exchanging respiratory systems. He clutches my back and pulls me toward him, so now we're horizontal, my face buried in the musky vanilla scent of his neck, his face, his chest. His hands are caressing my back, slowly, gently, almost hypnotically, and suddenly, all I hear is a rushing wind, some thunderous pounding of blood blocking out any other sound, any sense—

Now, as this happens, there is a part of me screaming and jumping up and down. I see her clearly in my mind: She's scared and lonely, and wears baggy pajamas all the time. Her hair is never combed. Even as I search Fletcher's mouth hungrily, this other Shelby is pounding on the inside of my head, telling me that I'm stupid and too young, and that boys all want one thing, and that everyone will know if we do anything.

As I watch this melodrama behind my eyes, another Shelby shows up. She's wearing fishnet stockings, a black leather mini, and high heels. Her midriff shows, and her breasts are encased in a fire-engine-red halter top. Her hair is even redder than mine, and her makeup is more expertly applied. She simply kicks the pajama-wearing Shelby behind the knees and shoves her aside. Grinning, she says, "Go for it, girl. You're only young once." Sexy saxophone music starts to pulse in my brain, with a hypnotic electronica beat, and my mental Shelby starts to dance a sensuous belly dance.

"Shelby?" Fletcher's muffled voice brings me back to reality. He's got me by the wrists, and he's holding me at arm's length. "Uh, what are we doing?"

"Hmm?" The music in my head abruptly scratches to a stop, like the needle being pulled from a vinyl album on an old turntable.

I focus on Fletcher and notice that I am sitting on top of him. In my skirt. Which is hiked up almost to my tummy. I am officially a slut.

I jump off of him as if I've been touching a live wire in a full bathtub. "Hey," I say weakly.

Fletcher looks stunned and confused. "What—" he starts to ask, but the front door opens and his sister, Denise, clumps into the house.

I pull my skirt down so it looks more respectable (although I don't deserve respect) and I smooth out my wild hair (although it doesn't deserve to be smoothed). I don't even know what to say.

"Hi, Denise," Fletcher says too loudly. His sister, who's ten, glances at us, grunts, and heads for the PlayStation parked in front of the television. "Shelby, can we go outside for a minute?"

I nod numbly. I pack up my crazy pajama Shelby and my fishnet slutty Shelby and the three of us walk out the front door, embarrassed beyond belief.

Fletcher discreetly waits until we're outside before he addresses my obvious insanity. "What were you doing?" he says, half laughing. Scratching his head in bewilderment, he chucks me on the shoulder like a buddy. "Not fair, you know. You're too sexy to try stuff like that as a joke."

"I wasn't joking," I blurt out before I can stop myself. Geez, even with three of me I can't stop from saying stupid things.

I see the smile fade from Fletcher's face, and in his eyes I see that he gets it. He understands that I was serious. "Oh."

Words tumble out of my mouth. "I know what we said, that we wanted to go slow and everything." I stop and breathe, kind of choking on it. "But lately, it's like I can't stop touching you, I can't stop thinking about you, about how you smell, how you look, your arms, your hands. It's like I've got some disease."

"Thanks, that's very flattering." He sits down on a red porch swing, stares at the well-manicured lawn, and kicks against the banister. "A disease, huh? You do know how to make a guy feel good."

I flop down next to him on the swing. "No, I didn't mean . . . well, I did sort of, but what I meant was that lately, with all this stuff about the prom and deciding who to stand by, I can't stop thinking about you, about us. It's confusing me."

He turns and arches a red eyebrow at me. "Confuses you?"

"I just always felt like I could stop caring about you whenever I felt like it. But lately, it's like there are three of me, and one is afraid of you, and one wants to do awful, wonderful things to you, and then there's me. And I don't know what I want."

"Maybe I could just have a meeting with the one who wants to do the awful, wonderful stuff with me," he muses, rubbing his chin thoughtfully. I slap him on the arm. "Ow."

"I'm serious!"

He laughs, puts an arm around my shoulder, and then gets quiet. "I know you're serious, Shelby. I do understand how you feel, too. I've felt like that about you since we met. But . . ." His words trail off, and he swings gently, staring out at the street again.

"But what?"

Fletcher sighs heavily, as if I've just placed some incredible burden on his shoulders. "But I don't want you to . . . to make a mistake for the wrong reason."

"What would the wrong reason be?" I ask, feeling my face getting hotter. Slutty Shelby stands, hands on hips, defiant.

He doesn't look me in the eye, but studies his tennies. "It feels like this sudden change in temperature is due to the fact that you don't want this conflict between you, me, and Becca. So, you figure if you do something really drastic, that will take care of it. You won't have to choose. The choice will be made for you."

Pajama Shelby throws her hands over her head in a victory gesture, dances around in bunny slippers, and throws a bucket of cold water over slutty Shelby's head. I, meanwhile, choke back tears. "So, what are you saying?"

Fletcher closes his eyes, hits his head against the back of the porch swing numerous times, and then says, "I can't believe I'm saying this, but I think we should wait on anything physical until you're sure about why you want to go there."

"Why I want to go there?" I screech. I jump off the swing, a woman scorned. "I guess it doesn't occur to you that I just want you, does it? Or maybe you don't want me. That's it, isn't it? You're just trying to find a kind way to let me know that you like me, but not that way."

"Hey." His head snaps up, and he puts one hand up in a calming gesture. "Wait a minute. I never said—"

I kick at the swing and march off the porch, tears stinging my eyes. "Just leave me alone."

"Hey. Hey!" He runs after me, trying to catch up to me as I dash down the path and out to the street. His legs are longer, and despite the fuel of intense embarrassment, he outruns me within a few paces. He grabs my shoulders, turns me around, and peers into my face. "You think I'm not attracted to you?"

I don't say anything. What other answer could there be? I practically throw myself at him in the heat of passion and he doesn't take advantage of me. Obviously, he isn't interested.

"Could it possibly be that I respect you, and don't want to take advantage of you in a weak moment?" he asks, touching my cheek to wipe away the dampness.

"That's what guys say when they just aren't interested," I mumble, turning and marching toward the street.

"Shelby. Shelby!" he calls after me. I hear him groan in frustration, and I feel him watch me as I clomp away in a big huff. After a few seconds, I hear his door slam shut.

Well, congratulations, all the Shelbies say. *You've managed once again to screw everything up for all of us.*

It takes me about twenty minutes to walk home, and the whole time I can feel my face glowing red hot with embarrassment. I wonder if anyone has ever caused a car accident because of excessively bright blushing? People could see me and think I'm some sort of radioactive material, or an emergency vehicle with a silent siren. An emergency vehicle wearing a skirt.

Obsessive, stupid thoughts actually occupy your mind pretty effectively as you walk, so I'm home in no time. Becca and Evie are sitting on my porch swing drinking iced tea.

"Hope you don't mind. We kind of invited ourselves over," Becca says. Euphoria whirs out onto the porch with another frosty glass of her brew, and waits for me to take it.

"Don't mind at all," I say casually, hoping the stain of my intense blush isn't still lingering on my cheeks.

"Took you a while to get home," Becca observes as she sips from her glass. I grab my own tea, and lean against the white banister in front of them, trying to look like I'm not lying, which I am about to do.

"I had to get some tutoring." Duh! I really need to practice lying. That was not a good one.

"Tutoring." Becca's eyes narrow slightly; she's a lie-detecting cat and I'm the pants-on-fire mouse. "In what?"

To buy some time, I take a big sip of tea and then pretend to choke on it. Neither Becca nor Evie looks particularly concerned. Some friends they are; I could've died. After I've milked the fake choke as much as I can, I reply: "No, *I* was tutoring." Good save! I did do tutoring last year, even though I was a freshman. Maybe Becca won't remember that I absolutely refused to do it again this year since it mostly amounted to kids wanting me to do their homework for them.

"I thought you quit tutoring."

I look to Evie for some sort of support, but her face is a blank canvas. Finally, she says, "Good tea."

Becca jams the swing to a stop with one lime-green Converse-covered foot. "Stop the crap. I know you were at Fletcher's. I saw you walking to his house. You were in enemy territory."

"He's not the enemy." I feel my jaw set defiantly. Who is she to decide who is the enemy and who isn't? "And why shouldn't I go to his house?"

"Maybe I should just go . . ." Evie says timidly. Obviously, she isn't keen on being in the middle of a Queen Geek civil war. Neither am I, actually.

"It's okay. Stay." I sigh heavily, take another drink of tea, and rub the cool condensation from the glass on my hot forehead. "Here's the thing: I just attacked Fletcher. I mean, I practically assaulted him. I was like a she-devil of lust angling for fresh meat."

The jaws of both girls drop simultaneously like something from an old Looney Tunes cartoon. If their eyeballs could zip out on little springs, they would.

"She-devil of lust?" Becca asks, all trace of resentment gone. Juicy gossip is much more fun than an internal feud. "What happened? Did he start it?"

Evie shakes her head, and shifts uncomfortably. "Maybe I really should go. I don't think I'm old enough for this conversation."

"Nothing happened!" I screech, a bit too loudly. "But that wasn't because of me. I jumped him and had him in a lip-lock that could've bruised his tonsils!"

Becca shakes her head and eyes me quizzically. "You attacked him? At his house? This just doesn't sound right."

I explain to them about the theory of the three Shelbies, and how the one in the fishnets was really the one who did all the lusty pouncing.

"I don't think having multiple personalities is going to be a form of birth control or anything," Becca says dryly. "Even if it was that other girl's fault, it's your body. I'd suggest you gag her and put her in a closet somewhere." She pauses and sips. "But was it good?"

I can't deny it. "It felt like blue electricity was zipping around my arms and legs and head, and even though my brain knew that it wasn't a good idea, something inside me just kept pushing. If he hadn't stopped me, I don't know what would've happened. And then he totally insulted me. And I left."

This gets Evie's attention. "He insulted you? What did he say?"

I explain Fletcher's theory of how I jumped him just so I could have some decision made and some choice taken away or something. "Isn't that stupid?"

Becca shakes her head wisely. "Ah, Grasshopper, not so stupid. I think he might be right. But we can't simply discount the fact that your hormones have a mind of their own." She stretches her long legs and says, "Let's go in the house and forage for food. And go over our plans for Operation Spider-web."

Anything that begins with the word "Operation" always makes my stomach churn. It means that whatever plan we were working on just got bigger. By bigger, I mean that there are large pieces of paper (like the kind on easels at business meetings) with elaborate charts in various serious-looking colors. The dining room looks like the central staging area for the rebel attack in *Star Wars*, minus the talking aliens.

"Uh . . . don't you think we should wait until we have everyone together to go over this?" I ask lamely, hoping for a reprieve. Euphoria rolls in with a plate of little sandwiches minus the crusts. "Egg salad," she sings. Evie and Becca hungrily gulp down a couple of the miniature munchies.

"How long have you guys been working on this?" It's incredibly detailed; there's one spreadsheet filled with names and e-mail addresses of people from all over the world, and what looks like some kind of mechanical diagram with technical notes that I am unable to read. "Are we planning to overthrow the government or something? If we are, I need to go shopping for better shoes."

"Planning is critical to something like this," Evie says with her Australian spy voice. "In order to make it a success, we need to coordinate events in various locations exactly. And we need our contacts to organize on their ends as well."

"I'd love to see them all organizing on their ends," I joke lamely. Nobody laughs.

Becca and Evie are embroiled in the diabolical planning of this Operation Spiderweb, and their enthusiasm washes over me like lukewarm bathwater. I just can't get revved up about anything after the way I behaved. I mean, if I am so weak that I actually attack Fletcher once I get him alone, it means that maybe Becca is right. Maybe I am letting my hormones walk all over me. Is that even physically possible?

"Earth to Shelby." Becca waves a silver-ringed hand in front of my face. "What do you think?"

"About what?" I squint at her, fuzzy around the edges from too much pondering.

She sighs heavily, letting me know that my preoccupation with my psychotic lust is putting a crimp in her day. "Let it go, already," she snaps. "You are not the first girl whose judgment has been impaired by boy sweat. I, myself, have been tempted to stray from the path of righteousness and onto the road of ruin and lost panties. However, I have not acted on this, and neither will you."

"What about Carl?" I ask, trying to change the subject.

"What about him?" she asks casually as she scribbles with a red marker, filling in a portion of a pie chart.

"Were you ever really tempted to . . . to attack him?" I ask. Evie, who is leaning over a poster paper bubble graph of what looks like every country in the world, snickers slightly, then turns it into a cough. "And what are you laughing at?" I ask frostily.

Evie looks up, her dark eyes peering over the tops of her rectangular glasses. "I just think it's funny how you all pretend that you are so strong and above the whole male-dependence thing, but look what we're spending our time talking about! I think the perfect cure for this obsession is to focus on the task at hand: How to create a worldwide event that will blow everything else out of the water, prom-wise."

I turn to Becca. "Have you sucked out her brain and made her your zombie? She sounds just like you."

"Hey," Evie says, less hurt than amused. "That's not fair. I've always been like this. It just happens that I ran into all of you and now I have someone to share my insanity with."

I suppose she's right. If we were really all that free of boy obsession, we wouldn't be spending so much time talking about them, thinking about them, dreaming about them, imagining them in tight Speedos. Okay, maybe that last part is just me. The point is, I realize that I've been so focused on trying to prove that Fletcher is no big deal that I've made him a big deal. What if he's right? What if my attraction to him is simply a way to distance myself from my friends so I don't have to take sides? So they'd reject me instead of me *not* choosing them? How is it possible that my psychology is this twisted before I hit twenty? Some therapist is going to make a lot of money on me someday.

"Fine," I say to no one in particular. "What is my job, Queen Geek?"

Becca slings an arm around my shoulder and sits me down in front of her laptop. "Your job, oh Princess of Lust, is to do a search on Web technology and find out where we can purchase the items on this list." She hands me a legal pad with three cramped pages of writing.

"You seriously think there's any way we can buy any, not to mention all, of this stuff?" I laugh. "Okay, so who's delusional now?"

Evie and Becca share a glance that makes me extremely uncomfortable. I suddenly feel like the odd geek out, like they're part of some supersecret subgroup and I'm not cool enough to be in the loop. Last year, I was one of the people in the supersecret loop. I don't like being loopless.

"Paying for the equipment shouldn't be a problem," Becca says breezily.

"And why is that? Have you sold a kidney or something?"

"No need." Becca grins with the satisfaction usually only seen on the faces of cats after they eat someone's pet parakeet. "I've got Melvin."

I stare blankly at her. "Melvin."

"Melvin." Becca plops onto my sofa and puts her hands behind her blond-spiked head, leaning back like someone who has just been told they never need to worry about anything ever again. "I told you he's in town."

"Yeah, but you hate him," I say a bit more forcefully than I intend to. "Would you seriously borrow money from him?"

"Nope," she says, the cat-grin spreading so that it seems to eat up her ears. "He's giving it to me. Free. No strings attached."

"Listen to yourself," I snap at her. " 'No strings attached.' There's no such thing!"

"Now wait a minute," Evie interrupts. "Maybe he's just realized how valuable his relationship with his daughter is. Would you consider any favor a father does for his daughter to have 'strings attached'? Maybe he's just trying to rebuild their relationship."

I'm ready to bean her with a rotten kiwi, I swear. I try to keep my temper though. "Listen," I say through clenched teeth. "Sure, parents do favors for their kids. But he's clearly trying to buy off Becca. Of course, I don't know how he thinks he's going to rebuild his family when he lives in Hollywood and hardly ever sees either of them."

"Well, he did rent an apartment a block away from the house," Becca says quietly, not meeting my eyes.

"And why would he do that?" I ask, not really wanting to know.

"Because," she says, her eyes flashing at me defiantly, "he wants Mom back for some ridiculous reason. And I intend to benefit from that."

6

SOUL-SUCKING DEVIL DADDY

(or Foolish Film Folly)

The day you realize that your best friend has actually sold her soul (or given it away, or traded it) is a sad day. Innocence is lost on such a day. And the likelihood of eating high-calorie foods rises exponentially.

After Becca drops the bombshell that Melvin has squatted in her neighborhood and is stalking Thea, I don't say much else. We work on the graphs for a while, but then I think they sense that I'm detached, and they both realize they have some phantom homework assignment looming, so Becca decides to go with Evie over to Briley's house next door to work on the phantom homework. I realize that this is just code for trying to ditch me.

They leave, and as the door swings shut, silence closes in around me like a noose. In order to make the noose looser, I head for the kitchen and dig out a carton of ice cream (thank the gods of dairy!) and a big spoon. After considering leaving off the fudge sauce (but only for a half second), I spoon a bunch of the gooey brown sweetness directly into the carton of butter pecan and eat from the container. It's an eat-from-the-container kind of day.

Becca's dad is trying to get back with her mom. My dad is in like (or in love) with Becca's mom. There is some seriously nasty geometry forming here that makes the Bermuda Triangle look like something Elmo drew on *Sesame Street*. My dad will be heartbroken, of course; he hasn't been seriously interested in anyone since my mom died, and now that he's really considered giving his heart to someone, he's going to get it ripped out. Ripped out, stomped on, and paid for.

The naive section of my mind argues that Becca has nothing to do with this. The grown-ups make their own decisions; she can't really influence who likes whom any more than our parents can influence who we feel attracted to. But if Melvin has moved in somewhere and is hovering like a big hairy spider, and Becca is planning on getting money out of it, doesn't that sort of imply that she's going to help him? And that she's going to basically stab my dad in the heart with a steak knife?

The shock of the whole thing wears off a bit with the cold slap of ice cream. I pick up my cell and ring Becca, but she doesn't answer. I know she's next door; I'd just have to go over there and face her, but I can't. I just feel like somebody punched me in the gut or stabbed *me* in the heart with a steak knife.

Euphoria rolls in with the dirty dishes and notices that I'm not my usual chipper self. "Something wrong?" she asks casually, pretending like she's not fishing for information.

"Why?" I ask, trying to form words around the mounds of melting ice cream.

She wordlessly picks up the half-empty carton, and, in mute disapproval, waves it at me.

"I was hungry," I say defensively as I retrieve the container from her claw.

"What happened?" She scoots away on her rollers so I can't quite grab the ice cream. "I'm not giving this back until you talk."

"Fine!" Blackmailing robots. That just fits my life perfectly. I tell her the whole story, and end with, "And now I feel like we've all been stabbed in the heart with steak knives."

"That's a bit of an exaggeration," she replies. "But I see your point." She rolls back and forth across the kitchen floor (her version of pacing) and I hear her processors humming. "I know what you should do."

"You do?" I feel hopeful until I remember her previous bit of advice, which was to just ignore the problem until it was too late to do anything, and then run for a bomb shelter to avoid the emotional fallout.

"You tell your father that this Melvin person is in town and is trying to steal his woman."

"I don't think Thea is *his* woman," I say, shuddering. "That sounds so caveman."

"Regardless of what you call it, men all have a need to protect what belongs to them. If he considers her his woman, then he'll try to protect her. So, as I said before you interrupted, you tell your father about this other man. You lead him to believe that Becca's mother is not interested, but that he won't leave her alone. He will be moved to protect her, and a confrontation will occur." I wait for her brilliant ending to this amazing scenario. She says nothing more, just sits there buzzing happily.

"And?"

"And what?" She opens a cupboard and begins to inventory our cereals. "We need Cheerios."

"Listen, Euphoria, I appreciate your advice, but it would be even more helpful if you actually finished a thought!" I sound nastier than I intend to, but I'm frustrated. And on a sugar high. "What happens after this confrontation?"

"Special K," she murmurs as she closes the cupboard and turns to me. "Well, of course, the woman must choose. And if you think Becca is trying to manipulate her mother for personal gain, then it's your duty to make sure your father wins, otherwise true love dies."

I should never let her listen to pop radio. She starts sounding like Celine Dion if she spends too much time hearing sappy song lyrics. I swear, I think she believes that's how human beings really go about dealing with relationships. She has no idea that it's much messier and makes much less sense.

"So you think I should tip off my dad and get him to scare Melvin back to Los Angeles," I muse out loud.

"It might not be such a bad idea," she says, trying to shrug her nonexistent shoulders.

I throw the container of ice cream away and stalk off to my room to brood alone. Lying on my bed, I stare up at the Day-Glo stars plastered on my ceiling, and I remember when Dad and I put them up, one or two every night, trying to make the patterns of constellations. There's the constellation Mickey Mouse, and there's the constellation Peanut Butter Sandwich. Oh, those parents grow up so fast.

My cell buzzes in my pocket, shocking me out of reliving the good old days of my recent childhood. "Yes?" I answer coldly.

"So, what is with you?" Becca's voice crackles with anger. "If you have a problem with me, just tell me what it is."

"Are you alone? I don't want Evie in our private conversations about our parents' sex lives."

Becca snorts. "Never say 'sex' and 'parents' in the same sentence. You'll go to hell." She pauses, sighs, and adds, "Okay, so just tell me. I really want to know."

"Okay." I swallow, knowing that what I'm about to say could get me banished from the Queen Geeks forever. Or for at least as long as Becca decides to remember she's mad at me. "I think it's wrong of you to take money from Melvin when you hate him."

Silence on the other end. I hear her sigh. "Yeah, I know."

"So why are you doing it?"

A pause again. "I guess because I feel like he owes me. Bigtime."

"And so you're going to reclaim your inheritance by screwing with my dad's love life?"

"Hey, wait a minute," she snaps. "Don't forget it was me who told you about the thing between our parents. God, that sounds *so* wrong."

"Right. But if Melvin is back in the picture, my dad will probably get booted to the curb, right?"

"Well, you don't have a lot of faith in your dad's sex appeal. And again, that sounds *so* wrong." Becca laughs, a slight chuckle in place of her donkey honk, gut-buster laugh. The situation, after all, isn't all that funny. "Honestly, I know it's sleazy, but I'm just playing Melvin for money. I know that Thea will have absolutely nothing to do with him. She is so angry with him that she doesn't even want his chi poisoning her hallway, let alone her bedroom."

"Chi?"

"You know, spiritual energy. All that stuff she's into with the Sufi dancing and feng shui and tofu."

"I eat tofu. Does that mean I have chi?"

Becca sighs, trying to be patient with me, the innocent, ignorant friend. "We all have chi, Shelby. You really need to take a world cultures class or watch the Travel Channel or something."

"Which doesn't change the fact that we have a problem here. And you're being sleazy." I never thought I'd have the opportunity to call my best friend "sleazy," but here we are. "And how does Melvin propose to pay you off, anyway? And for what?"

I hear Becca crinkling the Oreo package again on the other end of the line. "It's for the greater good, Shelby. He's going to help us finance Geek Prom by sponsoring a fund-raiser."

"A fund-raiser." I was kind of thinking he would write a blank check, but now I see that would be too obvious. Fund-raiser implies that there will be work, and lots of it. And guess who will be doing the heavy lifting? Not Becca. "A fund-raiser?"

Becca laughs, a conspiratorial giggle that she uses to try to make me feel like I'm on the inside of some great scheme. The truth is, I just feel like she's telling me just so I don't mess it up. "He's going to have a movie coming out in a couple of weeks, so he's going to designate one screening as our fund-raiser. And when it's all over, he'll realize it was pointless, and that neither my mom nor I like him at all, and he'll zip back to Los Angeles in a huff. He'll probably start dating one of the Olsen twins or something to get back at us."

"And in the meantime, all the people you love just get screwed, and that's okay because it's for the greater good?"

I hear her shifting position on the bed, springs squeaking slightly, Oreo wrappers crinkling in protest. "In the end, it won't hurt anybody, and it will help us do what we want to do. All I need is for you to support me on this, even if you don't to-tally agree. I'm asking you, as your best friend: Will you please just help and not blab about the whole thing to your dad?"

She's pulled the best friend card, which means I have no choice but to agree, or lose the position as official best friend. Am I ready to do that? We've been through a lot together, Becca and I: She's the only person I've ever met who I feel really under-stands me, and I'd never really had any good friends before I met her. Isn't that worth taking a risk? And honestly, how hurt could my dad be by this? Wouldn't he just laugh at stupid Melvin and his overflowing wallet? And Thea. She's not a total idiot or any-thing. She'd see through this in a heartbeat, and ignore Melvin's feeble attempt to get her back. So, all in all, things would be back to the way they were, but we'd have accomplished our goal, and Becca would be happy (at least until the next big thing comes along).

Reluctantly, I agree. "Okay. I'll keep my mouth shut. I'll help with the fund-raiser. I'll even help with Geek Prom. But I don't want my dad to get hurt. He's been through enough already. If it looks like that's happening, I'm going to spill my guts and he's going to find out everything."

"Hey, no big deal," she says, her voice bright and cheery. "Like I said, Thea will never fall for it, and so they'll probably just have a good laugh over it anyway while Melvin worships from afar with his Visa card." She sighs again, as if she's winding up to say something important, but then there's just a big chasm of silence between us. We never have nothing to say to each other; since we met, we've been talking nonstop. But here we are, phone line crackling, and no conversation to deaden the noise.

"Were you going to say something?"

"Uh . . . no. I guess I'll just see you tomorrow, huh?"

The silence again, and something unspoken between us. I'm not brave enough to mention that I've noticed it. "Yeah. To-morrow."

"Queen Geek meeting Friday, don't forget." The cell goes dead. I go back to picking out lonely constellations on my ceiling, the same thing I did before I met Becca and actually had someone to talk to.

I spend the next few days avoiding my dad at home and Fletcher at school. If I don't see Dad, I figure I don't have to keep secret any crucial information on his love life. This isn't that tough to do, because he's hardly home at all. Euphoria notices that I'm out of the house quite a bit, and by Friday morning, she's so suspicious that she corners me between the toaster and the low-fat milk.

"What is going on?" she demands, green eye lights blinking angrily. Okay, well I probably just read that anger into the blinks, but she still looks pissed.

I stuff a whole piece of toast in my mouth and motion that I can't talk because my mouth's too full. Then I point to the kitchen clock, shrug my shoulders, and seem regretful that I have to leave before I have a chance to engage in what will probably be a very uncomfortable conversation.

As I try to muscle past her, she blocks my way with one steel claw. "Oh, no. You're not going anywhere until you tell me what is going on."

I swallow the dry toast, and resign myself to the fact that my robot is a big snoop. "I promised Becca I wouldn't talk about Melvin. Dad isn't supposed to know about it. So I've been hanging out at the library after school, and then at different coffee places, hoping I won't run into anyone I know. May I be excused?"

Euphoria considers my explanation and slowly retracts her claw. "You can't avoid him forever, you know. And what about Fletcher? I haven't heard you talk about him, and I haven't seen him all week."

I shrug uncomfortably. The truth is, I have been studiously avoiding him, too. After that full-frontal assault I staged at his house, I turn scarlet just thinking about him. Joining a witness protection program starts to seem like a great idea. Maybe a witless protection program would be more my speed.

I grab an apple from the counter, and rub the little bridge between my eyes where a headache is already starting to form. "Fletcher's been very busy. He just hasn't had time to see me."

"That's funny, considering he's called several times and actually came over here yesterday while you were hiding out."

"He did?" My heart skips a beat involuntarily. It doesn't know enough to be embarrassed by my lust-driven pouncing. "Did he leave a message or anything?"

"Hmmm." Euphoria just pivots on her wheels and rolls toward the dishes. Even somebody made of metal with no real emotions finds me infuriating. I have no chance with real people.

I barely arrive on time to school, which is just as well since then I don't have to run into anyone who might ask me something I don't want to answer. As lunch rolls around, though, my stomach starts doing flip-flops, and it has nothing to do with hunger. The Queen Geek meeting will be a real test of my ability to keep a poker face, and I have a feeling I suck at poker.

The room is already crowded by the time I arrive, so I sneak to the back. The regulars are there: Amitha, Caroline, Claudette, and about twenty or so other girls, most of whom I've seen before. Becca, Amber, and Evie are clumped at the front of the classroom while Elisa passes out some mint-green papers to every row of girls. I snag one as the stack comes back toward me. *Geek Prom Movie Night,* the flier reads. A big picture of a filmstrip with some B-list horror movie is centered in the middle of the flier, and underneath, somebody has written a description of the "fun-raiser." Fun-raiser? That's like something the Student Senate would put on their fliers, not us.

"Hey," Becca shouts above the din. "Let's get started. Shelby, come up front!" So much for going incognito.

As I shove past now-listening girl bodies up to the front of the room, Becca continues. "This will be the most awesome fund-raiser ever. We have a rich benefactor in the film industry who is going to designate one screening of his upcoming movie as our fund-raiser, with tickets selling for twenty dollars. With that money, we can buy or rent the equipment we need to do our remote setups for Geek Prom. We're inviting geeks from all over the world, and we are shooting for having the most people virtually to attend a prom ever!"

"Has anyone ever virtually attended a prom at all?" a mousy girl in front asks.

"Uh," Becca stammers, looking to Evie to field the question.

Evie jumps in as if she's been planning planetary takeovers all her life. "As far as I know, the only virtual proms have been on websites where people have avatars, alternative identities, and they chat and dance with characters. Nobody has ever done a virtual prom like this, as far as I can tell. Maybe we'll be the first! We're calling Guinness World Records for this one. And the fund-raiser will be a great way to publicize the event."

"Why doesn't this rich benefactor just give us the money instead of making us work for it?" Amitha, an Indian girl whose brother dates Elisa, pipes up.

"Maybe he wants us to build character," Elisa answers absently as she punches numbers into Wembley, her ever-present electronic personal data computer. "And actually, if we sell all the tickets we could sell, we'll make a lot more than he's going to spend to sponsor us with the film screening."

"How's that possible?" Amitha continues to prod. I guess maybe she doesn't like movies or something.

"Because the financial angel is a movie director. He has connections, and so he's sponsoring the screening in exchange for the publicity. We'll probably get national coverage."

The level of excitement and possibility has risen to where it's almost something you could touch. This happens every time Becca introduces some new, weird scheme that seems impossible, but given her track record, the Queen Geeks have now come to expect that no matter how crazy the idea sounds, she'll pull it off. I think if she told them she was going to plant a magic bean in the football field and that it would grow into a stalk that would poke a hole in a giant's jewelry box, they'd show up with buckets to collect the falling gemstones.

Amber raises her bangled arm to silence the chatter. Amazingly, it stops. Amber has clearly been working on her Emo superpowers. "Our goal is Geek Prom. With this fund-raiser, we'll be able to let people know about it, plus attract attention away from the stupid 'regular' prom."

"What's so bad about the real prom?" a blonde with oversized glasses and one wandering eye mutters. Unfortunately, she says it during one of those awkward pauses where no one is talking, so all eyes focus on her with varying degrees of contempt.

For a second, it looks like Becca is ready to unleash her spike-haired fury at wandering-eye girl, but then she stops and reconsiders. A lot of times, yelling at people you're asking to help you isn't a good personnel strategy. "What's your name?" Becca asks sweetly.

"Karen," the blonde answers, blinking slowly, lips pursing slightly as if she's readying an answer to an onslaught of questions.

"Karen," Becca repeats. "Well, Karen, here's what's bad about this so-called real prom: A lot of girls won't get to go. Guys won't ask them, and sure, they could go alone, but who wants to spend all that money on a stupid formal dress and then hang out by the snack bar all night alone?"

"I'd go with my friends," Karen says quietly, defiant. "I don't need a date to have a good time."

This is something of a major blow to Becca. I mean, one reason the Queen Geeks has become so popular is because one of our main focuses has been on the fact that we don't need guys to be happy or fulfilled. Of course, since I recently tried to tongue-maul my boyfriend against his will, I'm not sure whether I can still be in any group with that philosophy. I wonder if it shows? Do I have a scarlet letter above my lips or something? Anyway, the argument that the "real" prom hinges on dating rings kind of hollow.

Becca's lips have turned a bit white around the edges, a sure sign that she's getting pissed. She really doesn't like people questioning her brilliant, diabolical plans. But just when I think she might blow, Evie jumps in. "You could go to the regular prom without a date, sure," Evie says, nodding. "But can you wear your Skechers? Can you dye your hair any way you want? Can you party with people from Australia, and England, and Japan?

Can you pick the music and the food? Can it be *your* dance, and not something someone else planned?" A soft murmur in the room rises to a full-on chatter, and the girls are all in animated conversations, discussing whether or not they'd want Vienna sausages or sushi, punk or old school. Becca smiles triumphantly.

"Great," she says. "Now, if we could just have each one of you get into one of our groups to help with the planning . . . publicity is over there in the back with me, tech stuff is in front with Evie, Amitha is dealing with decorations by the door over there, and Elisa is working on music and food."

"I brought snacks, too," Elisa pipes up. "So, you'll all want to work for me. I take care of my minions."

The tide has turned; the members of the Queen Geek Social Club have decided that they do, indeed, plan to make the Geek Prom an event to remember. Little clusters of girls scatter to various corners to plot and plan the details that will make Geek Prom the amazing, memorable craziness that they've come to expect from Becca.

Before she heads back to the publicity group, Becca spares me a minute. "I didn't hear from you, so I didn't assign you anything particular to do." That statement kind of lingers in the air; we both know there's more to it than just the words. She softens a bit, and says, "Want to help with publicity?"

"Sure." I follow her to the back of the room, where she immediately takes command like a field general whipping troops into a frenzy. Meanwhile, I sort of hover at the back of the pack. Mostly, I'm thinking about Fletcher, which seems to be all I'm able to do lately. I drift away mentally, and see myself at a drive-in movie, parked in an old '57 Chevy convertible. Next to me is Fletcher, wearing a rolled up white T-shirt and jeans. His long legs are folded up over the shiny red vinyl steering wheel, and he leans against his freckly arms folded behind his head. "Great flick," he says, motioning toward the screen.

In my mind, I look up at the movie and notice that it's us. *We're* the movie. I see myself cornering Fletcher in his room, except that I'm wearing some sort of hookeresque blue tube top and a white lace miniskirt. White makes my hips look big, I notice. Even in a daydream I have a crappy body image.

"I don't think I own a white lace miniskirt," I mention as my dream Fletcher slips an arm around my shoulders. Back in the Chevy, I look down and notice I'm wearing some Doris Day–pink cardigan sweater, the kind with the little gold chain linking it below the neck. I am also wearing a poodle skirt, but instead of a poodle, there's a penguin stitched into it. The penguin winks at me, then goes back to being embroidery.

Now, in the movie in my mind, I've got Fletcher pinned to the floor, both my hands (manicured in Corvette red) anchoring both his hands to the rust shag carpeting. For the record, nobody has rust shag carpeting. I think it's just the one thing that should be featured on Tackiest Rooms in America, and since I've besmirched Fletcher's honor by attacking him, I guess rust shag carpet is what I deserve, rugburn-wise.

The mental movie shows a close-up of my big, fat, sucking lips trying to devour Fletcher's head. "Yuck!" I say, squeamish. Watching your own lips up close is kind of like studying those sucker fish who live in the cold, dark part of the ocean. You kind of know the things exist, but you really don't want to come face-to-face with them. "How did you stand it?"

Dream Fletcher laughs and turns to me. "It's not all black-and-white, you know." He motions to the penguin on my skirt. "Right?"

"Yep," the penguin says, nodding. This is extremely hard for it to do since it is in two dimensions. "Except for penguins, nothing is really black-and-white."

"And even you have an orange bill," Fletcher points out helpfully.

The penguin snorts, offended.

"So, what do you think?" Becca is saying to me. I focus, and her facial expression communicates that she thinks I'm a joker short of a full deck. Or a penguin short of a poodle skirt. Or something. "Are you with us?"

"In what sense?" I ask. The other girls in the group, including Caroline and Claudette, are all frowning at me, studying me for signs of dangerous insanity. "I'm fine. What were we talking about?"

After ten more minutes of frantic arguments over whether green or pink paper would be best for fliers, the bell mercifully rings. As I sling my backpack over my shoulder, Becca puts me in a friendly chokehold and noogies my head. "Where were you?"

"Hmm?"

"Back there, at the meeting. You were physically here, but mentally on vacation."

"Believe me," I reply as I head for the door, "I would not have chosen that particular daydream as a vacation spot."

I try to get away, but she falls in beside me. "Shelby, we really need to talk."

Hmm. Probably she's right. But I don't want to do it, not right now. "How about tomorrow?" I ask as we dodge the sea of babbling teenagers rushing to class, riding a nacho-and-energy-drink high that would last just until the next period started.

She ducks an empty milk carton that sails toward a trash can. "How about after school?"

I realize I can't get out of this, unless I want to torpedo whatever friendship we have left. "Okay." I sigh, stopping at my next class. "By the Rock."

"You sound so excited," she says, trying to sound light. I can tell, though, that there's something heavy between us, and so can she.

7

THE COW JUMPED OVER THE MELVIN

(or All Is Dangerous in Love and Art)

All through the afternoon, my stomach feels like it's home to a herd of caffeinated butterflies doing a conga line. The meeting with Becca makes me nervous. Isn't that screwed up? I mean, hanging with my best friend should be a treat, something to look forward to. But instead, I've got these stupid bugs dancing in my tummy.

When the bell signaling the end of school rings, I take a long time packing up my stuff. The teacher is actually ready to leave, and kind of shuffles papers on her desk while eyeing me suspiciously. Maybe she knows about the butterflies and she's afraid they might get loose and leave butterfly poop on her carpet or something.

I finally take off, waving halfheartedly as I swing out the door. Becca's leaning against the Rock, and the campus is pretty empty. I guess I took a really long time packing up.

"Hey," I say, in my cheerful, what-could-be-wrong voice.

"Hey," she answers back in her absolutely-nothing-could-be-wrong voice.

"I guess we're going to my house?" I trudge toward the street, head down, a plaid-skirted traitor in the game of friendship.

She skips toward me, and falls into step beside me. She's wearing high-top yellow Converse that clomp as she plants her big feet, one after the other, next to my smaller, less interesting appendages. "Your feet kind of look like aggressive bananas," I offer lamely.

"Thanks?" She grins at me, and I grin back. It feels very awkward.

We walk in silence for a couple of blocks, talking only to make fun of a giant billboard advertising a sports car that, apparently, will turn you into a blond goddess with ponderous cleavage if you buy it.

We get to my house, and take up residence on the old porch swing. I don't see Dad's car, so I guess he's out stalking Thea or something.

Becca swings her long legs out toward the banister, kicking against it with her banana-colored shoes. "So?" she finally says, still swinging.

"So?" I answer.

She abruptly shoves her foot against the rail and stops the swing. "Cut this out," she commands, her voice harsh.

"Cut what out?"

She turns to me, eyes blazing. "You've been acting like . . . like you're phoning it in. Like nothing matters to you anymore. Now, this can't just be about Fletcher. I know that's bugging you, but there's something else." She purses her lips and stares out at my magnolia tree before releasing the swing from its foot-anchor. "There's something going on with us."

I lick my lips and stare off into the yard also, trying to figure out how to say what I want to say. There's no good way to express it. I mean, the bottom line is that I think Becca's doing something kind of immoral, I guess. Immoral? Is that something that should even bother me? It's not my dad who's getting screwed over. Or maybe it is . . .

"Hello?" she asks, tapping my skull. "Would you like to involve anyone else in that conversation in your head?"

I swat at her hand as if it's a big, silver-ringed gnat annoying me. "I don't think I want to tell you what I'm thinking," I finally say.

"Why not?"

I sigh heavily, knowing that no matter how I handle it, this conversation will not end well. But what am I supposed to do? She wants the truth, and I guess I kind of owe her that, don't I? "Okay," I say quietly. "The whole thing with Melvin really bothers me."

For a second, she doesn't say anything at all. I feel a shocked silence occupying the space between us. "Melvin?"

I nod.

"What does he have to do with anything?" She aggressively stamps her foot at the banister, causing little flakes of paint to float to the floor.

"You're using him just to get what you want. I mean, I know you don't like him, and that he really treated you and your mom badly, but doing something like this is just . . . just . . ."

"This again?" Her voice gets louder, more angry. "What could you know about it, Miss Righteous? I mean, you've never had to deal with a parent who totally screws you over for money, so I guess you wouldn't understand."

"You're right, I don't understand." I feel my face turning a violent shade of red, and anger starts bubbling up from my gut. "I don't understand how someone who claims to be all about equality and fairness and helping people can turn around and manipulate her own father just so she can get something she wants!"

"Oh, and I'm the first kid who's ever done *that!*" she yells.

"Whether or not you're the first doesn't matter," I yell back. "*You're* doing it. And it's wrong, and I know that if you weren't blind because of your stupid obsession with being cooler and better than everyone else, you'd see it, too." She's fuming silently. "And another thing. We both know that my dad is starting to really like Thea. So, you're just going to encourage another guy to go after her, disregarding how my dad will feel."

"Another guy?" she squeals. "He's my father, Shelby! I guess it never occurred to you that maybe I'd want my parents to be together—" She stops as if someone has thrown an iron ball at her stomach and squished all the air out of her lungs.

"You . . . you want them to get back together?" I stare in disbelief. "So, this isn't just about the movie screening?"

Becca swings silently, her jaw set at a defiant angle. "I want a normal family. That's all. I'm sick of having no parents. Thea is like . . . like a dysfunctional big sister. I thought that if Melvin did something for me, maybe he really had changed, and maybe he really does want her back. And then, if he does, maybe we could actually have a normal family. And I also know this all sounds crazy, because knowing both of them, it could never be normal."

I'm blown away by this revelation. Becca wants to be . . . normal? I glance sideways at her blond spiky hair, her long calf with its dragon tattoo, her hip, edgy clothes, and I realize that, as in most things, I've been making assumptions that aren't necessarily correct. "I didn't know."

"I know you didn't." She sighs heavily, stands up, and leans against the porch pillar. "I'm a total mess."

"So, is the Geek Prom thing somehow linked to this new desire to be normal?"

Her eyes open wide, and she blinks at me, bewildered. "What? No, of course not. That's just because I want global domination."

"Good," I mutter. "At least my whole world hasn't disintegrated."

We decide to take a walk, so we are less likely to run into

any parental units or boyfriends. Moving targets are tougher to hit, you know. Cruising down the neat sidewalks in front of the perfectly manicured lawns, I wonder about why Becca would want to be "normal." I mean, this whole suburban perfection thing is like a stifling mask on who people really are, right? Why would someone like Becca want that?

"So, do you want Thea and Melvin to get remarried?" I finally ask as we kick a pebble back and forth down the sidewalk.

"I don't know," she moans. "He seems different now. He seems like he understands how to be—I don't know—a person."

"What was he before? A stalk of asparagus?"

"Ha." She flicks me on the head with her giant-sized fingers. "I mean that he's acting like a *decent* person. Trying to help his kid. Paying attention to Thea, and trying to help her with her art stuff. And they're a lot alike, really; she's artistic, and so is he, even though he makes schlocky horror films. I mean, it's still creative. Your dad is more scientific, and flaky, and I love him, but I just don't see them having a future together. I don't think he is Mr. Right as much as he is Mr. Right Here."

Mr. Right Here?! That's so insulting, but I don't say anything. In my mind, I'm wondering why Becca thinks she should decide who has a future with whom. I also have a really bad feeling in the pit of my stomach about all of this, and I'm afraid that it will all blow up in her face. But, being the chicken in a skirt that I am, I don't say anything.

After several awkward moments of studying the various gardening styles of my neighbors (those little lawn angels are really popular, I notice), I decide to change the subject. "What's with you and Carl?"

She growls. "He's still insisting on me going to that stupid prom with him." She aims her banana-shoe missile at an innocent pinecone lying in her path. "We haven't even seen each other for a week. He's called, but I never call back."

"Well, that's a great way to keep the magic happening," I say sarcastically.

"And what about you and Fletcher?" she snipes. "Have you talked to him about your full-frontal assault?"

A violent blush creeps up my cheeks without my permission. "I just haven't really run into him at school, to be honest."

She laughs mockingly. "Haven't run into him? You've been acting like he's got leprosy and you're afraid your lips will fall off if you even talk to him. I saw you run, *literally run*, across campus the other day when he waved at you. Don't you think he's getting a little suspicious of your Olympic-caliber avoidance?"

The sound of tires squealing breaks the peace of my boring neighborhood, and an engine revs until Thea screeches to a stop next to us. "Mom?" Becca tilts her head like a confused puppy who sees its sock puppet driving.

"Get in!" she yells over the knockety-knock of the untuned Jeep engine. Becca shrugs at me, and we head for the Jeep. It's better than continuing our pointless sarcastic battle.

Thea brushes stray strands of hair from her eyes, tucking them back under a lemon-yellow bandanna tied around her head. "Euphoria told me you were walking," she yells over the grind of the idling engine. "Melvin's in the hospital."

"What?" Becca's face goes pale. "What happened? Is he okay?"

"I think so," she says nervously. "He was trying to help me crate up a wall-sized abstract cow mosaic, and it fell on him. He lost his balance and fell, then hit his head on my African fertility sculpture. I don't think he broke anything, but he was knocked out for a couple of minutes, so I drove him to the emergency room—"

"Well, if he made it through the drive and never regained consciousness, I'm sure he's fine," Becca jokes.

"Just get in!" Thea screeches as Becca climbs into the front seat.

"Want to meet Melvin?" Becca asks, shrugging. "Come on. We could use the moral support." Why not? Although I'm not a big fan of hospitals, it might be a good way to check the likelihood of a Melvin/Thea reunion. I pull myself into the backseat.

Thea revs the Jeep and drives off down the street. "I feel so bad. He might have a broken rib or something! My art is dangerous."

Becca rolls her eyes and turns to give me a look of amused disgust. "Why was Melvin helping you with your cow mosaic, anyway?" she asks.

"Uh . . ." Thea stops at a red light and fiddles with the radio. "Want to hear some punk music?"

Becca covers Thea's hand with her own. "Mom?" she asks again.

The light changes, and Thea peels out. "I needed some help, and he was around, so I called him," she answers defensively.

"Hmm." From the backseat, I can see Becca smile slightly.

Thea takes us on Mr. Toad's Wild Ride to the ER, trying, I guess, to make sure there are more injured people for them to work on when we get there. Seriously, she is the worst driver I've ever seen, and I've ridden with teenagers. After several close brushes with death (one of which involves a petroleum tanker and a big sign advising DO NOT TAILGATE that I could read clearly while we were tailgating), we zoom into the hospital parking lot. I'm still vibrating, trying to navigate the parking garage on buzzy, wobbly legs.

Thea rushes to the elevator, and Becca is close behind. I'm trailing, since I can't feel my feet. They impatiently hold the door for me, and once I'm in, we start upward with a sterile swoosh and a blast of Metallica retooled to be elevator music. "That should not be legal," Becca mutters, gesturing to the speakers set into the walls.

Thea fidgets, watches the red digital numbers change from floor to floor, and finally we arrive at Floor 8, Home for Psychotic Victims of Ceramic Cow Attacks. (Actually, it's the orthopedic floor, but I like my name better.) "He's already been admitted?" Becca asks. "When did this happen, anyway?"

"This morning," Thea mumbles as she marches purposefully out of the Metallica music box.

Becca throws me a startled glance. "Does that mean—"

I shrug. "I don't know. Let's not assume." We follow Thea's

scent trail of paint thinner and patchouli until we reach a corner room, the bed hidden by a gray-and-pink curtain patterned with randomly formed amoeba shapes. (I kind of doubt that "amoeba" is a pattern they were going for, but I've taken enough science not to be fooled by attempts to make bacteria look stylish.) Thea reaches the room almost thirty seconds before we do, because she practically sprints to it.

When we part the amoeba curtain, she's grasping a man's thick, hairy paw in her own delicate, silver-ringed hand. She's removed the yellow bandanna, and her hair hangs in damp little curls around her flushed face. She looks like an English heroine in a tragic novel, except for the Chinese tattoo on her left bicep.

"How are you feeling?" she croons, utterly disgusting. Becca's face cringes in obvious pain.

"Ah, better," the man answers. Dark black hair pokes out from a large white bandage wrapped around his head. One leg is strung up and in a plaster cast. "They got me a little doped." I assume he's Melvin, and he's really nothing like I thought.

I'd pictured Melvin as this suave, kind of girl-crazy player cruising the Hollywood scene in search of loose women and fast-acting substances. I figured he had a lot of money, probably a goatee, maybe even a pierced ear, and even though Becca had said he was short, I figured he was one of those short, wiry guys, like the wrestlers—all compact muscle.

But the guy in the bed is nothing like that. The real Melvin is short, that's true; but I couldn't see anything that could really be defined as a muscle exactly. And there's no goatee; instead, he has this stubbly white-gray, steel-wool kind of beard that looks like it's afraid to really sprout. His face is thinner than I'd pictured, and his hazel eyes are kinder than I thought they'd be. I kind of want to hate him, but he actually looks nice, like a grandfather. A grandfather who steals your dad's girlfriend. It's no wonder I'm messed up.

"He's old, I know," Becca hisses in my ear. I swat at her to be quiet so I can hear the gripping dialogue.

"I feel *so* bad, Mel," Thea says softly. Her expression is . . . well . . . genuine, not like she usually looks. She looks like she really means it, as opposed to most of the time when she's talking to my dad and seems to be trying too hard. I feel a little stab in my tummy, a stab of worry and pain, and the unmistakable knowledge that someone I love is going to have his heart ripped out.

Becca's dad (he quickly becomes that in my mind) closes his eyes and laughs softly. "Yeah, yeah, I know. Your art is dangerous, honey. I should've known better." He has a slight accent, maybe New York, but since I've never left California it's kind of hard to be sure. He turns to me, winces in pain, and then winks. "And this must be Shelby. I'd shake your hand, but I'm not supposed to move. Forgive my rudeness."

"No problem." I awkwardly stand there, wondering if I'm supposed to shake his fingers, wave, or curtsy like Shirley Temple. I opt for a smile and a nod. That works for everything except getting arrested.

"Becks, sorry about this," he says, and it takes me a second to figure out he's talking about Becca.

"Becks?!" I blurt out. Becca gives me the glare of death, and I know absolutely that if I breathe a word of this nickname, I will no longer be able to feed myself.

"I'm just glad there wasn't more damage," Thea says, pushing a plastic cup full of water and a straw toward Melvin. She turns toward us. "A broken ankle, and the doctor said the skull X-ray they did in the ER looked pretty good, but they're keeping him so they can do a CAT scan, just to be sure there's no swelling."

"Probably just a little fracture," Melvin says, dismissing it with the wave of a hand. "I've got a pretty thick skull. But a broken ankle? That's like a girl injury."

"No comment," Becca mutters.

"I heard that," he answers, grinning slightly. "I can still throw things. Remember that."

"Assault with a deadly bedpan?" Becca looks humorously unconcerned. "I'm not all that worried. You have lousy aim. You'd probably hit Shelby."

"Gee, thanks," I answer. After a semi-awkward silence, Thea and Melvin start talking about the ceramic cow and its amazing power to inspire, and Becca tugs at my arm and motions toward the hallway.

"What do you think?" she whispers when we're out of earshot.

"Let's go get coffee. Maybe you should ask if they want—"

"No! I mean, what do you think about him?" She links arms with me, her bangles jingling, and walks me rapidly down the hospital corridor. "I'm so glad she hit him."

"That just sounds wrong." I check to see if any of the nurses or doctors hear her basically confess to witnessing a crime. "She didn't hit him, exactly."

"No, no," she says, waving my thought away. "I know. I mean, I'm glad they had this little accident. It will bring them closer together."

"Is that what you want?"

She stops walking, turns to me, and says, solemnly, "If you could have your mom back, wouldn't you want that?"

I feel like she's punched me in the gut, and I stagger for a minute, recovering. I can't even say anything.

"I know it's not the same, exactly," she continues softly as she leans against the wall. "And I don't say it to make you feel bad or anything. But look at it from my perspective: If they could be together again, and be happy . . . well . . . that would be something great."

She turns to continue our long walk to the cafeteria, but I'm mentally elsewhere. This throws a whole new twist into something that was already contorted beyond recognition. I look into other people's rooms as I walk a couple of steps behind Becca; one holds an old woman with paper-thin skin, her mouth hanging open as she lies unconscious. A second room holds a hound-faced middle-aged man with short-cropped black hair; he stares at the wall above the door, not blinking, not reacting. I wonder if maybe these people are in the hospital alone because somebody ditched them. Can you literally die of a broken heart?

After grabbing some burnt coffee, we head back to Melvin's

room. I don't say anything, which makes Becca suspicious. "You're mad about this, aren't you?" she finally asks as she juggles a plastic cup and two little plastic containers of faux cream.

"No." That's not totally a lie, really; I don't know if I'm mad, scared, unhappy. My emotional life is like the Wheel of Fortune. I feel like I'm going to hit Lose a Turn at any moment.

"I understand why you'd be worried," she goes on brightly, as if we're discussing the efficiency of makeup remover. "But this will be better for everyone. Your dad will get over it."

"How do you know what my dad will get over?" I blurt out angrily.

She stops in her tracks, turns on the banana-yellow rubber heels of her tennies, and sloshes molten coffee onto the linoleum floor. "Whoa. I really didn't know you were going to take it like this." The expression on her face is puzzled.

"How else would I take it? My dad has started to like spending time with Thea, and now all of a sudden, here comes this guy—"

"*This guy* is my dad, Shelby."

"I thought you hated him!" I realize I'm shouting when a neat blond nurse in teddy bear scrubs gives me the pantomime for shut up. More quietly, I say, "I mean, didn't you always tell me he was a jerk?"

Becca stands, mouth open, staring at me as if I'm an alien that just landed, plop, in the middle of the hospital corridor. "Shelby, that is a horrible thing to say about someone's father."

I growl with frustration, throw my hands in the air, and march away from her. Unfortunately, I only make it to the lobby because

I have no car and I'm depending on Becca's mom for a ride. That sort of thing really makes it tough to make a great exit.

I collapse into a magenta chair made of some nubbly fabric that feels like it will leave dents in my thighs. Head in my hands, I study the teal and mauve carpet of the waiting room, trying to find some meaning in the black gum stains and the bits of lint. Becca follows me, her banana shoes slapping against the white linoleum until the carpet pads her footsteps. Then the banana feet are there, interrupting the linty beauty of the carpet.

"Can I sit down?"

I look up at her and nod. She eases into a teal chair next to me and says nothing for a minute. I just hear our breath coming in, going out, and the drone of some television talk show featuring a Southern-drawl psychologist and several women who have unnatural attachments to their panty hose. Maybe I should go on the show and get help.

"Shelby," Becca says, her tone much more gentle. "None of this is easy. I know it, believe me. But isn't the best thing for everyone to be happy?"

"My dad won't be happy," I whisper.

We sit there for about ten years, and finally Thea shows up, flushed with excitement. "They're going to keep him for tonight, but they think he might be released tomorrow. Isn't that great? I'm so relieved that my art didn't cause him permanent damage."

Becca stands, puts an arm around Thea, and gives her a little hug. "Let's take Shelby home," she says.

It's dark when Thea pulls into my driveway. I realize I haven't checked my cell phone, and when I do look at it, there are seven messages from Dad. Thea leaves the engine running as I contort myself out of the Jeep. "See you tomorrow?" Becca asks.

"I'll call you." I skip up the front steps as the Jeep's amber lights throw weird shadows onto the porch.

"Shelby?" Euphoria calls from the hallway. She zips around to the foyer, her green eye lights blinking rapidly. "Where have you been? We've been so worried."

Dad follows a minute later. "What happened?" His hair looks more disheveled than usual, as if it's been surprised by something. Maybe bad news, like his almost-girlfriend is dumping him for Baldy McMovieguy.

"Didn't Thea tell you that we went to the hospital?" I toss my purse into a corner of the hallway. "Melvin was injured in the line of duty."

"Melvin?" Poor Dad, poor naive Dad. He studies me quizzically, as if I'm speaking Chinese.

"Melvin. Becca's dad." I gravitate toward my beautiful purple velvet sofa, which suddenly feels like an oasis of comfort. Flopping facedown onto the soft cushions, I can sort of pretend that I'm not in the middle of some stupid personal dating crisis involving my dad.

The cushions sag slightly as Dad sits down next to me and strokes my hair. "Honey, why are you so upset? Was he badly hurt?"

As I so often do, I react in a totally inappropriate way: I start laughing like a hyena on crack. I almost choke, I'm laughing so hard. Euphoria slaps my back with her claw, which doesn't stop the choking laughter, but does cause a little abrasion where my bra strap rubs against my skin. She's stronger than she thinks she is. Anyway, it snaps me out of my hysteria.

When I come up for air, I see Dad glancing desperately at Euphoria as if he's looking for answers in her sensors. "Sorry," I say, still laughing a little.

Dad seems relieved that I haven't totally lost it. "So, was he really hurt?"

"Not too bad," I manage to say without laughing. Why a man's concussion and possible broken bones is funny, I can't say. Maybe it's the irony of my dad inquiring about the health of a guy who is totally destroying my dad's life. Yeah, that's probably it.

I manage to get to bed without any more cross-examination, claiming female problems. (Again, this has to be used sparingly; if my dad catches on that I use this excuse whenever I want to ditch him, I won't be able to use it again.) Unfortunately, Euphoria is another story entirely. She has a perfect memory of every excuse I've ever used, and she knows it's not possible for me to have three periods a month.

"What's going on?" she drawls as she shuts my bedroom door behind her. I'm lying in the dark, staring at my ceiling, picking out constellations: The Lying Goat, the Cheating Man, the Heartbroken Father, the Daughter Who Wishes She Could Join the Peace Corps But She's Too Young. "Shelby, I know something is going on. What happened with Becca's father?"

"I don't want to talk about it."

"Well, that's just too bad." Euphoria doesn't bend at the waist very easily, but she makes an attempt, easing her ponderous bulk onto the edge of my mattress. Springs groan, complaining. "I don't want to see you moping around for the rest of your life, so spill your beans, young lady."

I sit up, stripping off my shirt as I do. I suddenly feel hot, and just want to lie naked under my ceiling fan. Maybe I caught some disease at the hospital. "I have no beans to spill, Euphoria."

I toss my dirty clothes in the corner, which I suspect might distract Euphoria. She hates when I'm messy. But she doesn't buy it. "What happened with Becca's father?" she repeats. "I'll use my Taser if I have to."

"Oooh. Threats from my robot. That's something *Cosmo Girl* doesn't usually write about."

Euphoria remains silent, the only sound a whirring where her processors are analyzing my speech patterns, perspiration, and the pitch of my voice. "Did he hurt Becca?"

"No!" I sputter. "Nothing like that."

"He hurt Becca's mother, then."

I sigh, exasperated. "No, he didn't hurt anyone. A cow mosaic fell on him. He was helping Thea."

The whirring gets louder, and her lights blink more rapidly. After a minute, she says, "It's exactly what I said before. He's trying to win her back, isn't he?"

"Nobody calls it that anymore" is the only thing I can spit at her. I can't deny it, because my robot can tell when I'm lying.

"And he's injured, which means that Becca's mother feels ob-ligated to nurse him back to health, leaving your father—" Eu-phoria turns toward the bedroom door and says quietly, "Oh."

"Exactly." I sit up, hugging my knees to my bra-swaddled chest. "What do we do?"

8

INSIDE JOKES

(or How to Keep People
Away with Humor)

It seems like every Saturday morning, my phone rings way too early. Today, it's the cell chirping at me like a torturous canary. "Hello?" I grumble.

"Shelby? It's Fletcher." My heart jumps, does a backflip, and sticks to the roof of my mouth, making it tough to speak. "Are you there? Hello?"

"I'm here," I mumble thickly.

"Can I come over?" It's way too early for this kind of thing; I had expected maybe a note, a text message, a MySpace comment, but never direct confrontation. I feel myself blush at the thought of Fletcher being within ten miles of me.

"Aren't you afraid I'll attack you again?" I chuckle, a deep, throaty chuckle that I think the movie queens would use, except that I sort of choke and sound like I have a hair ball. So much for glamour.

Thankfully, he laughs. "I'll take my chances. Be right over."

Only minutes to look human on a Saturday morning? I gulp. "Sure."

After I hang up, I spring out of bed (okay, maybe spring is an exaggeration), wash my face, pull a comb through my hair, and throw on eight or ten outfits before deciding that nothing I own looks good.

"Jeans? Shorts? Skirt?" I hold up blue denim, khaki, and a hippie-dippy daisy-flowered peasant skirt. "If only I could go naked!"

Euphoria, who always manages to be around whenever I say something embarrassing, rolls in. "Naked? Did you say naked?"

"Yep." I choose the jeans, always a safe bet. As I pull on a green linen camp shirt and begin to button frantically, I slide past Euphoria and dig into my shoe cupboard for a pair of sandals. Toe nakedness, always a turn-on. But not as aggressive as full-on nakedness.

"Shelby, is someone coming over?" She seems to primp in front of my mirror, even though I don't think she has anything to actually primp.

"Fletcher just called." I shove in behind her and pull a brush through my hair again, hoping to make it look full and movie-starlike. As I snap on the silver bracelet, the one he gave me for Christmas, I answer her unasked question. "We're going to have a serious talk."

"About what?"

Dad knocks on the door just then, opens it, and pokes his disheveled head inside my room. "Honey, have you heard from

Becca's mom? I've tried calling her all morning, and can't get an answer."

Guilt rises up like a puke-flavored tidal wave. Should I tell him? Should I try to pretend I no longer speak English? I pretend to be looking in my jewelry box for something so I don't have to meet his worried gaze. "No, I haven't heard anything. Maybe she's at the hospital. You know, to be sure Becca's dad is okay." I glance up to see if he accepts this sort-of probably true explanation.

He looks relieved. "Oh, yeah. That's probably why. You have to turn your cell phone off in hospitals." He notices that I'm applying mascara, a sure sign that something is going on. "You're dressed before noon. What's the occasion?"

Euphoria butts in. "Fletcher is coming over!" she sounds so excited I'm afraid she might blow a circuit board or something. "I think a reconciliation is in the air!"

"Were you having a problem I didn't know about?" Dad eases into the room a bit and puts on his concerned-dad eyebrows. "What happened this time?"

"Nothing, nothing." I apply lipstick and mentally will my dad to disappear. I do not want to tell him why Fletcher and I haven't been talking. How would that conversation go? *Well, Dad, I tried to jump Fletcher in his own house, and when he fended off my slobbery advances, I ran, embarrassed, and have avoided him ever since. Your daughter is officially a slut puppy.* Yes, I'm sure that would ease his mind.

Euphoria starts to talk, but then the doorbell rings, and she rolls off to answer it. "He's here? What, was he parked around the corner at the 7-Eleven?" I hiss as I finish with a spritz of perfume. Dad moves out of my way to avoid being trampled.

Fletcher is standing in the hall, casual in shorts and a white T-shirt. My pulse starts to pound when I see him, as if he's a double espresso shot dripped directly into my heart. "Hey," I say softly, shyly.

He meets me halfway and flicks me in the head.

"Ow!" I rub the spot where he finger-assaulted me. "What was that for?"

"For being such a clueless doof." He steps back from me, folds his arms, and gives me a freckly smile. "Why didn't you think you could talk to me?"

Euphoria and Dad are standing, observing, like we're playing the home version of a cheesy soap opera. "Could we have a little privacy?" I ask pointedly.

"Hmm?" Dad asks, bewildered.

Fletcher rolls his eyes and grabs my arm gently. "How about we go somewhere for a little bit? Would that be okay?" He looks at my dad, who nods. Then he turns to me, a twinkle in his eye, and says, "Can I trust you to behave yourself?"

I aim a slap at his shoulder, but he's too quick and ducks it. That's the downside of knowing someone well. They anticipate your every act of violence.

Thankfully, Dad doesn't understand the "behave yourself" remark, and just tosses me a confused, dadlike look. "Is it okay if we go out for a while?" I ask, trying to keep my distance from

Fletcher. I wonder if my dad can see the intense rush of heat that seems to have engulfed my face. Guess not, because he just nods and shuffles off to the kitchen to forage for food.

We walk to the car silently, keeping a space bubble between us so that we can't touch and suddenly ignite the magnolia tree in the front yard. Fletcher opens the passenger door of his old car for me, then scoots quickly around to the other side.

"Where are we going?" I ask as he backs down the driveway.

"Someplace where we can talk uninterrupted."

"In public, I hope?" I don't meet his eyes. Just in case that was an inappropriate remark, I want to be spared the look of disapproval. But he just laughs.

"Yes, in public." He stares intently at the freeway traffic, never glancing at me.

We just keep driving and driving, fifteen minutes, half an hour, forty-five minutes. "Geez, where are you taking me? Tijuana?" I finally ask.

"Unless Earth has shifted polarity or something, I'd say no. We're headed north." He chuckles smugly to himself. I refuse to give him any more opportunities to skewer me with his laser-sharp wit, so I just shut up for the rest of the trip to nowhere.

We come around a bend in the road and I see a gorgeous site—the crashing blue-green waves of the Pacific Ocean. Now, you'd think since I live in Southern California that I'd live at the beach, that I'd have a surfboard and personal bikini wax technician and all, but that's not true. I hardly ever get to the coast, even though it's not that far away. This explains why, when I see the ocean, I act like a five-year-old going to Disneyland.

"Oooh! Are we going to walk in the sand?" I squeal. "Make a sand castle? Go clam digging?"

"Something like that." He parks the car and starts walking up a steep asphalt path. A sign reads TORREY PINES STATE BEACH. I've never been here before. The park smells like pine car air fresheners, only more real, and the sound of the surf pounding on the sand in the distance mingles with the call of birds and the screaming of toddlers frightened by biting sand flies.

Bottlebrush limbs slap me as I crouch, nearly doubled over, trying to catch up to Fletcher's maniacal hiking; as I've said before, I get winded licking a stamp. "Why did you bring me here?" I wheeze.

He doesn't say anything, just keeps climbing up the mountainous road. (To be truthful, it's not that steep. Three little kids with light-up Elmo tennis shoes run past me as we trek upward. I'm just a wimp.) He disappears around a curve in the trail, so I put on a burst of turtlelike speed to catch up to him.

When I round the corner, I see something that takes my breath away (even though I really don't have any breath at this point, so I'm speaking metaphorically). Fletcher is standing on an outcropping of sand-colored rock, framed by two towering gray-barked pine trees. The wind whispers through the waving limbs, mixing the sea-salt smell with the dark evergreen scent.

There's a weathered wooden bench parked next to one of the trees, and he sits on it; he motions for me to sit next to him, so

I do. He puts his arm around my shoulders and gestures majestically toward the ocean below us. "I give this all to you."

"I was hoping for jewelry," I murmur, hoping to hide the fact that I'm perspiring, and it's not because of the exercise.

"See?" he says, flicking me on the head again. "You ruin the moment." I scoot away from him just an inch, and he notices, drops his arm, and faces me, grinning. "I mean, you are just terrified we might have an actual meaningful conversation, huh?"

"You promising me the sky and the sea isn't exactly what I'd classify as meaningful—" I begin, but before I get any further, he puts a finger on my lips.

"I brought you here to make a bet with you."

A bet? Hmm. "Okay. What is it?"

"I bet you can't have a conversation with me while we're here that doesn't involve a joke."

I wait for the real reason we're here, but he just sits there. "Seriously," I finally say. "Let's start over. Why did you bring me here?"

He laughs and looks out at the ocean, the wind ruffling his penny-colored hair. "You even think my bet is a joke. See? You can't have a conversation that doesn't involve jokes."

"What's wrong with that?" I follow his gaze and focus on the whitecaps, little moveable meringues on a big blue-green cake. "You love my sense of humor."

"Yeah, I do." He faces me again. "But you keep me away with it."

Okay, now this is starting to sound like one of those Hallmark specials where one person tells the other one that they have toenail cancer or something, and they want to be sure their relationship is secure before the time of trial begins. I start giggling, thinking about the possibility that Fletcher has toenail cancer.

"See?" He shakes his head at me. "You're doing it right now."

"I didn't say anything!" I protest.

"You're saying it in your head! I can almost hear it! I bet if you repeated what you were just thinking, there would be a joke in there. Am I right?"

"No," I lie, tracing the shape of a cancerous toenail in the sandy dirt.

"Okay." He sighs. "Here's why I brought you up here, really. I wanted to get you away from Becca, from Euphoria, your dad, everybody, and I wanted to make you talk to me. I mean, really talk. About what's buried under all the jokes."

"I—" I begin but he gestures for me to stop.

"I'll talk first, uninterrupted, and then you can answer, as long as you don't do it with a joke. Deal?" I nod. Of course I can do this. What does he think I am, an idiot? Who can't go through a whole conversation without joking? Maybe it's the toenail cancer . . . maybe it's spread to his sense of humor. Oops. I just did it, huh? Maybe it will be harder than I think.

He gazes out at the ocean for a minute before speaking again. "We've been through conflicts, breakups, reunions, karaoke. We've been through a lot. Obviously, there's something here, or we wouldn't keep coming back to each other." He glances at me for confirmation of this: I just nod. I nod seriously, with no jokes attached.

"Okay," he continues. "But I've noticed that whenever we start really getting close to each other, I mean where we get past the jokes and the stupid pranks, that you do something to screw it up."

"I—" I try to interrupt, but he shushes me.

"Let's look at the evidence," he says, sounding like one of those guys with the spray-on hair from Court TV. "Last year, you decided that I liked Samantha Singer instead of you, and you avoided me like I had leprosy with a touch of black plague. After I tricked you at the dance, you gave me another shot. In the fall, we went on that date at the Italian restaurant and you stacked sugar packets instead of looking at me. Then you created a conflict between me and Becca that meant you'd have to 'choose' between us, causing you to conveniently give up the boyfriend for the best friend to preserve your independence."

"But I—"

"Not done." He shakes his head at me like a granny giving a lecture on good hygiene. "When I wanted to include you in my life and my friends' lives, you acted like a spoiled brat, insulted my friends, ran away from the party, and told your dad we were all boozing it up, and then walked around school for a week wearing a Jamaican Rasta wig so I couldn't find you."

Okay, he's got me on the Rasta thing. I mean, that was really pretty extreme.

"And finally, we have the other day." He leans forward, puts his elbows on his knees and stares at the gravel path as if he hopes some answer will be spelled out in the tiny pebbles. "For lack of a better term, you jumped me. In my own house. With

my little sister nearby. She could've been severely damaged, you
know." He winks at me.

"You just made a joke," I say in a strangled voice.

"I'm allowed to make jokes." He sits back, folds his arms
imperiously over his chest. "I don't have a problem with keeping people away with my jokes."

"That's because they're not very good," I mumble.

"I'll let that one go because I set you up." The breeze ruffles
his hair, making him look like a model in a sportswear commercial. Well, if sportswear commercials featured geeky red-
haired guys with toenail cancer. Joke alert! I did it again! He's
right: I am hopeless. "Anyway, I think all of those incidents, including the spontaneous jumping, were all ways to keep me
from really getting close to you."

"How can I be more close to you than when I have my tongue
in your mouth?" I screech too loudly. I know it's too loudly because a troop of Brownies nearby is shooed away from me by
their shocked-looking leader.

"I know, I know, it sounds crazy." He gazes into my eyes,
strokes my hair, and I feel myself starting to melt. "And don't
think I didn't like it. But I think you did it for the wrong reason."

For once, I don't make a smart remark. I just slump there
against the rough wooden bench, letting the tiniest spark of an
idea flare up from some midnight-dark place in the basement of
my mind. Could he be right? Is that what I do, keep people
away? And with him, the physical thing—could that be a way
for me to concentrate on something other than the feelings I
have for him?

God, I so want to make a joke about it.

Which means, I guess, that he's right.

For the third time today, he flicks the side of my head. "Hello? Anybody home?"

"Stop it," I say. My voice sounds flat, like a balloon with all the air blown out.

Fletcher hugs me closer, and leans his head against mine. "Stop what, the flicking or the indecent emotional exposure?"

"You made a joke." I huddle into him, for the first time really feeling the soft-rubbed texture of his shirt, and the slightly scratchy stubble on his face, smelling the vanilla-flower musk of his skin, hearing a constant heartbeat that I've rarely been quiet enough to hear. Damn, it's kind of nice when I shut up.

For a change, I say hardly anything as we walk back down to the car arm in arm. Without my own constant chatter, I actually enjoy the sky, the birds, the skin-lacerating pine needles that slap me whenever Fletcher ducks under a branch and it flips back too fast for me to avoid it.

"Can I ask you about something?" I say. He opens the car door and cocks his head at me, waiting. "It's about my dad."

We get in and he starts the car, pulls out of the lot, and we wave good-bye to the beautiful beach. Then he says, "What about your dad?"

"He's in love, or in like or something, with Thea."

"Becca's mom?" he squawks. "Wow. That's kind of *Twilight Zone*. I mean, she's a flaky-artsy-moon worshipper and he's Mr. Science. How did that happen? Mind-altering mushrooms?"

"It's not funny. He really has a thing for her, and now she's kind of back with Becca's dad, Melvin, and Melvin's probably just jealous because Dad showed an interest in his ex-wife. And now Becca's all happy because she secretly wanted her family back together, even though she hated Melvin for choosing the art over her in a custody battle. And now Dad has no clue."

"Uh, neither do I," Fletcher says, shaking his head. "I think you just read off the script summary for a daytime soap opera."

"I know." I groan. "So much unnecessary drama! And aren't parents the ones who are supposed to be sensible?"

Fletcher shrugs as he guides the car into another lane of traffic. "I guess they're just big teenagers."

"But what do I do about it? Do I just not tell my dad anything? Hope it will work out? Stay out of it? I don't know what to do." That's an understatement. Not only do I not know what to do, I'm afraid if I do anything I'll make things worse. If that's possible.

Fletcher squints into the sun and says, "Maybe Melvin will just go away. You said he was injured, right? He'll probably have to go back home and recuperate."

"I guess." Watching the blur of scenery outside the car window, I am reminded of the intense pace of my life: Here I am, sixteen (and unable to drive!), I've lost one parent, thought I was getting another one, then found out I wasn't, thought I was getting a sister, now I'm not. Had a boyfriend, didn't have him, had him again, distanced myself, got myself closer. If I could get frequent-flier points for my emotional mileage, I could probably go to the moon on the space shuttle. First class.

When Fletcher pulls into my driveway, Dad is sitting on the

porch, which sort of screws up my chances for a really good kiss. I just can't suck face in front of my dad. Fletcher sees it, too, and shrugs his shoulders, satisfying himself with a peck on the cheek before getting out of the car. "Hey, Mr. C." He waves as he comes around to my side and waits for me to get out, and then we walk up the steps together.

Dad waves halfheartedly. I skip up and give him a kiss, but he doesn't even react. "What's up?" I ask, perching on the swing next to him.

He gives me a sheepish grin, then shrugs back against the green wooden slats of the glider. "I'm a chump."

"Chump?" Fletcher parks on the topmost step. "Why do you say that?"

Dad laughs, a melancholy, in-desperate-need-of-Prozac laugh, and says, "Thea. She's had Melvin move in to her place."

"What?" I screech.

"He's living there?" Fletcher asks, shaking his head. "Aw, that's bad."

Dad nods. Even his salt-and-pepper hair looks sad. "He's hurt, you know. She said she felt obligated to nurse him back to health since her art knocked him over. But," he says, wagging his finger, "I think there's more to it than that. Euphoria thinks so, too."

As if on cue, Euphoria slams open the screen door and rolls onto the porch. Somehow, she's gotten herself all decked out in black clothing—an oversized T-shirt, a black beret, and Velcroed armbands emblazoned with grinning white skulls. She presses a button on her midsection and the theme song from the 007 movies starts blaring. Then she says, "The name is Bolts . . . Jane Bolts."

Fletcher almost falls off the porch laughing, but I am more speechless than anything. "What happened to you?" I ask as I walk slowly around the travesty that was my robot.

Euphoria beeps, then sends a thin, red laser light zapping against the white porch banister. "I've been upgraded," she informs us.

"Crap," Fletcher mutters, moving a little farther away from the laser. "Is that thing loaded?"

"No, no," Dad says, keying in a sequence on Euphoria's keypad (discreetly covered by one of the cute little skull bands). "It was her idea. I already told you, Euphoria, that there will be no covert operations."

If a robot can fume (I mean emotionally, not mechanically), Euphoria does it. "Mr. Chapelle, don't stop me from fulfilling my true destiny. You need inside information. I can provide it. I promise, no one will know I'm there. I'll be a flea on the wall."

Fletcher chokes off a laugh, pretending to cough. It's not a good idea to insult a robot on a mission.

Dad rubs the spot between his eyebrows, the spot where headaches are born. "I do appreciate it, really. But Thea is a grown woman. If she wants to get back together with someone who obviously has no regard for her happiness, and only wants to ruin whatever chances for a decent life she might have had, that's her choice, isn't it?" He pats Euphoria on the arm. "You'd have a little problem blending in, too."

"I'm sure I could hook up with a utility pole that could assist me." Euphoria seems to nod knowingly. "I understand it's a risk, but I'm willing to take it."

My cell chirps at that moment. "Spies R Us," I say, but before I can laugh at my own lame joke, Becca is babbling in low, hushed tones.

"Get over here," she whispers.

"What's up?" I take a few steps toward the edge of the porch to pretend I have some privacy. "Why do I need to come over?"

"Well, first of all," she hisses, "Carl and I broke up, and second, Evie and I are planning the best way to fling all human males on a catapult to the sun."

"Ah," I say, looking at Fletcher and Dad, wondering how they'd feel about a one-way trip to the center of the solar system. Probably not enough sunscreen for that, unless you ordered the swimming pool–sized bottles. "I could probably come over, but I'd have to get a ride from someone of the male persuasion."

"Just don't let them get out of the car," she snaps, then hangs up.

Fletcher has been tracking my conversation while trying to look like he's not listening. "So, who was that?" he asks as if he already knows the answer.

"Becca," I answer as if he already knows who it was. "Can I get a ride to her house?"

Dad sighs, a big heavy outflow of breath spiced with disappointment. "Hope you have fun."

I give him a big kiss and hug. "Maybe I could make sure another fertility statue falls on his head."

He grins without much enthusiasm and swings listlessly as we skip down the stairs and to the car.

Fletcher opens the door for me. "What's up with Becca?"

"She says she and Carl broke up."

He whistles as he backs down the driveway and into the street. "That's going to make things tough for you."

"Huh?"

"Think about it. Do you think she's going to want you to be dating me if she's not dating anyone?"

"That's pretty unfair," I start to say, but then realize that he's probably right. She did talk about hurling all boys/men into the sun, and I suppose that's an indication that she will want her first lieutenants to be boy-free. But she wouldn't ask me to simply break it off with Fletcher because of *her* dismal love life, would she?

We travel in silence the rest of the way, and when he pulls into Becca's circular driveway, I unbuckle my seat belt before he can kill the motor. "See you," I say as I try to hustle out of the passenger seat.

"Hang on," he says, grabbing my arm. He pulls me to him, holds my face in his hands, and gives me a long, smoldering kiss that makes me forget about the sun, the moon, and any catapults that might be injured in the course of our activities. "All right then. Go on about your business."

I wave to him as he pulls away, feeling like a dopey Miss America winner minus the roses and tiara. Apparently Becca hears the motor, because she and Evie bolt out the front door, grab my arms, and drag me into the house.

"I am able to walk, you know," I sputter as I try to swat against them.

"We're going to my room and we're staying there until we deprogram you," Becca says resolutely.

That doesn't sound like much fun on a Saturday afternoon. Especially after a mind-warping lip-lock.

9

SILVER SCREEN SCHEME

(or Fifty Feet of Celluloid Doom)

When you are alone with your girlfriends, a couple of things happen pretty consistently. First, you always gripe about the boys in your life, and if you have no boys in your life, you complain about that. The second thing that is most consistent is the presence of chocolate, preferably dark.

After Becca and Evie swoop into the yard and drag me up to Becca's room, they shove me onto the bed. "Here," Becca says, all business, as she tosses a heart-shaped box of truffles at me. "We already ate most of the good ones, but I did save you the coconut."

I peer into the box. "You already took a bite out of it," I observe, hoping I don't sound ungrateful. It is, after all, chocolate.

"Well, how else would I know what it was?" Becca asks, clearly annoyed at my lack of understanding about her teeth marks on my candy. I eat it anyway.

"Fletcher brought you over," Evie states.

I nod, unable to speak because of the gooey rush of sugar.

Becca sits on the bed beside me and picks a half-eaten nut thing from its stiff paper nest. She crunches into it, rolls her eyes ecstatically, and leans against a fluffy pink pillow. "Carl and I broke up."

"Yeah, you just told me that. Want to give me some more details?" An orange cream calls to me, and I do not ignore it.

Evie sits down on the rug, sighing. "It was kind of ugly," she says slowly, her Australian accent slightly flavored with the scent of raspberry truffle. "He came over this morning, apparently, and demanded to know whether or not Becca intended to buy a dress, and if so, what color it was." Evie looks horrified, as if Carl had asked Becca to loan him a vital organ.

"And then," Becca says, pausing for dramatic effect, "he informed me that he plans to wear a kilt to the prom. A *kilt!*" She shakes her head and reaches for another piece of chocolate.

As for me, I am totally unsure of why any of this is a crisis, and I wonder if maybe the two of them have gone into a diabetic hallucination or something. "And you broke up with him because of a Scottish skirt?"

"Well, it obviously wasn't just that!" she spits. "He also told me that our Geek Prom was a stupid idea, and that he didn't want to be involved, and that if I insisted on doing it, he'd never speak to me again."

"Uh-huh." Now, I'm not a big expert on guys or anything, and I certainly don't know Carl really well, but I can't really see him pitching a fit about anything, let alone whether or not

Becca would or would not do something. "Is there more to it than that?"

"What do you mean?" Becca's blond spikes poke at the wall behind her head as she stretches against the headboard.

"I mean, what led up to that part of the conversation?"

Evie, who has been studying me over the dark plastic frames of her glasses, speaks up. "Are you implying that Becca had something to do with it?"

Hey. Who is she? I don't remember anybody voting for her to be Becca's watchdog and anti-boyfriend posse leader. That used to be my job, anyway. I don't answer her.

Becca watches the two of us with something like amusement. It sort of irritates me, actually; it's like she enjoys seeing us squabble over who has more insight into her self-destructive relationship patterns. "What do you mean, Shelby? Do you mean, did I do something to make Carl run away with his skirt between his legs?" She stretches and reaches for another chocolate, then meets Evie's gaze and giggles. "I guess maybe I did."

The two of them laugh, and in my mind, it sounds kind of maniacal, like the evil villains hanging out in the grotto below Gotham City waiting for Batman to get a run in his tights. Kind of mean. That's probably just because I'm overstimulated by the candy, I suppose. "So, can you kind of tell me what the actual conversation was about?"

Becca stops cackling long enough to sit up, tuck her legs underneath her, and get serious. "Okay, here's what happened. He came over this morning, and Evie spent the night, so—"

Hang on. Evie spent the night? I don't even hear the rest of the story, because I'm engulfed in a roaring tide of insecurity. My best friend had *someone else* stay over? I realize this sounds like a huge overreaction, but high school is very competitive. And it took me fifteen years to find Becca, and she is the only best friend I've ever had, so realizing that this Australian dingo girl could be bumping me off the best friend roster . . . well, it's just not something I can accept easily. Unfortunately, because of my momentary wave of paranoia, I miss most of what Becca says. Some best friend I am.

"So, that's what happened," she finishes, sighing.

Evie is watching me, looking for signs of weakness, I suppose. "What do you think?" she asks. Clever girl.

"Oh, I don't know," I say, faking my way through the conversation. "I think it's obvious. Don't you?"

Becca frowns at me, then looks at Evie. "Huh?"

Damn. Now I'm caught. Better think of something noncommittal yet meaningful to say. "I mean, clearly he isn't right for you on a deeper level."

"Yeah," Becca says, squinting at me. "But how about what he said about Melvin and Thea?"

Wow. I must have been gone for a while, mentally. I totally missed that part of the conversation. "Uh . . . I guess everyone has an opinion?"

"Sure, but they're not his parents," Becca says snidely. "He comes from this perfect little two-parent home with no wrinkles and no problems and no dangerous art. But does that give him the right to criticize my mom's weird relationship dynamics? It's like with us—I'm your friend and I could totally tell you that your hair sucks, but I wouldn't want some outsider telling you your hair sucks. It's just wrong."

"Does my hair suck?" I self-consciously pull at a strand, trying to stretch it out so I can see it without a mirror.

Becca sighs. "The point is, he doesn't understand. That's the bottom line. I can't be with someone who doesn't really get me." She crosses her arms and leans back, as if that's all settled.

Evie grabs a clipboard and thrusts it at me. "Check this out."

On the clipboard is a chart. On the chart are many colors. Other than that, I'm not really sure why I'm looking at it. I squint at her. "Pretty?"

"Don't you know what that is?" she squeaks, indignantly retrieving the clipboard and chart that I so callously didn't understand. "It's a schematic."

"A what?"

Evie rolls her eyes as if I've just asked how to breathe. "Schematic. It's a plan for how we're going to network all the various Web proms so we can have the biggest virtual prom ever. See," she says, pointing to a red bar floating under a blue sphere, "this is Scotland, and France is here, and New York is over here. We're trying to get Japan, too, and of course, Australia. It's not all settled yet, but it's looking good." She proudly points to a green column at the end of the chart. "This shows how we need to hook up our equipment in order to be sure we have enough power and bandwidth to receive all those signals at the same time."

She might as well be speaking Chinese. I'm not a total loser at technology, but my experience is pretty much limited to web pages and chatting and such. Becca starts yammering away with Evie about how they can effectively connect a designated server to be the master, and then make some slaves obey it. It just gets really confusing, and sounds kind of illegal, but I just nod and smile and pretend that I understand.

"Your job," Becca says, clapping her hands on my shoulders, "is to recruit people to attend."

"Oh, that's great. I'm supposed to just go up to people and say, 'Hey, want to come to this cool alternative prom? It's cheap, and there will be computers!' That does sound like a real appealing pitch." I reach for another piece of candy. I hope I don't get a zit, but at this point, it's really the least of my worries.

"It's all in how you spin it," Becca reminds me. "We just need to make it something people want to do. So we need to play up the strengths." She looks at me, then at Evie. "So, what are they? Let's make a list."

Evie whips open her laptop and starts to tap-tap it into submission. "Okay, go ahead." She sits, poised to record any brilliant comments that fly out of my mouth. Unfortunately, I only manage to cough a little. "So? Strengths?"

"Okay, I'll start," Becca says, exasperated at the slowness of my response. "Cheaper. Our ticket prices will be half of what the zombie prom will cost."

"Zombie prom?"

"Oh, yeah. We call it that because only the brainless, sheeplike followers will go to that one." Becca taps me on the head with one large finger. "Hopefully your brains are still intact."

"To be honest, I think a zombie prom sounds pretty fun." I

know I'm going to regret saying it, but I can't help it. Evie's rabid typing and that stupid chart have made me cranky and uncooperative. "If that's a way to get people to go to the other dance, it's a good idea."

"You're not helping." Becca stands up, paces the room, and stares at the ceiling as if looking for a flash of inspiration to come from above. "Okay, so, cheaper. Obviously, the record-breaking aspect of the thing should be pretty cool."

"Comfortable shoes," Evie mutters, typing furiously.

"But we still need something else," Becca murmurs, her back to me as she gazes out her window. "We need something that nobody else has ever done."

"Well, this whole virtual prom thing sounds pretty much like uncharted territory." I hesitate to mention that maybe nobody will actually care, because most people who go to a dance pretty much want to be concerned with themselves and the person they're dating. But I don't want to burst her bubble and risk a nosebleed. "But if you want something different, what about location?"

Becca turns, her face transformed. Her eyes are wide, pupils dilated, almost as if she'd just returned from a trip to the eye doctor where they put in those nasty drops. I'm probably exaggerating, but she really does look excited. "Location," she whispers.

At that moment, the bedroom door flies open, and Amber and Elisa swoop into the room. "We got your message," Amber says, swinging her hair dramatically. "We came as soon as we could."

"So, where are we?" Elisa arches an eyebrow and peers over

Evie's shoulder. I see a glint of disappointment in her eyes; after all, Wembley had been our electronic note keeper for the past year, and now he (it?) was being replaced by a newer model. I know how he (it?) feels.

Becca brings them up to speed, finishing where they came in: "We need to think of a stunning, unusual, amazing, mind-blowing location."

"And we need to have good food," Elisa mentions, tapping Evie on the shoulder and motioning toward the laptop. Dutifully, Evie taps away.

Amber sits cross-legged on the floor, Elisa continues to hover over Evie, and Becca has migrated back to the bed. "Location," she whispers again. It's like a chant. Or a curse. Or a CD that skips.

After several uncomfortable minutes of no one having any good ideas, Becca growls, frustrated, and says, "We need a change of scenery. Let's go get a latte or something."

Caffeine sounds great to me. As we file down the stairs, Thea comes into the foyer. "Honey, where are you all going?" Her hands are covered in some guacamole-green gook. "I was going to ask if you could help me with my new organic clay mixture."

"Uh, maybe later," Becca says, frowning at the stinky green stuff. "We really need to go run an errand. Can Meredith help you?" Meredith is their live-in maid who is too classy to actually do much real work.

"Meredith refuses to do anything that has to do with art," Thea complains. "She says it's a liability thing."

"Thea!" From somewhere toward the back of the house (it is

a mansion, after all), Melvin's voice echoes. "Thea, I need that special tea. Hurry up! I'm supposed to do it every hour!"

"Men," Thea says, laughing uncomfortably.

Becca shoots her a bemused look, darts into the kitchen, and returns with an oversized rag towel, and dabs at Thea's hands, a look of disgust on her face. "You shouldn't let him order you around like that."

"He's hurt," Thea says defensively.

"Hmm." Becca hands the towel to her mom. "There you go. We're off to get wired. Want anything?"

Thea frowns and waves at us. She doesn't approve of caffeine.

Lucky for us, a coffee place opened up a couple of blocks from Becca's house earlier in the year, but we've hardly been there at all. We cover the two blocks in no time, everybody chattering at once about food, clothes, dance music, and of course, the unidentifiable mystery location that needs to be revealed.

The Endless Pot is a bad name for a coffeehouse, especially if teenagers go near it. The person who started the place must have had one too many cups of espresso is all I can think. But anyway, the place is nice, walls painted a dark bloodred, mismatched chairs and sofas left over from somebody's garage sale, art on the walls, and a sleek black granite counter speckled with white paper fortunes born from discarded cookies. I think the owner used to run a Chinese restaurant and had to get rid of the cookies, because no matter what you order, you get one.

We get our drinks (and fortune cookies) and find a circle of ratty furniture to occupy. I get a ridiculously low gold brocade chair that makes it impossible to eat or drink without contorting my body into torturous positions.

Amber cracks open the cookie she gets with her double soy cappuccino, then unrolls the crinkly white paper. "Hmm. Says here that I am 'well respected by my *pears*.'" She looks up over the soup bowl–sized blue mug, and says, "Guess that one should have been Shelby's. She's the vegetarian."

Elisa is already munching her cookie, and has discarded the fortune. "Mine always says the same thing: Made in China."

"You're reading the wrong side." Becca picks it up off the floor and shows her. "See? Yours actually says, 'There were three bears, one died, the other was very bad.'"

Elisa stares at her, snatches the slip of paper, crumples it, and throws it back to the floor. "I think the other side makes more sense. That's why I always read it."

"Enough of this, ladies." Becca sighs, sipping her iced coffee. "Location, remember? We need a place to hold our prom."

"How about here?" Amber asks, gesturing at the pieces of abstract art in dazzling blue, garish red, and bio-hazard yellow. "This place has character."

"If by character you mean art that would make Picasso puke, I agree. So no, that's not going to work for most people. Besides, it's way too small." Becca leans against her leopard-printed sofa.

"Too small?" Elisa squeaks. "How many people do you think are going to come to this shindig?"

"At least three hundred," Becca says breezily, as if she's talking about a bowling team instead of a sizeable chunk of the school population.

As she says this, I am gracelessly trying to sip from my latte, but when I hear the number she has in mind, I just end up blowing steamed milk foam up my nose. As I blot it away, I say in a strangled voice, "Are you kidding? Are you delusional? Three hundred?"

Becca eyes me coldly. "Shelby, if you're going to rain on my parade, you'd better bring a damn big umbrella."

Everyone pauses, and Elisa says, "Becca, what did that mean, exactly?"

"I don't know, but I've always wanted to say it. Now, let's drink up and get the creative juices moving."

Several coffees and trips to the bathroom later, we still have no brilliant ideas. "Maybe my fifth cookie will hold some ancient Chinese wisdom," Evie says wryly, cracking open yet another dry, cardboardlike confection. "Yep. Here it is: 'Look to your father for enlightenment and to drive a path out of the darkness.'" She balls it up and tosses it to the floor with all the others. "Somebody gets paid to write that crap. Can you believe it?"

While the other girls chatter, I notice a change in Becca's expression. It's the same maniacal gleam she always has when she gets an impossible idea. She sits up slowly, slowly sets her cup on the chipped wooden coffee table, and slams her hands down so hard the ceramic mugs shake in their little saucers. "I've got it!"

"I don't want it," Elisa mumbles, rescuing her drink from certain sloshing.

"You've figured it out?" Evie asks eagerly. "The location?"

"Yes. 'Look to your father for enlightenment and to drive a path out of the darkness.' That's it." She gazes at each of us, expecting a cheer or at least a response of some kind. We all stare blankly. "Don't you get it?"

Elisa clears her throat and says, "I think I speak for all of us when I say this, Becca. What the hell was in your coffee?"

Becca growls her most frustrated growl and puts her arms over her head, as if shielding her brain from the draining effects of hanging out with us morons. "God, it's so obvious! Father, enlightenment, drive, path out of darkness . . ."

"A church? We're going to have our prom in a church?" Amber asks doubtfully. "It would have to be one of those really liberal ones. Maybe the Unitarians—"

"No!" Becca jumps up, does a little happy dance (which is actually a pretty big happy dance since she's taller than most people) and she starts chanting in a singsong voice, "The drive-in, the drive-in, the drive-in!" She sits back down abruptly as a cranky manager gives her a disapproving glare. "We can rent out the drive-in movie theater and do the screening of my dad's crappy horror film, but instead of that being our fund-raiser, we have the geek prom there after the movie. It will *be* the event."

Nobody says anything for a minute, since we're all stunned at the impossibility of the task. Becca turns to Evie like an excited puppy and squeaks, "Isn't it brilliant?"

Evie smiles, pushes up her dark-framed glasses, and says, "Um, yes. Brilliant. How in the bloody hell do you expect us to rent a drive-in movie theater and power it for several computers and video setups?"

Becca seems slightly deflated by reality, but still perky. "Okay, I guess there are some small details to work out," she says as everyone else groans. "But I just know it's a great idea. Picture it: Kids in funky formal wear moving under the stars on a huge dance floor surrounded by huge video monitors. Above it all is the white screen of the drive-in, where a first-time screening of a famous director's horror film will start the evening. After that, the dance kicks in, and we have the whole thing catered with amazing food, and have an awesome DJ providing the tunes, maybe even a light show on the movie screen!" She leans back against the leopard cushions, a coffeehouse goddess in her own delusional world.

The rest of us share glances ranging in emotion from disbelief to panic. Becca notices our less-than-enthusiastic responses, purses her lips tightly, and huffs back against the sofa, disgusted. As the best friend, I guess it's my duty to say what everyone else is thinking: "Becca, it's a fantastic idea, but it's not doable. Even if we all want to do it, there are so many things getting in the way. How would we rent a drive-in? How would we get the equipment and power to do the virtual prom? How could we decorate a gravel parking lot to look like the bayfront Hyatt? Who's going to want to spend prom night shuffling through stones, old cigarette butts, and discarded Good & Plenty boxes? Drive-ins don't exactly scream elegance." The other girls are nodding, except for Evie, who glares at me. The truth hurts.

Becca, though, seems energized by my list of obstacles. "Is that all?" she squeals. "Oh, all that stuff is simple. Simple!"

"Really?" Elisa asks, amused. "Do you happen to have several thousand dollars sitting around doing nothing?"

"No," Becca says proudly, "but my dad does."

As the realization dawns on us, the temperature in the room changes noticeably, and it's not just because a bunch of people ordered steamed milk drinks. Suddenly Amber is chattering, and Elisa is calculating, and Evie is animated, tapping on her laptop. I'm the only one who's not blown away by the fact that Becca plans to tap her estranged dad for mass amounts of capital.

"So?" she asks, gesturing to me. "Now are you on board?"

What do I say to that? Here's what's going on in my head: Fletcher kissed me, I'm still kind of tingly, I don't want to have a fight with him, and I was counting on not being able to pay for Becca's grand scheme; I figured that at some point, it would fizzle out, and that would be that. She's apparently broken up with Carl, which means any move on my part to be friendly to Fletcher will be seen as treason. My best friend status is already in jeopardy because of kangaroo girl, so I can't risk going against Becca on this unless I'm okay with losing her friendship. The whole lack of money thing was totally going to save me from any of this. And now Melvin is screwing up my life with his movie millions. I knew I didn't like him.

That whole internal conversation really doesn't take as long as it seems, because a second or two later Becca is still glaring expectantly at me, waiting for a response. "Uh . . ." is what I say. I'm very eloquent under pressure.

"What does that mean, 'uh?' Are you helping us or not?" She folds her arms across her chest, defying me to defy her.

"Uh . . ." I say again. I realize this won't work a third time, but I'm still hoping some brilliant idea will strike my brain. Think, think, think little cerebral cortex. Pay for all that space you take up between my ears! Before I am aware of it, I say, "Of course I'm on board. Duh." Way to go, brain. You're dumber than I thought. I may have to evict you and send you to live on the street with all the other useless globs of gray matter, with your little cardboard brain suitcase filled with all the memories of things we used to do together. I'll miss you.

With Melvin's money fueling the project, I guess Geek Prom will be a success. My role is still unclear, of course; I feel an overwhelming need to have a heart-to-heart with my robot. Or my dad. I excuse myself and head for the bathroom, call my dad on the cell, and wait for him to pick up. "Hi. What's up?"

"Can you come get me? I'm at the coffee shop by Becca's house and I really need a ride home. I need to talk to you." I don't mention that I considered confiding in Euphoria first. No need to be hurtful.

"Conflict within the ranks?" he asks, laughing.

"Sort of. Can you come get me?" I glance around the pillar separating the bathroom waiting area from the rest of the place, to see if they're still gabbing and congratulating each other, which they are. They don't even notice I'm gone, really.

"I suppose. Want to go get some food?"

"Sure."

"I'll be there in about fifteen." The line clicks dead. I flip the phone shut and tuck it back into my pocket. I put on my best disappointed face and return to the gaggle of schemers.

"Wow, what happened in the bathroom?" Elisa asks. "You look so sad."

"My dad called. I have to go home, so he's picking me up in

about fifteen minutes." I try to look disappointed as I plop back down into the hip-sucking gold brocade.

"The dance floor should be elegant-looking, maybe that wooden panel stuff that clicks together," Amber is saying as she stirs whipped cream into her drink. "And we need some good lighting, too. Decorations. Should it be a theme, or just classy?"

"How classy can you make a drive-in?" I blurt out. Stupid brain again, saying what it thinks.

Becca bristles a bit at my naysaying. "With the right lighting and decorations, anything can look great. I was reading this magazine about entertaining, and—"

"Whoa. You were reading a magazine about *entertaining*?" I choke on what's left of the dusty fortune cookie I'd been gnawing on.

"I was in the eye doctor's waiting room," she says defensively. "The point is, they had a story in there about this guy who threw parties all over the world, in these really obscure locations. One was in Beijing, China, and he rented part of the Great Wall."

"Thank God you didn't suggest *that*," Elisa grumbles.

Becca ignores her. "Anyway, the guy rented part of the Great Wall, brought up a string quartet, a generator, sheep roasting on a spit, crystal tablecloths and silverware, fine wine, and it was the most elegant thing ever, right in the middle of this ancient, crusty stone ruin."

"Ruins have class," Elisa says. "They have that history thing going for them. Drive-ins are mostly associated with dancing popcorn and getting groped by the football team." Everyone kind of stares at her, and she blushes. "Not like I know from firsthand experience or anything."

"My point is we'll have as much money as we need to make it fantastic." Becca stares up at the ceiling intently. "I wonder if there's a way to hang a chandelier if you don't have a roof?"

"Are you sure about the money thing?" Amber asks hesitantly, wary of getting her head cut off for being a party pooper. "Have you asked your dad about it? What if he says no?"

Becca laughs her donkey honk laugh and slaps the back of the leopard sofa, which emits a cloud of antique dust and scone crumbs. "Are you kidding? He is *so* wanting to buy me off. I could ask him for an island in the South Pacific and he'd ask how big." I think I see a fleeting hint of insecurity cross her face, but then it's gone. "Don't worry about that. He's trying to get back with my mom, and he's willing to do whatever it takes to weasel his way back into the family."

"And you intend to soak him for all he's worth?" Elisa asks, shaking her head. "Sounds very *Brady Bunch*."

Becca fumes a bit at the comment, but then comes out of it quickly enough. After another ten minutes of delusional chatter, I see my dad's Volvo pull up outside the coffee shop, so I choose that moment to depart before I get asked to give an opinion that might get me in trouble. "So, I'll talk to you tomorrow?" Becca asks, rising to walk me out.

"Yeah, I guess." I bolt ahead of her, hoping we won't have time for a one-on-one conversation.

"Hey." She touches my shoulder as we reach the door, and turns me around to face her. "What's going on with you?"

"What do you mean?" I wave to my dad as if I know he's pressed for time.

"I mean," she says, getting closer and whispering slightly, "that you are doing everything you can to avoid having anything to do with this. Is it because of Fletcher? You can tell me." Her eyes are all sympathy.

But I'm still afraid. If I don't give her the answer she wants, will I be permanently booted from the Queen Geeks? And how would I feel about that? It's too complicated to figure out in the doorway of the Endless Pot, so I just laugh it off. "Look, honestly, I've got a ton of homework to do, and Dad's waiting . . . can I call you later?"

She studies me; her lip twitches slightly, the only indication that she might not truly believe me. "Sure," she says, smiling her most dazzling coffee goddess smile. "Call me later."

I climb into the car next to my dad and burst into tears. Stupid brain.

10

AN EASY LESSON IN CLONING

(or How to Be Your Own Twin)

"And I think Fletcher's right, I mean, I do always make jokes. But if I really try to stop it, am I just pretending to be something I'm not? And what about Becca? I feel like I'm letting her down by simply *having* a relationship at all. And now there's this whole Evie thing." I pause for breath and look at my dad's glazed expression as he sips his third glass of iced tea through a mangled straw. (He chews on them when he's nervous; so do I.)

He slurps a last gulp, then wipes his lips on a napkin, eyeing me with a puzzled expression. "Honestly, Shelby, I really have no idea what you're talking about."

"Great!" I throw my napkin down. "I just poured my heart out to you, and you have no idea what I said. Fantastic!"

"Hang on, hang on," he says, motioning toward the waitress.

"Let's get dessert and we'll try it again. Maybe my blood sugar is still too low." He motions to our waitress, a middle-aged woman with jet-black hair that looks like those Halloween wigs you buy for ten bucks at the drugstore.

"Hi there," she oozes at my dad, trying to shove her squeezed-up breasts over her "Trudy" name tag. "See anything you like?"

Dad blushes and studies the menu as if he's reading the Bible. He orders us two slices of cheesecake, and Trudy leaves, disappointed that he didn't order something more personal.

He leans back against the fake blue leather of the booth. "It's like they smell blood in the water," he murmurs, glancing secretively at Trudy's retreating rear. "I think I'm going to become a hermit."

"You tried that. It didn't work," I remind him. "But let's get back to me. Can't you give me some adult wisdom or something?"

"I really am trying, honey. It's just so . . . detailed."

"I know." Honestly, *I* don't even understand my life or my various crisis situations. "Okay. Let's take one thing at a time. What should I do about Fletcher?"

Dad sighs and rubs his headache spot again. "Why do you need to do anything? Can't you just let things flow as they do?"

Oh, that makes sense. Just let life take its course, and hope for the best? Doesn't he know that the only way you can truly be happy is to totally manipulate details in your life so they all line up perfectly, like little white pins waiting to be knocked down by God's big cosmic bowling ball? What I say is, "Fletcher wants us to be a real couple. I mean, he wants us to have a meaningful relationship, not just some dumb, casual, let's-go-to-the-malt-shop thing."

"Do people still go to the malt shop?"

"Not really. But my point is, he isn't going to be okay with me treating it like it's just casual."

Dad shrugs in his seat, squirming like he's sat on a spring or something. "I'm not really sure what you mean by 'meaningful' and 'casual.' Could you go into detail on that? So I don't have a heart attack?"

"Dad," I whine, frustrated. "I'm not talking about sex!" Of course, the very second I say that, everyone has stopped talking, so there is a huge, silent gap in conversation that is conveniently filled by my voice. People turn and stare at me in various stages of trying to look like they're actually ignoring me. One little girl squeaks, "What's sex, Mommy?" and I feel myself turning a bright, bright red.

Dad is sort of laughing, trying to look concerned. Trudy brings our dessert and shoots me a conspiratorial grin, as if she and I understand each other. Yuck.

The discussion sort of ends after that, and we occupy our mouths with cheesecake instead of embarrassing personal conversation. Dad picks up the check that Trudy the waitress drops in his lap, and cringes. "She left me her phone number and her bra size," he says, disgusted. "I pray to God I have exact change."

Thankfully, he does, so we wait until Trudy is occupied in the kitchen and we make a run for the door. We don't stop until we get to the car, just in case the desperate waitress decides to throw some frozen peas under our feet to stop us so she can molest my dad. "Women are confusing," Dad says as he maneuvers the car out of the parking lot.

"Why is it that guys think women are confusing, but women think guys are confusing? Shouldn't there be some kind of dictionary or something to help us translate for each other?"

Dad laughs sadly as he brakes to a stop at a light. "I'm a lot older than you, and I clearly don't get it. I mean, look at Thea. I thought we . . . well, I thought maybe . . ." He glances sideways at me. "I guess I thought she might be someone I could be interested in. But now, with Melvin . . . I guess I just misread it."

I gaze absently out the window as we pass groups of people already starting their Saturday night. "I don't know, Dad. I think she likes you. But she has history with Melvin, you know."

"And a daughter," he adds. "I don't want to get in the middle of that. I guess I should just admit defeat and build something else."

My cell buzzes in my pocket. "Hi, Becca."

"So, are you finished with your dad yet?" From the sound of it, the girls have migrated from the coffee shop to an arcade or something; electronic pings and buzzes and bleeps make it hard to hear.

"Not quite," I lie. "We're just heading home now."

"We're coming over." Becca says something to someone else in the room with her, then comes back to the phone. "We're trying to get a ride over. Thea's being difficult, but Amber's mom might be able to pick us up. Honestly, you need to get your driver's license. Anyway, we got a few more ideas we want to tell you about, and I need you to help with a couple of things."

I guess I'm going to be involved whether I want to be or not. "Okay," I say lamely, minus my spine.

Dad can sense my deflation. "So? Further complications?" We're stopped at a light, and a group of punk rock girls shuffles across the street smoking cigarettes. "I'm just glad you're not out doing stuff like that," he says as he gestures toward the girls. "Your problems are relatively minor compared to substance abuse and tattoos."

"Hey, Becca has a tattoo," I remind him. "And maybe I should get one, too."

He flinches. "Please don't. I don't want to have to spend your college fund on laser removal." We're only a couple of blocks from home, and Dad knows that the moment of reckoning is at hand for me. "So, what are you going to tell her? Are you going to help or not?"

"Seems like an easy question," I answer. I start sweating more the closer we get to home. "Maybe I should do what Euphoria said. Just help them plan it and then don't show up."

"Is that what she said?" Dad pulls into our driveway, and thankfully no one else is there yet. "She's pretty smart. I'd help you out myself, but I'm going to be gone that weekend. There's a conference in Santa Barbara."

And that's when it hits me, the solution to all my problems, conflicts, and issues: I will just be in two places at once. It's a great plan! I'll help plan the Geek Prom, work on it as if I'll be attending, then on the night of the event, I'll show up to help them set up, forget something, and go to the real prom with Fletcher. I'll just duck back and forth all night, and everyone will be happy. Nobody will know I went to the other event, and no one will be mad at me, and I'll have a boyfriend *and* a best friend, and everything will be super swell.

I am a genius. I can't wait to tell Euphoria.

Becca and the girls arrive about ten minutes later, and Dad makes sure he's nowhere to be found just in case Thea exits the car for a change. Fired up about my new plan, I am all smiles, cheery, perky even. "Wow, you're in a good mood all of a sudden," Elisa notices as we flop over various pieces of furniture in the living room.

"Why shouldn't I be?"

Becca frowns suspiciously. "An hour ago you were the face of doom, and now you're bordering on manic. What happened?"

"Nothing." I produce a clipboard filled optimistically with lined paper. "I just want to get going on this project. Now, what's my job?"

No one says anything at first; Amber finally pipes up. "We just thought you didn't want to have anything to do with it, to be honest." She peers out from behind her long, shiny hair. "Because of Fletcher and all."

"Fletcher!" I yell a bit too loudly. Everyone looks startled, so I tone it down. "Ha! What, do you think he owns me? That he can tell me what to do or something? I'm not his sidekick, his geisha, his trained pet monkey."

"Uh, I don't think anyone accused you of being a trained pet monkey—" Elisa starts, but I interrupt. I'm on a roll.

"I'm nobody's girl. I work for myself. I'm independent, a free thinker, somebody who makes her own decisions and blows whichever way the wind takes her." I'm out of breath at that point, so I just shut up.

"Well," Becca says, clapping slowly. "And the Academy Award goes to . . ."

"No, really," I say, a bit more subdued. "I don't belong to Fletcher. I like him, of course, but I make my own decisions."

Becca squints at me as if trying to decide if I'm telling the truth or simply telling her what she wants to hear. I guess she decides I'm being honest, because her face relaxes into a wide-open smile. "Great," she says, grinning. "We're glad to count you in."

Even as she says it, though, I get this little gray thundercloud feeling in the bottom of my stomach. You know the spot: It's where the part of you that knows best goes to hide when the irrational person running your brain tries to chop them up with an axe. Pen poised over clipboard, I chirp, "So, what am I going to be doing?"

"Have you lost your mind?" Euphoria squawks at me in the comfort of my room. Everyone has gone and I've confided to her my entire crazy plan. "There is no way you can carry it off!"

"But you told me to go with it . . . remember? Just make each person believe that I was on their side, and then they'd never know the difference until the night of the event. But this way, they'll *never* know." I sip the delicious hot chocolate she's made for me and wiggle my bunny slippers. Pajamas are the best; I believe everyone should wear them all the time and then there would be no war.

Euphoria buries her metallic head in her claws. "Oh, Shelby," she moans. "I've failed you."

"What?"

"Don't you see?" She beeps and rolls toward the door and back, her version of pacing. "This is a classic failed scheme from some old television show. You try to be in two places at once. You begin the evening fairly well, but things happen: Traffic stops. You lose a shoe. A black hole opens up between the space/time continuum. Something. And there you are, trapped between the two events, participating in neither, and both your friends are angry and will never forgive you, and you'll end up becoming scrap at some auto yard south of the railroad tracks." She rewinds the conversation in her head, chirps, then says, "Well, probably not the scrap part. That would be me. But you will alienate all of your friends."

Wiping the chocolate milk mustache from my lips, I contentedly lean back against my headboard and sigh. "Nothing can bring me down. I know this will work."

"What about transportation?" Euphoria crosses her arms, *click-click*, and stands there blinking at me self-righteously. "How do you plan to get from the drive-in to the hotel and back?"

My bunny slippers droop, disappointed. "I hadn't thought of that," I admit slowly. "I'll just get my permit before then. And I'll get Dad to let me borrow the car." I smile triumphantly. Crisis averted.

"He won't let you borrow the car!" she screeches. "Are you insane?"

"Oh. Yeah, you're right." I bite the inside of my cheek, something I do whenever I have a particularly difficult puzzle to solve. "I guess I'll make copies of the car keys."

Euphoria doesn't say anything; she rolls out of my room and down the hallway toward the kitchen. "Mark my words," she moans like some movie-set ghost. Nobody seems to have confidence in wildly unworkable plans anymore.

It turns out that my job for Geek Prom is going to be the food. That's actually perfect, because I can order it, have it delivered, show up to set it up early, and then ditch out to meet Fletcher at the hotel where the real prom is being held. (I realize the hypocrisy that goes with me calling it the "real" prom, but it's the shortest description I could think of. Saying "consumeristic overpriced formal event" is a real mouthful.) I spend most of Sunday calling various restaurants to find out if they cater, and how much it will be, and whether or not they have vegetarian dishes in addition to pigs in a blanket.

In the midst of my telephone frenzy, Fletcher calls. "So?" he asks as if I should know the answer to that question.

"So what?" I answer as I finish jotting down prices for the Fancy Clam Seafood Buffet.

"Did you have some time to think about our little outing yesterday?" I hear him munching over the phone. "I'm having pizza, by the way, if you'd like to come over and share it with me."

I gulp involuntarily. Go to his house? The site of my most recent major embarrassment? "Uh . . . Pizza sounds really tempting, but I have some homework to finish before tomorrow."

"Ah." He sounds disappointed, but not upset. "Anyway, the other thing I wanted to ask about is what you're wearing. To prom."

"Uh . . ." Again with the eloquent comments. "Hey, do you know why Becca and Carl broke up?"

"Oh, do I know. Yeah, he told me the whole story. But I'll tell you after you tell me what you're wearing. I don't want to clash."

Dang. I tried the old evasive maneuver and was shot down. "I really haven't found anything yet."

"Color? Could you just pick one?"

"Why don't you pick?" I flip through my notes and notice that the cost for the Fancy Clam would be twice as much as buying tofu and veggie platters from The Naked Fruit, my favorite health food store. See, vegetarianism is better for you *and* cheaper. I'm not entirely sure I can sell the other Queen Geeks on soy burgers, but we'll see.

"Blue?" he says.

"Fine. Blue it is."

He stops chewing. "Really? That was easy. Okay, then. I'll be looking for something with blue in it. That's great. Oh, and what happened with Becca and Carl was that he asked her again if she'd please go with him to the prom and just have her thing on another night, and she said no, and he asked her why, and she said it was none of his business, and then I guess there was some throwing of pillows or something, and Carl finally just decided enough was enough, and he split." He clears his throat and says pointedly, "I'm sure glad we didn't end up having a big blowup like that. I think Becca's a little too stubborn, don't you?"

I stop myself from defending her; after all, if my evil plan is going to work, I have to keep it on the down low or everything will be ruined. Excessive standing up for friends might tip Fletcher off, so I play meek and mild: "I guess." Well, I wasn't about to give him more than that; I do have some dignity to maintain, even if it is slightly tarnished.

After I hang up, I feel overwhelmed by all the stuff I have to do. Checking the calendar (a cute one with big-eyed dogs and cats morphed into disturbing shapes), I see that I have exactly four weeks before P-Day (prom day, for those who couldn't figure it out). I know I can take the classroom portion of the driver's ed stuff online, and then I can get a learner's permit, and I can get Dad to take me out driving so I can get some experience before the big day.

Euphoria notices that I'm frantically surfing the Web looking for driving courses. "Shelby, I hope you know that you're not allowed to drive by yourself," she clucks over my shoulder. "Even if you do get your learner's permit, you have to have an adult in the car with you at all times."

"What's your definition of an adult?" I ask, tapping away.

"Uh . . . an adult? Someone older than you are, someone with more experience." I turn and grin at her. "Oh, no. I'm not going. Don't drag me into this."

"Euphoria, you're my only hope. Dad will never help me with this. He'll think it's stupid and dishonest and dangerous."

"Which it is."

"Yeah, I know." I groan. "But it's the only way I can see to keep everyone happy." I flutter my eyes at her, putting on my biggest, baddest puppy peepers to get her to do what I want. "Please? Euphoria, you're kind of like my other parent, you know."

She sort of chokes up a little, which sounds like rusty metal filings grating on a tin roof, and if she had tear ducts, I think she'd have cried. "Oh, Shelby," she says softly. "That's the sweetest thing anyone has ever said to me."

I feel a little bit bad for manipulating her like that, but I ignore it and the feeling passes. I mean, it's not like she can really get in trouble; she's not a person, so I don't think she can go to jail. And if I dress her up, I could probably pass her off as my old aunt Effie or something. Anyway, probably no one will stop me and so it won't be an issue. But first, I have to get over the hurdle that is Dad.

I find him tinkering in his studio/lab/workshop in the converted garage. This is where I usually find him, if he's not depressed and swinging on the front porch. No boring doorknobs for my dad; he has a door that swooshes open, like the ones in the old *Star Trek*. The room looks as if an auto shop, a factory, and Microsoft headquarters were sucked into a black hole and set back down in random order.

"Dad?" I ask cautiously. You don't want to surprise my dad when he's in the studio; he's liable to electrocute you or himself, or blow something up. "Dad? I need to ask you something."

"Hmm?" His eyes are covered by huge plastic safety goggles, and he's hunched over a circuit board, staring at it through an oversized magnifying lamp. "Hang on." He solders something and the smell of burning metal and silicone slices into the air. He straightens up, pushes the goggles out of the way, and looks at me expectantly.

"I need to get my learner's permit. For driving." He says nothing, so I continue. "There's an online course I can take to do the classroom portion of it, so all I need is your credit card, and then you can teach me to drive. How's that sound?"

"Uh . . . bad?" He shakes his head. "I'm not ready for you to drive. You've only been sixteen since January, only a few weeks, Shelby."

"A few months, Dad," I say, a little more snotty than I should be. "And besides, wouldn't it be great if you didn't have to haul me around everywhere I need to go?"

"I kind of like hauling you around. I get to see more of you." He nudges the still-smoking circuit board with a latex-gloved hand. "I don't know, honey. Why do we have to do it now?"

"Well, to be honest . . . I've been thinking of doing volunteer work. At the orphanage." Oh, boy. I am surely going to burn in hell.

"Do we *have* an orphanage?"

To distract myself, I start picking up bits of discarded wire and plastic off the floor, putting them in his trash can. "Sure. I know it sounds strange, but colleges really look at that kind of stuff. I need to start racking up some community service. And I need to be mobile to do that." I don't look at him; I'm kind of ashamed of how easy it is for me to lie about orphans who don't exist.

"College, huh?" He rubs his stubbly chin and thinks about it for a minute, then sighs. "Okay. I guess it has to happen sooner or later. Let's go set up the class online, and we'll get you started. But schoolwork still comes first."

"Sure." I give him a big hug. "Thanks, Daddy." I'm a horrible person. But it's all for a good cause, I remind myself: saving me from being totally and utterly alone.

Later, I call Becca to tell her the good news. "My dad is letting me get my permit," I squeal.

"Awesome!" she squeals back. "How soon before you can drive us all around?"

"Legally? I think I have to wait till I'm, like, twenty-one or something." I am sitting on my bed, making my bunny slippers do ballet. "Of course, off the record . . ."

"Oooh. You are bad." Becca chuckles an evil little laugh. "Of course, that's one of the reasons I like you."

I don't want her to think I've totally become corrupted, though, so I add, "Of course, I'd only transport people my own age in an emergency. You know, like if we needed to go to a study session or something like that."

"Right." Becca sighs into the phone, and I hear her making squeaky stretching sounds. "Oh, by the way, Melvin is totally in. I convinced him that helping us with our event would be good for his career, too. I mean, he hasn't really had a hit since 1995, so he could use the publicity."

"Was that the year he did *Killer Pumpkin*?" Boy, that was a stinker, I'll tell you. But a lot of people liked it, I guess. It fed everyone's secret fear of jack-o'-lanterns and getting fat on mini-Snickers. "Is that the movie he wants to show?"

"I don't know yet. He's been talking about screening it again, a retrospective sort of thing. He also has a new movie coming out that he's thinking he might premiere at our event."

"Brand-new? That would be cool." The bunny slippers look fatigued, so I let them take five. "What's the new movie about?"

"It's *The Drainpeople*. It takes place under this old house, where a whole race of mutants lives in the sewer, and they come up out of people's toilets to wreak havoc on the population."

"And I suppose too much two-ply toilet paper got them mad?"

"Not sure he goes into the details that much," she answers. "It's mostly just an excuse for gory scenes in people's bathrooms and girls in wet T-shirts."

"A piece of art."

"Indeed." She yawns. "Gotta go. Meet me at lunch tomorrow, under the tree. Good night."

I flip my phone closed and smile contentedly. I hope nobody pops out of my toilet unannounced. That would kind of ruin my good mood.

When I finally get to our designated lunch spot the next day, everybody's already there, and things look a little tense. Becca's fuming, Evie looks miserable, and Amber and Elisa are sitting between them, looking like they expect machine-gun fire to erupt at any moment. "So, hey," I call as cheerily as possible.

Becca waves halfheartedly. Evie says nothing. Elisa explains: "Carl asked Evie to the prom."

"What?"

Amber nods. "Yep. He called her and actually asked her to go."

"And she said . . ."

"I said no, obviously!" Evie shouts. "But some people"—she shoots a malicious look at Becca—"don't seem to understand that I cannot control what her former boyfriend does."

Amitha and Naveen show up and Elisa goes all wet noodle. "Hi, honey," she says, so sweet I feel a diabetic coma coming on. "I'm so glad we're not fighting."

"Yeah, it's quite a relief," Naveen answers as he grabs Elisa around the waist and gives her a squeeze. Amitha rolls her eyes and plops down on the grass. "My sister is here to report on her progress regarding decorations," Naveen says.

Becca perks up a little, momentarily distracted from her disastrous love life. "That's great, Amitha. What have you figured out?"

"I want to do the whole thing in silver and black, like an old movie," she says, eyes shining. "Maybe even some big silver statues, like the Oscars. Very classy."

"That would be good except that the movie we're going to show is about as far from Oscar material as a health-class sex ed film," Elisa grumbles as she nuzzles Naveen's neck.

"Some of those are actually pretty entertaining," Naveen answers, grinning. Elisa smacks him as Amber blushes violently behind her hair. "Where's Jon, Amber? Isn't he part of the Geek Prom posse?"

"Yeah, he's helping, but he had to go to the photo darkroom to develop some pictures for his class." Amber leans against the tree and stares wistfully in the direction of the photo lab. "He shot a whole roll of black-and-white photos of garbage. It's really artistic."

"So, are we going with the drive-in?" Naveen asks.

Becca clears her throat noisily. "As a matter of fact, my dad has already made arrangements for it. He had to pay twice the regular price because they already had some event booked there that night, but once they heard he'd be screening a premiere of a new movie, they jumped."

"And how are the plans for global domination coming, Evie?" Elisa asks. "The computers and such."

"Dad is renting all that equipment, too," Becca answers instead. "We just have to get it hooked up and make sure the people in the other parts of the world are on board." Evie just sulks.

"And my most important concern—food?" Elisa asks as she munches on a chicken salad sandwich.

"I called a bunch of places yesterday," I answer, "but I still don't know which one is best. We'll get something together, though, don't worry."

"Are we all going together to look for clothes at some point?"

Amber asks. "I think it'd be fun. Especially since we don't have to wear stupid taffeta dresses and heels."

"But I was really looking forward to that," Naveen protests. "I look *great* in taffeta."

The conversation drifts into details of Geek Prom–related things, but my mind is elsewhere, specifically with Fletcher. I don't know where he is, but I suspect he's comforting Carl after his painful breakup. I'm going to need two outfits, I realize; one blue thing for the real prom, and something else kind of funky for Geek Prom. I guess maybe I'd better get Euphoria to Velcro everything so I can make like Superman and change in a phone booth. Or in the back of the Volvo.

"He only asked me out so he could get you to pay attention," Evie blurts out. Everybody stops chewing. "He really likes *you*, Becca. Why are you mad at me?" She's practically crying. "I've done everything you've asked, and I've put tons of time into this project. You're going to punish me for something I have no control over?"

Becca's clenched jaw relaxes just a bit, and I see her soften. "I know you can't help it if he picks up the phone and calls you. But why did he call *you*? I guess what I keep coming back to is that you must have done something to make him think you might go with him." With that out in the open, she chomps down on a big apple violently and challenges Evie to prove her wrong.

Evie grabs her bag, throws it over her shoulder, and stands up in the graceful, tornadolike way only a really pissed-off girl can manage. "Listen, if I wanted your stupid boyfriend, I'd already

have him. I'll talk to you again after you've figured that out."
She trudges angrily across the grassy lawn.

"Harmony reigns supreme," Elisa says sarcastically. "No
wonder we have a hard time getting things done."

11

DRESS TO CONFESS

(or The Secret Lives of Liars)

"Watch the curb. Watch the curb!" Dad screams and covers his face. So much for having a calm, seasoned driving instructor.

"I wasn't going to hit it," I reason with him. In fact, I missed it by at least a portion of an inch. I'm steering the Volvo down our tree-lined street, and I have to say I'm getting the feel for driving. I'm a natural at it. It's like I'm one with the car, a glorious blending of girl and machine, and intuitively I can feel the power of the beast beneath me, raring to go, wanting to put on a burst of speed. Unfortunately, Dad doesn't understand cars like I do. He gets mad if I go over the speed limit.

I took the online driving course, and it was so easy that it makes me worry about other people driving, to be honest. It's supposed to take thirty hours, but I did it in a lot less time (a *lot* less). Within a couple of days I got my certificate of completion, and we took that down to the DMV, which I believe stands for the Department of the Monumentally Vague. Nobody could answer any questions I had unless I got into at least three lines and waited for at least twenty minutes in each one. I usually ended up back in the original line with the same vague person behind the counter, and once I'd done the line shuffle, the person was able to help me. It's kind of like a ritual or something. Maybe if I'd brought a chicken to sacrifice, I could have saved myself some time. Either way, I find out that I have to wait for my official learner's permit to come in the mail.

Anyway, Dad and I are driving on a beautiful Saturday morning after a grueling week of schoolwork and the prolonged silent treatment between Becca and Evie. I'm kind of concerned that if they don't patch it up, the whole Geek Prom thing will fall apart (which wouldn't be so bad, I guess). I'm driving over to pick up Becca and Amber and Elisa so we can go shop for Geek Prom clothes. I'll have to go separately to get my traditional stuff, since I'm not really supposed to be going to the real prom. I may have to bust out my trunkful of disguises in order to shop incognito.

"Okay, now, slowly apply your foot to the brake," Dad says evenly. I jam my foot down and the car lurches forward as if an invisible hand has grabbed the back end. Tires screech and I smell burning rubber, so I throw Dad my most dazzling smile. He just pops another Tums and breathes deeply.

As I pull into Becca's circular driveway, I honk a little pattern to let her know we're there. Dad slumps down in his seat, hoping, I guess, that Thea doesn't see him, or that he doesn't see her (or, more important, her and Melvin). Becca races out of the front door, a backpack slung over her shoulder, and she opens the back door as I get out to let Dad take over.

"So, how—" I don't get further than that because Becca stands, grinning, at the open door of the car, her long fingers pointing to her now unspiked hair. "What happened?" I gasp.

"I decided I needed a new look for the event." She does a little twirl, showing off the short, gold-blond pixie cut that has replaced the signature white spikes. "What do you think?"

We climb into the backseat, and I can't take my eyes off the hair. "I think it's good," I mumble. It just seems so strange to see it different, since she's worn it the same way ever since I met her during our freshman year. "It really makes your eyes stand out."

"Yeah," she says, fluttering her eyelashes. "I plan to get an extremely funky outfit to match."

Meanwhile, Dad is driving as fast as he legally can away from Becca's house, and doesn't seem to mind playing chauffeur. When we pick up Amber and Elisa, they shove into the backseat while I take the front, then squeal simultaneously when they see Becca's new do. "Wow," Elisa says. "You look shorter now. I feel closer to you."

"I guess that's a plus," Becca says, shrugging.

Dad graciously drives us to Parklane Mall and also graciously hands over a wad of cash so I can buy my necessaries. "See you in two hours," he says as he gives me a peck on the cheek and then pulls away.

"Shelby was driving when they got to my house," Becca says casually.

"What?" Amber slaps me on the arm, a little too hard. "You didn't tell us you could drive!"

"Technically, I can't. I'm supposed to wait until I get my official learner's permit, but Dad is letting me try it out, just on our streets and near the house and stuff."

"Is it fun?" Elisa asks as we shove through the double doors of Silver Buckle, one of my favorite stores. "Driving, I mean?"

"Yeah. What's most fun is knowing that at some point I won't have to depend on my dad for rides." Amber has already zipped across the store and is waving frantically for us to come over.

"Look what I found, right off the bat!" She holds up a faux leather waistcoat trimmed with red velvet. "Isn't this awesome?"

"If you want to dress up like Dracula's French maid, I guess," Elisa snorts. "But for you, I suppose that would work. I, on the other hand, will need something for the more vertically challenged." Elisa putts over to the petite section.

I'm still staring at Becca's hair; I can't help it. She does look a little less tall, but somehow older, and the deeper platinum blond sets off her pale skin and eyes. "You look like a model," I tell her.

To ruin the magical modeling moment, she does her donkey-honk laugh, makes a horrific, contorted goofy face, and picks up a fuchsia-colored corset with lime-green ties. "What about this?"

"Only if you want to be in *Rocky Horror Picture Show*." I browse through racks of fancy dresses, little black dresses, slinky dresses, and dresses so skimpy they really shouldn't be called dresses, but cocktail napkins. "What are you looking for exactly?"

Her face squinting in concentration, she bites her lips as she considers a turquoise blue satin jacket with a matching scarf. "Something with a lot of color. Something glamorous but not prommy."

"Prommy? Congratulations, Mrs. Webster. You've just hatched a new word."

And then I find it.

I expect a golden light and a choir of angels to sing a power chord as I pull this exquisite outfit off the rack. It's a shining sage green sleeveless mini, slit from knee to mid-thigh. It comes with a pair of black capri tights, and I can't wait to try it on. In the dressing room, I peel off my clothes like they're on fire, and then reverently unzip the dress.

When I slip it over my head, it feels like I've just met the dress I will spend the rest of my life with. I mean, it fits tightly in all the right places but doesn't hug too close to anything. The slits in the skirt hit at just the perfect place, and the neckline is cut just low enough to be revealing but not low enough to be slutty. The fabric, soft and cool as a cloudy summer morning, clings to me and seems to energize every inch of skin it comes into contact with. In short, I want to marry this dress.

I slip into the tights and check myself in the mirror. Dazzling. I walk outside so I can share my gorgeousness with everyone else.

Standing in front of the full-length mirror, Elisa picks and pulls at a cobalt blue pantsuit trimmed with fake diamond buttons. "I look like the mother of the bride," she moans. She looks at my reflection standing behind hers, and her eyes go wide.

"Holy God, that's the most gorgeous dress I've ever seen!" she gasps.

Becca and Amber hear her and come dashing out of the dressing room in various stages of decency, but no one else is in the store, so it doesn't matter. They all coo and ooh and ahh over my perfect dress, just like normal girls. "Of course," Becca says as she heads back toward her cubicle, "you'll have to wear tennies with it."

"Tennies?" I gasp, faking drama. "This dress cannot be worn with tennies. It will explode."

The rest of the girls eventually find something formal yet funky to wear, and it's kind of fun to spend some time just doing what other girls do, namely, primping and squealing about clothes. We hardly ever do it, which is fine, but today it feels good. I also eyeball a really traditional blue gown that I might be able to come back for later to form the basis of my super-secret real prom getup.

"We still have about an hour before my dad picks us up," I say. "Let's go over to the bread place." The bread place is a restaurant where they have amazing French bread and soup and stuff, and they play classic jazz and have soft lighting. Plus, it's less crowded than the food court.

We drag our bags into the restaurant, find a cozy booth, order food, and park. "This is going to be the best event ever," Amber says between sips of iced tea. "Is Evie still going to work out the details of linking it to places around the world?"

Becca's expression goes sour at the mention of Evie. "I don't know. Maybe we'll just do our own little local thing and forget about the rest of the world. I don't know if I can trust her."

"Just because Carl is using her to get to you?" Elisa asks. "That's not really fair. Look at how you'd feel if the roles were reversed."

"Well, I know I'd just tell the guy to eat dirt," Becca snaps. "I certainly wouldn't spend time discussing it."

"Do you even know what happened?" I ask. "Did she actually encourage this or did Carl just think of it on his own?"

"I can't believe Carl would think of anything on his own," Becca answers snottily. "But of course, no, I really haven't researched it."

"Then it's not very fair of you to be mad at Evie." Amber grabs a breadstick from a black basket in the middle of the table and chomps off the end. "I always thought friendships were more important than guys."

Caught in an obvious paradox of reason, Becca chooses to choke on her iced tea rather than answer. Elisa claps her on the back (a little too hard, I think) until Becca waves her away with serious swatting action. "I'd rather die from choking than be beaten to death by Shorty McViolent!" Becca says in a strangled voice.

"I was just trying to save your life," Elisa says, sulking. "Sorry. Next time I'll let you croak." She turns to me, ignoring Becca. "So, Shelby, how's the driving coming?"

"Fine." Of course, I don't tell them about my super-secret plot to be in two places at once with the help of my trusty

Volvo. "I'm starting to get the hang of it. I think I could actually drive by myself."

"When can we find out?" Becca asks, suddenly interested.

"I can't drive any of you until I get my actual license. If I got caught my license would be suspended until I'm thirty or something, and I'd probably go to jail."

"I hear there are some nice-looking guys in jail," Amber says casually. Everyone looks at her like she's nuts. "Well, I'm just saying. They can't be really picky, so I think they'd be extremely loyal."

"Yeah, and Shelby could go and stage a jailbreak for her new boyfriend," Elisa says, laughing. "I can see your dad's face when you bring home a stray felon."

A tall pimply boy is suddenly standing over us. We all look up and I imagine we look like a pack of puppies with our heads cocked to one side, puzzled looks on our puppy faces. "Yes?" Becca asks.

"Are you Becca Gallagher?" Pimply guy scratches his neck.

"Maybe. Who wants to know?" Becca eases back against the booth, eyeing the stranger, considering, I suppose, whether she'll have to bust out her fake karate moves on him.

"Dude, chill. I just have a message for you." He tosses an envelope onto the table, grabs a breadstick, grins, and chomps the end off it as he walks away. "Later."

Becca opens the envelope, slips a letter out of it, and begins to read out loud. "Dear Becca, I know you think I am trying to go out with Evie and that I want to ditch you. In fact, you are in error. I would very much like to talk to you about what's going on. If you ever thought there was anything between us, please meet me in front of Game Rage at five. Sincerely, Carl." Becca looks up at us and shrugs her shoulders. "So? Paper's cheap."

Amber sighs, exasperated. "Becca, just go talk to him. What do you have to lose?"

Becca bites her lower lip, and rubs the letter between her thumb and forefinger as if some secret message in Braille will float to the surface and she'll get some divine answer. "Okay," she says finally. "But I want the three of you watching from somewhere to see if he tries to abduct me."

"Abduct you?" Elisa snorts. "We're not in one of your dad's movies, Becca. Carl isn't the abducting type."

Becca shoots her a withering look. "And I suppose you know all about the abducting type?"

"I read," Elisa says loftily. A bit more softly she says, "Anyway, we'll be glad to watch. Just in case you need reinforcements."

The meeting Carl has set up is in about half an hour, so we walk casually over to the area of the mall where Game Rage, the mega video-and-board-game store, is located. "I think the best vantage point will probably be the bookstore," Elisa says as she calculates the shortest distance between two points. "We can get a really good look at what's going on as long as you keep him in front of the *Star Wars* display. Don't go behind Darth Vader or we won't be able to see you."

"I'll make sure I keep him away from all supervillains," Becca promises. "Just don't bury your heads in books and forget to watch."

Becca heads over to Game Rage while we prowl around the shelves of the bookstore. In order to keep an eye on the game store, we're unfortunately stuck behind a display of cheesy romance novels. Amber picks one up, opens it, begins to read, and makes a disgusted face. "Okay, listen to this: *Jane Faraday worked a normal job behind the counter at the quaint diner and butcher shop in a quaint mountain town. Her life was calm and simple until one day, a lumberjack named Asher Merrywind appears and orders the Blue Plate Special with a side of romance. Amidst the majestic backdrop of the towering Redwoods, Jane and Asher find love and passion can heat up even in the subzero temperatures of the meat locker.*" Amber closes the book with distaste and slams it back onto the shelf. "That sounds totally perverted."

"Where did you put it?" Elisa asks, nosing through the titles in front of Amber.

"Elisa, you don't want to read trash like that!" Amber exclaims.

Elisa turns to her and blushes. "Oh, right. Of course I don't." As we drift down the aisle, I notice that Elisa grabs the novel and tucks it into her pocket. I don't say anything.

Amber suddenly ducks down below the romance novels (so our eyes are even with the heaving bodices and rippling pecs of countless fictional lovers) and hisses, "He's here! I see him!"

Elisa and I automatically crouch down next to her. "Why are we whispering?" Elisa whispers.

"Oh." Amber straightens up just a bit so only her eyes are peeping over the tops of the shelves. "Yeah, I guess he probably can't hear us."

Becca stands with arms across her chest, like an Amazon warrior girl ready to defend her territory. Carl, who stands a few inches taller, hunches like a dog waiting to be slapped with a rolled-up newspaper. Becca's gesturing now, and her face is getting redder, and Carl is starting to talk back. The two of them begin to look like two storks having a pecking war. Carl reaches into his pocket and pulls something out, shows it to her, and she slaps it out of his hand.

"I don't think it's going well," Amber says worriedly.

"At least nobody's gotten violent—" Elisa says as Becca slaps Carl across the face so hard it rings off the mall's marble fountain. "Oops. Spoke too soon."

"We'd better get over there before she does something to get herself arrested," I say, leading the charge.

We hustle out of the bookstore, momentarily delayed because Elisa sets off the book sensor with the meat locker romance in her pocket. She turns a violent shade of red and plucks it out of her pocket, tossing it across the floor as if it's infested with plague. "Sorry!" she yells to the manager, who watches, puzzled, from behind the counter.

"Hey, Carl!" I shout as we screech to a halt in front of a mess that looks like it could become World War III. "How's it going?" Lame. But what do you say to someone who's just been assaulted by your best friend? "Hey, did she draw blood?" Not very classy.

Breathless, Becca responds by kicking Carl in the shin. He howls in pain, and she runs into Game Rage, leaving us to clean up the mess.

"Are you okay?" Amber asks, bending over to check Carl's injuries.

"Did she draw blood?" Elisa asks, a gleam in her eye.

Carl bends at the waist, massaging his shin. "I don't know what is wrong with that girl. All I want to do is take her to a nice dance. Why is that so bad?" He rolls up the leg of his pants. "Geez, I think I *am* bleeding."

What do I say to him? I'd be in the same boat, I guess, if it weren't for my brilliant plan. I'd share it with Carl, but then he'd probably give it away, and I'd be ruined. Sometimes you have to think of self-preservation above other things. "I think it's best that you just stay away from her for a while," I say wisely, putting a comforting arm around Carl's elbow. (I can't reach his shoulder, so that's the best I can do.)

He gazes wistfully into the shelves of Game Rage, looking for his Amazon. "Yeah, I guess you're right," he says softly. Turning to go, he hunches, dejected, and shuffles off toward the exit. "Oh," he says, turning toward us forlornly. "Tell her she can keep the necklace."

The scene is so pathetic it really needs a tragic violin soundtrack. "Necklace?" Amber asks. She scans the floor and picks something up. "Look." It's a delicate silver chain, and looped onto it is a silver rabbit charm. "Aw . . . it's because they met when he was wearing the rabbit suit at Comic-Con," she says, choking up. "That's so sweet. Why is she being such a . . . a . . ."

"What was that?" Becca's suddenly standing right there, and we all jump. "Let me be clear, ladies: Carl is history. I want nothing to do with him. And you can throw that"—she gestures toward the jewelry—"in the trash."

She stalks off, leaving a trail of friends behind her scrambling to catch up. Amber gestures to me with the necklace, and I take it, put it in my pocket, and hope that at some point she might want it back. After all, how many guys do you meet who will wear a rabbit suit to get your attention?

The next day, Sunday, Becca calls me early. She sounds perky. "The Geek Prom is in three weeks. We need to advertise. I'm sending you a flier, so check it out." She hangs up and I go to my computer, get the file, and check it out.

It's a picture of a drive-in movie screen with the words G E E K   P R O M scrolled across it in horror movie lettering. A woman's terrified face looms over the screen, her hand clutched to her mouth as if stifling a scream. The ad reads:

Scared of high prom prices?
Terrified of uncomfortable clothes that you can't dance in?
Horrified at the thought of spending $80 for cocktail

weinies and an etched champagne glass when you can't even drink champagne?

Then go beyond the ordinary and ditch it all for

GEEK PROM!

Then the flier goes on to outline the great things you get for the $20 price of admission: the screening of renowned director Melvin Gallagher's newest horror film, *The Drainpeople,* fantastic food from the city's most famous eateries, and VIRTUAL PROM, where kids attending Geek Proms all over the world will network with ours via satellite. Plus DJ Jammin' Jon and the biggest outside dance floor under the stars! It does sound pretty fabulous.

I call her back. "Looks really good. I'd go."

"Well, of course you'd go. But will other people?"

"I think so."

"We have a couple of television stations from L.A. coming down to do a promo on the event." Becca sounds extremely pleased with herself.

"Wow, that's great. And local TV also?"

"Sure. People from all over town will be clamoring to go. People at Green Pines will be lucky if they can *get* tickets." She goes quiet for a moment, then says, "Shelby, I want you to know something. I understand what a sacrifice it is for you not to go to the regular prom with Fletcher. I get it, I really do. And the fact that you chose to stick with me instead of him means a lot." Cue churning stomach and guilty conscience.

"Yeah, well," I say weakly. "You are my best friend. Geeks before guys, right?" Change the subject, change the subject. "But you know, we really need to get Evie back on board if you want the virtual thing to happen. And honestly, based on what happened with Carl, I don't think any of it was her fault, do you?" I absently rub at Carl's silver rabbit charm lying on my desk. "He just wants you, that's all."

"I know." She sighs, exasperated. "Listen, could you be a great friend and go next door to talk to her? Or text her or something? I do feel bad about what I said, but I don't know if she'll even talk to me."

"Sure. I'll go over after we hang up. Call you later."

Euphoria has rolled into my room and pretends to be dusting when she's really eavesdropping. "So, have you given up this harebrained scheme of yours?"

"Nope. And you're still going with me, Aunt Effie." I pat her on her metallic shoulders. "I'll find you a nice flannel wrap so you don't catch cold or get rusty."

She shakes her head, her green eye lights flashing. "Nothing good will come of this."

I text a desperate message to Evie's cell, as promised. Within minutes, my phone chimes, and she's agreed to drop in.

While I wait for her to show up, I use the time to become less disgusting—you know, brush my teeth, comb my hair. Euphoria, however, just cannot leave me alone. "You should just come clean and confess," she whispers as she wipes down the bathroom counter for the third time.

"Euphoria, stop nagging me about it. The plan is good, and it will work, and my life will be fantastic and free of stress." The doorbell rings, and I plant a kiss on her cheek plate as I dash to answer it. "Have a positive attitude."

"I'm positive it will not work," she mutters.

Evie, wearing her trademark black glasses, shorts, and a brown T-shirt with a cream-colored skull on it, is leaning against the jamb when I open the door. "Well?"

"Come in?"

She looks over my shoulder, I guess to see if Becca is lurking behind brandishing a sharpened salad fork or something. Seeing nobody, she says, "Okay. But if this is about Queen Geeks—"

"Hey, let's just have some lemonade first." I gesture toward our living room where the big comfy couch awaits. Euphoria seamlessly takes the cue and heads for the kitchen, and Evie watches her as she rolls off.

"I still can't get over the fact that you have your own robot," she begins, but I stop her with an upraised hand.

"Don't call her a 'robot.' She's kind of sensitive about that." Evie shrugs, as if to question why a robot would be sensitive. And come to think of it, she kind of has a point, but I have more important things to talk about. "I asked you over because I need your help."

"*You* need my help?" Evie snorts, leaning against the soft velvet back of the sofa. "Or Becca needs my help?"

I have to play this just right if I want it to work. "I know she's been unreasonable. She knows it, too," I lied. Well, it was a little white lie, really, not totally untrue. She probably does know that she's unreasonable sometimes. I just think the times she thinks she's unreasonable and the times other people think she's unreasonable are often different. "Anyway, I want to remind you that there's a greater good here, a chance to really make your mark before you go back home. And none of us have the skills to make this happen."

"I didn't think you wanted it to happen." Evie takes a glass of lemonade from Euphoria, who has silently glided in with her silver tray and Southern hospitality.

"I hope y'all enjoy the libation," she drawls in an exaggerated accent. "I added a twist of mint to cool you off."

Evie just shoots her a crooked grin and sips the drink. "Lovely, thanks."

"Anyway, back to the situation." I take a drink, too, just to buy some time. "You know that Carl and Becca had problems, and he tried to get her back. He tried to get to her through you, which was a big mistake, and then they met again and had this huge fight at the mall. Kind of violent, actually. She gets it that it's not your fault, that it has nothing to do with you. And so now, I think she'll be thinking a little more clearly."

She shakes her head and stares forlornly at my carpet. "He really likes her, Shelby. That's the only reason he was even talking to me, to get to her. Why doesn't she see that?"

"She's blinded by her own ambition." As it comes out of my mouth, I realize it's true! Wow. What are the chances of *that* happening? "Anyway, now that they're not a couple anymore, she can concentrate on what she really wants: to conquer the world."

Evie nods, and looks relieved. "Well, I'm glad that at least it won't be so tense. To be honest, I've really missed everyone. Being stuck in the house with Briley is kind of a torture all its own. She tried to give me a makeover." She shudders, obviously replaying the hideous memory.

"Well, I'm glad you survived. So, what do you say? Back in the game?"

She smiles, and toasts me with her sweating glass of lemonade. "I'm your girl. Find me a power strip and I can do anything."

12

ANOTHER DAY, ANOTHER DRAMA

(or World Wide Web of Deceit)

Wednesday after school, Thea and Melvin pull into the circular campus driveway in a rented Hummer, a vehicle that could house a small family of grizzly bears. The purpose of the visit is to collect the Queen Geeks and take us to the drive-in we'll be renting for the event. When the mega-polluting vehicle shows up at school, Becca sees that I have Evie with me, and although she doesn't apologize, she doesn't look like she's going to kill an Aussie. Evie watches Becca for signs of violence, I guess, and I notice that she sits as far away as possible from her.

Since Melvin's still sort of immobile, Thea drives the dinosaur-burning monstrosity, and I consider, in the moments when my life is not flashing before my eyes, that we should advertise this as a thrill ride and sell tickets. Finally she careens into the gravel parking lot of the drive-in, sending dusty gray clouds of long-smoked cigarettes and swap-meet desperation into the air.

Amber, Elisa, Becca, Evie, and I climb out of the back of the skyscraper-on-wheels (I mean, you can see people's bald spots at stoplights!) and Melvin struggles to hoist his cement-shoed foot out of the car. I notice Thea liberally supporting his weight, and once again feel a pang of despair for my dad.

"So?" Becca says excitedly. "Isn't it perfect?"

Elisa nudges a crushed soda can with her foot. "If you're trying to collect recyclables for loose change."

"Don't be so negative." Amber shades her eyes (done up in full Cleopatra Goth makeup) and studies the screen looming behind us. "I think it will be amazing."

"Right over here." Melvin motions toward the screen as he shuffles, dragging his injured foot. "The world premiere of *The Drainpeople*. It's going to kick some serious ass."

"Dad!" Becca grimaces at him. "It's not all about you and your movie, you know."

"Sure, sure," he says, waving away her complaint. "The dance'll be great, too, honey, but think about it . . . how many of your friends have been able to attend a Hollywood premiere?"

Thea bounces up between them, the Earth Mama to their big ol' dysfunctional funky family. "Let's go inside and check it out."

We walk through the gates (lovely, classy, rusting aluminum fencing). We're approached by a skinny lady in blue hot pants, a daisy-print tube top, flip-flops, and a hat that proudly proclaims, "Honeymoon Reject." "Hi there," she says from behind bug-eye sunglasses, her strawlike, overprocessed hair whipping in the breeze. "I'm Maggie DeFranco. We spoke on the phone." She extends a wrinkly hand decorated with hot pink talons.

"Melvin Gallagher," Becca's dad says, extending a hairy paw.

"We're just thrilled to be hosting such a great event," Maggie DeFranco says, then gets caught up in a lung-busting bout of coughing. I get the feeling that a lot of that cigarette dust I saw earlier belongs to her. "Let me show you the electrical layout and the projection system."

Evie wordlessly follows her as she and Melvin hobble off talking about great old horror movies and dancing buckets of popcorn, and she only throws one resentful glance back at us. I don't blame her: Maggie DeFranco's leathery skin and tobacco smell would make me think twice about being with her in an enclosed space.

Becca grabs my arm and dashes off to the flat area right below the screen. "This is where the dance floor will be, after the movie screening. And we'll have food stations all along that fence, and after the movie, a bunch of music videos synched up by the DJ."

Amber and Elisa have trailed along, and Elisa hears that last comment. "If we do have a DJ, I am begging you, please, no rap music. It gives me a serious migraine."

"And please, none of that wannabe hip-hop stuff by kids under twelve," I say, putting in my two cents' worth. "If I see one more kid with a milk mustache playing drums on MTV, I will seriously throw myself under a bus."

Amber grins. "Don't worry. Jon's the DJ. He'll never commit serious crimes against music."

Thea flits around talking about the silver and black decorations, Amber and Elisa dish about what the crowd will be like and about how to get people to come to the event, and Becca looks on in satisfaction. I'm sort of apart from the whole thing, watching from a distance; I'm thinking about how I'll be shuttling myself back and forth on prom night, performing illegal driving moves with my robot guardian and my Velcro dress. Dresses, I should say. When Maggie Pink Talons and the power crew come back, I'm more than glad to be out of there, because honestly, the whole idea is starting to make me more than a little nervous.

That Friday we have a Queen Geek meeting, and general mayhem is the result. The Geeks are in a state of ecstasy over the rebel prom, and can't wait to paper the campus with multicolored fliers. Armed with tape and an attitude, the girls assemble to cover the campus like ants on a sugar donut. Becca stops them with one majestic wave of her hand. "Ladies, before you go out to do your work, I wanted to let you know that Panther TV will be doing a spot on Geek Prom next week, and"—she takes a breath for emphasis—"because of our Hollywood connections, E-Tube Television will be broadcasting live from Geek Prom!"

The screams of joy nearly take the asbestos-laden roof off the classroom. Gaggles of geeks rush out the door armed with information, leaving me and Becca alone in the now-silent room. "Well, that went well," she says as she tidies up.

"Are they really going to broadcast live?" I ask, skeptical. "Or did Melvin just tell you that to impress Thea?"

She shoots me a withering look. "Please. He doesn't need to impress Thea. She's like jelly. It's actually kind of disgusting."

She grabs a stack of fliers and a roll of tape and gestures to the door. "Shall we?"

We exit the relative quiet of the room and swim into the stream of ravenous high school students eating lunch. With only half an hour to eat, most kids will consume anything portable, which means most of them eat nasty hamburgers, fried chicken patties on white bread, or nachos that have never even heard of Mexico. I generally bring my lunch so I have more control over the crap I put into my body.

The place is also crammed full of kids trying to catch up on their social lives, which are horribly interrupted by school. Couples grope each other (as much as they can without getting scolded), friends sit on the concrete walkways talking, freshman boys gallop around like circus ponies on speed. We just try to maneuver around all these groups and find spots where we can tape in peace.

As Becca plasters hot pink and electric blue fliers all over the glass doors of the library, a large-knuckled hand bearing an oversized gold class ring slams, palm down, into the door next to her head. "What the—" She turns, furious, but before she can say anything else, an overstuffed upperclassman has stepped toward her, effectively wedging her between himself and the wall. He towers over Becca, which takes some serious height.

"Why are you screwing up Carl's life?" the guy rumbles at her. He's wearing a letterman jacket, and has the fine stubble of a potential beard roughing up his chin.

"Excuse me?" Becca says, in a tone that definitely doesn't

sound like she wants to be excused. She tries to shove her way past him, but he maintains his mountainous stance. "Please get out of my way, Goliath."

"Not until you explain to me what he ever did to you." The guy is immovable; I am afraid that this might come to physical violence (and we don't need a broken jock on our conscience or on our permanent records), so I butt in.

"Hey," I say, in as chirpy a manner as I can muster. "Maybe there's been some mistake?"

"I'm not talking to you," Athletic Guy snarls, then turns his attention back to Becca. "He's not concentrating, he's totally a mess. It's your fault." His tone does not sound as if he is inclined to forgive.

"What I do in my personal life is nobody else's business, least of all some Neanderthal who tries to push me through a plate-glass door," she spits. "Now move before I kick your ass."

But before any ass-kicking can occur, Athletic Guy is shoved backward onto the grass by someone who rockets out of the library doors. In a blur of muscle, someone is on top of him, and the two are rolling on the lawn, throwing punches here and there.

Stunned, Becca turns to me and says, "That's Carl. Quick, get him off there!" She dashes forward and grabs for Carl's jacket collar, but he jerks to the side and knocks her aside without even noticing. I see a campus supervisor in the distance who has picked up on the fight, and is using the radio to call for handcuffs or guard dogs or whatever they do. (I haven't been involved personally in any fights before, so I don't know the drill.) Becca leaps on top of Carl, grabs him around the neck, and squeezes for all she's worth until he starts to look a little blue and lets go of the jock.

"The narcs are coming!" Becca hisses to both of them and several supervisors begin to trot toward us. "Stop it right now or you'll both be doing community service on the side of the freeway!"

As the narcs surround the guys, they both act like they're playing, like nothing's really wrong. Magically, they're both grinning, with only a trace of hatred on their unibrows. Seeing the lack of a real fight, the supervisors mill around for a couple of minutes then disperse, talking importantly into their walkie-talkies.

When they're out of hearing range, the human mountain whirls on Carl. "What are you doing, jerk?"

"You were assaulting my girlfriend, jerk," Carl replies.

"I'm not your girlfriend anymore," Becca says, adding, "jerk."

Carl, his big blond head bowed in despair, lets a big tear drip down his cheek. "I know that," he whispers. My heart just about breaks.

How can Becca resist that? But she does. I look at her, and she's standing, arms folded, looking defiantly like a pissed-off goddess of wrath. "Don't try that crying stuff with me," she cautions. "It won't work."

"I'm not trying anything," Carl says, wiping his face on the sleeve of his basketball jersey. "I miss you."

"Sure," Becca says as Athletic Guy growls and walks away. She continues taping up fliers as if nothing has happened. "Don't try to manipulate me."

"I'm not," Carl says, hovering over her shoulder. "Let's try to find a way to make this work."

"Why don't you just go after Aussie Girl? I guess you have a taste for koala bear, huh?" she spits at him.

"I don't like Evie!" Carl whines. "I mean, she's nice, but she's not you. I was only trying to get her to tell me why you won't talk to me, Becca. C'mon. Why are you being so difficult?"

Becca turns on one heel, marches past him, thrusts a flier into his hands, and says, "You know what you have to do."

I follow in her wake, watching behind me as Carl stares despairingly at a lime green Geek Prom flier. "Don't you think that was a little harsh?" I ask.

"Not really," she says, her voice clipped. We spend the last ten minutes of lunch posting fliers all over campus, and I notice that they are drawing a bit of a crowd. I'm not sure if that's good or bad.

Fletcher's waiting outside my last class as I leave. "Hi there," he says, kissing me on the cheek. "What's up?" His arm fits nicely around my shoulders and we walk in an easy rhythm toward the front of the campus.

"Oh. Nothing."

We pass several of the Day-Glo fliers pasted on windows and walls, and Fletcher gestures to one as kids rush by. "I hear there was a little problem at lunch?"

"Kind of." What can I tell him? If I start talking about Geek Prom, I could give away my secret plan. But if I don't say anything, he might suspect. "Some basketball player kind of hassled Becca about breaking up with Carl, and then Carl tackled him, and then he cried, and then Becca kind of blew him off."

Fletcher stops in midstride and turns me around to face him. "Why is she being so mean to him? And how are you getting around doing this Geek Prom thing?"

Oh, boy. Here comes the true test of my acting ability: Can I lie to the face of the boy I think I love? I choose to look down at the fascinating cracks in the sidewalk. "I guess she's being mean because she wants him to do what she wants. You know how she is."

"Yes, I do." He continues walking, I guess satisfied by my answer. "But don't you think she's being unreasonable?"

"No comment." In order to draw attention away from the fliers, I turn Fletcher toward me and give him a big fat kiss on the lips. Usually kisses keep boys from thinking too much. We linger for a minute, and then the kiss extends into more of a lip-lock, and it starts to make me sweat, so I break away.

"Was that your way of distracting me?" he asks, stroking my hair as we hold each other.

"Did it work?"

"Uh . . . did what work?" He grins, and steers me toward the front of the school again, and we walk slowly. "Get your dress yet?"

"Oh." I thought we had successfully steered around any prom discussions! That's what I get for having a smart boyfriend. "I . . . uh . . . I found something I like, but I have to get it fitted. And it's bad luck for you to see it before the night of the dance."

He frowns. "I never heard that before."

"Sure," I say, waving away his ignorance of outdated fashion traditions. "Everybody knows that."

As we approach the Rock, I see Becca, Amber, Elisa, Evie, and a few other Queen Geeks gathered in animated discussion of something. "Maybe we should go our separate ways," I murmur.

"Ah." He shades his eyes and scans the group of chattering girls. "Yeah, I don't think I want to be in the middle of that at the moment. See you later." He pecks me on the cheek, sticks his hands in his jeans pockets, and walks in the opposite direction, whistling.

"It's two weeks away," Evie is saying frantically. "If we don't start getting the equipment together now, we might as well forget the virtual prom thing. And I've already been hooking up with friends all over the place who want to do it, so I think we'd be better off just getting it done."

"Melvin has everything coming down from L.A., and he'll have people helping us set it up," Becca says calmly. "It's two weeks away. The thing we need to work on right now is getting people there."

"Hey," I say. In their Geek Prom frenzy, no one notices me, and, better yet, they didn't notice me with Fletcher.

Elisa grabs my arm. "Food? What's the deal with food?"

"Uh . . . it's good to eat?"

She flicks me in the head. "What food are we having?"

We spend another ten minutes or so drowning in details about the prom, then people start scattering as their rides arrive. After a bit, only Becca, Evie, and I are left. "Listen, I didn't tell everyone else," Becca says conspiratorially as we walk toward my house. "But I've already given out about one hundred tickets."

"Given out? Aren't we selling them?" I ask.

She shakes her head, steps over an upraised crack in the sidewalk, and claps her hands like a little kid. "Guess you didn't actually read the latest flier! Nope, we aren't selling them. It's even better. Because Melvin is premiering his movie, he can write the whole thing off as a business expense, so all we have to do is get people to come. And who wouldn't rather come to a great *free* groundbreaking party instead of a stuffy, expensive, boring old prom?"

"What are you going to do about Carl?"

She stops walking. "What do you mean?" Glancing sideways at me, she tilts her head defiantly, daring me to tell her she was too harsh.

Evie, sensing the tension, fumbles in her backpack and says, "Oops. I forgot my geometry book. Gotta go back to get it. I'll see you guys later." She abruptly turns and starts to scoot back up the street.

"Hang on, hang on," Becca says, grabbing her arm. "Look, Carl told me that he only talked to you because he was trying to get to me. I'm sorry I reacted like such a . . . a jealous moron. I realize that he doesn't like you, and I'm sorry I treated you so badly."

Evie, whose face displays the mix of emotions someone would feel after being told they're not even remotely attractive to a guy, smiles crookedly, and says, "Uh, thanks, I guess. But either way,

I do have to get my book. I'll catch up with you all later." She shuffles, somewhat dejectedly I think, back toward school.

Now Becca has turned to me, arms crossed, and she's staring me down. "There, are you happy now? I made nice with the international contingent. Now, if we could just rescue you from Fletcher's attempts at mind control . . ."

"That's kind of insulting, you know," I answer as I begin walking again. "Like I can't think for myself."

"Well, I'm not saying you can't survive without him, but it does seem like you've become a little distant lately." She scuffs a stone with her pink tennis shoe, sends it skittering into somebody's yard where it sensibly takes shelter.

I hear footsteps pattering behind us, and two girls trot up beside us. "Hey, are you Becca?" one asks hesitantly.

"Yep." She crosses her arms, armored for battle just in case.

The taller of the two, a jockish blonde in a volleyball uniform, sighs with relief. "Cool. We wanted to get tickets to Geek Prom. Do you have any on you?"

Becca arches an eyebrow at me, then digs into her pocket, producing two tickets from a cardboard envelope. "Here you go. Hope you have a great time." The girls pocket the tickets, smile, and turn to go.

The friend of the volleyball girl stops and says, "Becca, I just want you to know . . . a lot of us think it's a great idea. No matter what the student government people say."

"Thanks," she says, genuinely warm. "I really appreciate that."

We walk on in silence, Becca beaming like a saint who's just been prayed to. "That's what I'm talking about. That's why I'm doing this. There are lots of kids who feel the same way about the established student government. We're just filling a need."

"Speaking of unfilled needs, why were you so bitchy to Carl?"

"*Why?*" This time her voice gets louder, and her cheeks go pink. "He's trying to ruin everything with his 'oh, poor me, I really like you' act. I'm trying to achieve something amazing, groundbreaking, something no one has done, and all he cares about is this stupid fascist dance party."

"Well, to be honest, it looks like all he cares about is you," I say softly. "I mean, the guy was crying."

"Oh, don't fall for that," she says bitterly. "He's just trying to manipulate me."

We walk on in silence, but what I'm really thinking is that she's actually trying to manipulate him. And possibly me.

Over the next two weeks, school is barely a footnote in my consciousness. I go through all the motions: homework (sometimes), eating lunch (always), Queen Geek meetings, occasional stolen kisses with Fletcher. Every once in a while I see Carl ambling across campus like a big, sad giant who's lost his beanstalk.

One other distraction to the complete importance of my high school education is the escalation of the ongoing civil war between the Queen Geeks and the student government kids. Obviously, the Samantha Singers of the world do not appreciate it when the little people butt in on their total domination of teenaged culture.

One day in the cafeteria, two unnamed cheerleaders manage to trip Elisa from behind so that her tray full of Cup-a-Soup and cheesy nachos goes airborne, and she plummets, facedown, onto the sticky linoleum. They pretend to help her get up, but I notice one of them rubbing some oily cheese sauce onto the back of her T-shirt. I scurry over, shoo away the zombie girls, and brush her off. "What was that about?" she asks, confused.

"I believe that was a terrorist plot to make sure you go hungry." I turn her around and dab at the cheese sauce between her shoulders. "I think the Geek Prom is really pissing some people off."

Becca continues to give out tickets, and since they're free, even kids who normally wouldn't come near us with a ten-foot cattle prod snatch up handfuls of passes. When I ask her about the obvious anger radiating from the Associated Student Body office, she shrugs and says, "It's like that sports cream you rub on sore muscles. When it's painfully hot, that's how you know it's working."

"If it gets much hotter, we might actually *need* sports cream. And bandages, and maybe even a cast or two," I mutter as we skillfully avoid a wad of nasty gum left purposefully in our path.

On my own, I practice driving with Dad after school, and armed with my learner's permit (finally!) I am feeling confident that my scheme will work. One night as I'm putting the finishing touches on my fancy "real" prom dress (shiny midnight blue poofy dress, full-length, trimmed with beads), Euphoria watches, making disapproving mechanical sounds.

"Shelby, please let me try to talk you out of this," she says for the millionth time. "It's a crazy idea. You know it won't work. Why do you insist on pushing it?"

She's sewing Velcro into the seams of the dress, but doing it in such a way that you can't see it. When she's finished, I should be able to shimmy into it, slap the Velcro shut, and be on my way. Just as easily, I'll be able to unfasten it, tuck it safely into the trunk of my car, and be ready underneath for anything the Geek Prom might throw at me.

"All right." Euphoria sighs, holding up the blue dress. "I think it's finished."

I give her a hug. "Thanks, fairy godmother. Now let's see if you turned the pumpkin into a golden carriage."

She bleeps, puzzled. "Just try it on."

With my extra cool, tight green dress underneath, I slip the blue dress on and run my hand up the part with the Velcro embedded in it. Looking in the mirror, it's almost impossible to tell I have two dresses on, except that my boobs look a little bigger. Side benefit. "The straps on the green dress show, but I'll wear a wrap, so no one will see them," I say, draping a gauzy oversized scarf across my shoulders as I prance in front of the mirror. "I am a genius."

As the magical day draws near, Fletcher calls almost every day, and so does Becca, even though I see both of them at school. "I'm really looking forward to the dance," Fletcher says one night over the speakerphone.

"Yeah, it'll be great," I agree as I paint my toenails a deep burgundy.

He clears his throat. "So, how have you handled the whole Geek Prom thing with Becca? Isn't she furious?"

I tip the bottle of polish over, and some of it drips on my carpet. Drat! "Uh . . . well, we just sort of compromised." Lame answer.

"Compromised, huh?" He snorts on the other end. "That I find hard to believe. But however you worked it out, I'm really glad you're coming with me. When should I pick you up, by the way?"

A cold stab goes through my heart. A flaw in my devious plan! Of course, guys always pick up their prom dates, give them dead flowers for their wrists and such. How could I forget such an important point? "Uh . . . you're breaking up over there," I say, trying to make my voice sound crackly. "Let me call you back . . . bad reception . . ." I flip the phone shut as if it's made of hot coals.

As if to taunt me, the stupid thing rings again. The screen reads: "Becca," so I flip it open. "Hello?"

"Oh my god, you will never believe it. We have now given out five hundred tickets—"

I nearly choke. "Did you say five *hundred*?"

"Yep." She whoops into the phone, which isn't a really pleasant experience for me. "People are getting on MySpace and asking how they can get in, people from everywhere! And I even saw them advertise it on E-Tube Television. This is amazing!"

"Yes, it is." Amazing that I haven't accidentally confessed to prom crimes real or imagined.

"So, you're going in the limo with us, right?"

"Huh?"

"Melvin rented us a huge limo. All you have to do is be at my house about two hours before the dance and we'll all drive over in style. Of course, we'll be spending the day getting the place ready, but I figured everyone can come back to my house to shower and whatever—" I don't even hear the rest of what she says, because I am stuck on the giant-sized limo that will be waiting for me.

"Oh, I gotta go, Becca. Dad's calling. Hang on, Dad!" I yell to make it sound convincing. "Call you back." I slam the phone shut again, senselessly taking out my frustration on wireless technology.

I throw myself onto the bed and bury my head in the pillow, hoping that I will be swallowed alive and never return to face the hideous mess I've made. But no matter how tightly I close my eyes, I'm still in my room.

Euphoria, who has been blessedly silent, says, "I believe I said something like this would happen."

I throw a pillow in her general direction but aim to miss.

About a week before prom day (or P-Day as I take to calling it because of similarities to the disaster of World War II), things at school start to turn nasty.

I keep getting dirty looks from jocks and prep girls, and people are tripping me for no reason in the halls. When I see Becca, she looks as if she's been suffering the same treatment. Evie trails along behind her a pace, like a secret service agent looking for would-be assassins. Or spit wad throwers.

"It's because the student government is mad that we're cutting into their business," Becca says, scoping the crowd during passing period for any likely foot trippers.

"Why is that, exactly?"

Evie elbows in between us. "It's probably because of the global presence."

"Huh?" I frown at her. "What do you mean?"

"I mean that we now have kids from several other countries who are going to be attending the prom virtually," she says, grinning. "Why would anybody pay a lot of money to wear tight shoes and go to a normal, boring hometown dance when they can party with people from around the world for free?"

Becca steers me by the elbow away from a mess of banana peels left purposefully in my path. "Student government hasn't sold a lot of tickets, and it's because of our event."

"Maybe it's because their event isn't as spectacular as ours," Evie murmurs as we reach her classroom. "Okay, see you all later. Watch your backs."

I thought that the lack of "regular prom" success would make me happy, but actually, I feel kind of bad about it. Maybe the whole thing was kind of a bad idea after all. But now, of course, it's too late.

They have voting during homeroom period for prom king and queen, and they show the court hopefuls on Panther TV. Each one has a chance to speak and explain why they would be so honored to wear a fake crown and cape and rule over meaningless high school rituals for a night.

While only half watching the monitor, I hear Fletcher's voice coming out of the TV screen. "Hi, I'm Fletcher Berkowitz. If you'd like a cheap alternative to expensive fuel, vote for me for prom king. Plus, my date, Shelby Chapelle, is exceedingly hot, so you should vote for me just so you can get a look at her in the spotlight."

My cheeks ignite and I try very hard to disappear, but my stupid, thankless molecules do not comply. Kids all around me laugh and poke me, and make silly noises while the teacher tries to shut them up.

Carl is next on the screen. He still looks sad. "Hi, I'm Carl Schwaiger," he rumbles. "Please don't vote for me for king. I don't have a queen and I'd rather just sit in the corner alone drinking myself into oblivion with Hawaiian Punch."

Everyone sort of squirms uncomfortably. Nobody likes to hear a guy threaten suicide by high fructose corn syrup.

What Fletcher says on Panther TV nearly blows my whole plan out of the water when, at lunch, Becca storms up to me and demands, "What's this about someone's exceedingly hot date, Shelby Chapelle?"

"Uh . . ." I stammer, hoping something brilliant will present itself. Something does.

Amber runs up and grabs me around the shoulders. "That was so amazing!"

"Uh . . . okay," I say, trying to shove her Gothness off me.

"I mean, how Fletcher talked about you on Panther TV. Everyone knows you're going to Geek Prom, so now they're all talking about how delusional the student government people are, how desperate they are to make us look bad! Isn't that awesome? How did you get him to do it?"

Ah. So now I've supposedly hypnotized Fletcher into saying I was going with him, only I'm not, and by mentioning me, the student government looks bad because they don't have the people they thought they'd have at their dance. I'm in so deep there is no way out, so I just stuff my mouth full of whole-grain crackers and pretend to choke.

13

DRIVING
MISS CRAZY

(or A Girl and Her Robot)

P-Day looms, and I want everything to go smoothly, so like any good evil genius, I need to rehearse my dastardly scheme. One afternoon when Dad has carpooled to a meeting with another geeky scientist, I make Euphoria go with me on a practice run.

Getting her into the Volvo is no easy task. For one, she's not so hot at the bending-at-the-waist thing, and you'd be surprised how necessary that is for getting into a car. We're in the driveway, and I've dressed her up in her Aunt Effie outfit: an old gray wig and purple pillbox hat (with a veil to cover up her eye lights), a large lavender caftan I found at the Salvation Army thrift shop for a Halloween costume a couple of years ago, and some elbow gloves trimmed with ostrich feathers.

"I gotta say, you're a vision, Euphoria," I tell her as I try yet another way to shove her into the front passenger seat. "Maybe we need some Vaseline or something to get you past the door."

"That would ruin my gown," she says haughtily. All of a sudden she's like the Queen Elizabeth of robots. Great.

"Yeah, well," I grunt as I push again, "something's gotta give." I adjust the front seat again, sliding it all the way back, and Euphoria tumbles into the car, legs askew. "Oh, and we probably need some shoes. If a cop stops us, he might be disturbed by your . . . prosthetics."

"I'd like a nice pair of flip-flops. I hear they're comfortable."

"You have to have toes to wear flip-flops, though. Maybe we should go with fuzzy slippers."

I pile into the front seat, and for a moment consider strapping Euphoria in with the seat belt, but then realize she's not a living person, so any auto crash would result in a trip to the body shop rather than the hospital. I, however, am a very careful driver, so I buckle up.

"Shelby, I really must object one more time," she says, her drawl getting thicker with the increased anxiety. "This is a foolish plan. If you're caught, we'll both be punished."

"Don't be an old lady, Aunt Effie. We're just going around the block." I back the car down the driveway, straighten it, and head down the street, feeling the sweet taste of freedom.

Euphoria has stabilized, and is able to look out the window. "My goodness, I've never ridden in a car like this before," she says, her voice full of wonder. "There are so many things to see. What are those devices poking out of the ground?"

"Mailboxes," I answer. "They're not devices, exactly. You just put letters in them, and you get bills and stuff."

As we drive past a two-story white house with black shutters, the smell of fresh-cut grass clippings fills the car, and the drone of a lawnmower becomes louder. Suddenly, Euphoria shouts, "Stop! Stop the car!"

I obey, since for all I know her super sensors have picked up a stray cat or an old lady walking across my path. "What is it?" I anxiously scan the street.

"Oh, Shelby." Euphoria's voice is full of sadness. "It's Eugene. Or part of him, at least."

Eugene was a failed project of my dad's, a lawnmower constructed to have a semi-functional processor and voice command. He was sort of Euphoria's dream man, but he never quite worked. It was kind of like her being in love with an institutionalized mental patient. A mental patient with rust.

The lawnmower that plows across our neighbor's yard is, indeed, partially Eugene. When he failed, Dad parted him out to various people, and I guess at least a few pieces stayed in the 'hood. "Oh, Eugene," Euphoria says, moaning softly. She turns away and says, "Drive on, Shelby. We can't dwell in the past."

"Yes, ma'am." I floor the car and we peel away from the site.

I take the car around the neighborhood a few more times, and start to feel pretty confident in my driving. "Now, the only challenge is really to navigate between locations. But you can help me with that, right? You're like a GPS satellite and nagging driving coach all rolled into one."

"Hmm." Euphoria sounds miffed, but I ignore that. By the time I pull the Volvo into the driveway, all is forgiven. "I just hope your father never finds out," she says as I struggle to free her from the car. "He'll gut me like he did Eugene."

"Euphoria! Don't say such a thing. He'd never do that to you." But then I think about it, and I consider that not only might he do it to Euphoria, but he might even do it to me if I get caught. I vow to be doubly careful.

On the Geek Prom front, Evie has turned into an evil computer genius tapping away on my computer until she has to go back to Briley's house for fear of being locked out. Her eyes are starting to take on the sallow look of somebody overexposed to pixels and pop-up ads.

One evening, she's tapping away while I'm making a lame attempt at homework, and she jumps and screams. "What's wrong?" I yelp, almost falling off my bed.

"Look at this." I scrape myself up off my carpet and scramble to peer over her shoulder. On the computer screen, her My-Space page comments are displayed, and one large one with a Japanese flag and a photo of a smiling girl has one word printed on it: *YES! It's on!*

"Does that mean that we have kids in Japan who are coming to our virtual prom?" I almost whisper. "Does that mean you actually did it?"

"Yes!" She jumps up, almost upends my desk, and we jump on my bed like we're two years old, screeching and whooping like we just won the Super Bowl. Euphoria rolls in, snaps a towel at me with deadly accuracy, and emits a sound equivalent to an air horn at a football game. It effectively stops our jumping and screeching.

"Did a herd of wildcats get loose in here?" she drawls.

"Sorry." I climb down from the bed. "We just managed a

hookup with Japan for the Geek Prom. It's just sort of an accomplishment."

"Sort of!" Evie snorts. "It's taken years off my life trying to set this up. I've had to help people scavenge machinery half a world away, get commitments from people I've never met, and work out the logistics of hooking up satellite signals from places I've never even seen. Sort of an accomplishment!"

Euphoria sniffs self-righteously. "Well, if you keep it down to a dull roar, I'd appreciate it." As she rolls out the door, she mutters, "You'd think no one had ever plugged anything in before, my goodness . . ."

I try to avoid Fletcher at school because every time I see him, he says something about prom. During passing period, he jumps out at me from an English classroom and says, "You're looking at the king of decorations. I've delegated every job to underlings, and now just have to look at the greatness of my genius. Oh, and did you like the interview on Panther TV?" he asks slyly as we change classes.

"Well, if you mean did I like you referring to me as hot, then I guess, yeah. But it was kind of embarrassing. And Carl's was just . . . well . . ."

"Pathetic?"

"Yeah."

He nods and squeezes my shoulders. "I'm glad we're not in that situation. I mean, he really cares about Becca, but she is so stubborn and wants her own way so much that she's ruined a good thing. Luckily, you have a much better head on your shoulders." He stops, leans over, and catches me in a deep kiss that causes other kids to make rude noises. "And it's a much better-looking head, too."

Dizzy from the kiss, I just sort of sway in the wind, hoping I don't fall over. But the functioning part of my brain is nagging at me, reminding me that I'm just as stubborn as Becca, just a better liar with a Volvo.

Green Pines is caught up in Prom Frenzy for the week. The theme of the regular prom is Mardi Gras, so everything at school oozes New Orleans charm (or at least what the mass producers of prom decorations think of as New Orleans charm). Purple, green, and gold trinkets seem to hang from every light pole and tree, and colorful posters featuring a masked woman on a white horse advertise a Night to Remember right next to our homemade Geek Prom fliers, which now look pretty homely.

Evie, Amber, and Elisa run toward me with a herd of geek girls at break one day, and I'm tempted to duck, but they're too fast. "Guess what, guess what!" Amber squeals. I've rarely, if ever, heard anything close to a squeal coming out of our dark poet, so it must be something squeal-worthy. "We got Scotland, Sydney, South Africa, and Canada. Can you believe it?"

"Are we talking about a game of Risk or what?" I ask, confused.

"No, doof. Evie got hookups for all those countries for the virtual prom!" Elisa grabs my arm and flops it up and down. It is unresponsive. "Look." Elisa pulls Wembley out of her pocket, but it doesn't look like Wembley. It's a shiny new device with a keyboard and a video screen.

"What's that?" I am shocked—shocked!—that she's parted with her Palm Pilot. "Where's your buddy?"

Elisa doesn't even look at me. "Times change. Affections change. I had to move on. This is Wembley II, complete with wireless Internet and video capabilities." She presses a few buttons and hands the device to Evie, who presses more buttons as the other girls hover around like bees waiting to suck on a flower.

"Look," Evie says triumphantly, handing me the Wembley II. On it, her MySpace is crammed full of comments and messages from people all over the world, people giving the details of how the amazing and seemingly impossible virtual prom will be made real.

"Wow," I say weakly as the other Queen Geeks chant Evie's name as if she's some virtual goddess. I, on the other hand, feel like hiding in a utility closet until it's all over, preferably one with no Internet access.

By Thursday, Becca is a nervous wreck. P-Day is Saturday, and she's given away more than six hundred tickets, but the Mardi Gras prom is starting to look pretty cool. "At least if people come to our event, they'll still be able to eat for the rest of the year," Becca grumbles as she pokes a finger at one of the posters announcing *Only $80 per couple! Includes soft drinks!*

Friday, the Queen Geeks gather for a last-minute huddle and pep talk. The room takes on the feeling of a football team strategizing before a big game, or a bunch of Christians waiting to be cleaned and dressed and sent out as a lion entrée. "Stop talking!" Becca shouts over the chattering. The conversations die down immediately.

"Okay, ladies. Tomorrow is the big day. E-Tube will be broadcasting live from Geek Prom, and who knows how many surprise Hollywood guests might show up? It's going to be a fantastic night, and it's all thanks to you. And let's give a big hand to Evie, the one who made the virtual prom part all possible." Becca beams at her as the other girls clap and cheer. "Make sure you show up early so you can get a good seat for the movie. Now, we do need help setting up the tables and chairs, putting up decorations, and such."

The conversation drifts into the nuts and bolts of running an event like this: when the food will be delivered, napkins, knives, cups, plates, crepe paper. I sort of tune out; my biggest concern is not with the decorations for the dance, but whether or not I can get to two events at the same time. My mind spins out into horrible scenarios: I drive to the regular prom, and my shoe gets stuck in an elevator; I drive to Geek Prom and get electrocuted by a stray neon light whose wire falls carelessly into my punch cup; I drive with Euphoria in the car, get stopped by the police, and have to explain why my aunt Effie has electrodes instead of warts.

The bell rings, signaling the end of lunch, and girls file out, all animated with the excitement of tomorrow's event. Becca hangs back, and grabs my arm. "Just a minute."

"Yeah?"

"Are you coming over to my house to ride in the limo?"

"Uh . . ." This would, of course, totally sink my plan. "No."

"You're not? Why?" Becca looks disappointed. I think she wanted to show off her dad's disposable money.

"I . . . want to do some stuff before Geek Prom. Secret stuff." Oh, that's brilliant. Now I'll have to figure out what the secret stuff is so I can tell another lie later on. I realize I'm digging myself a huge hole, but at some point, there's so much dirt all around you that you just sort of get used to it, I guess.

"Secret stuff. Right." She walks out with me into the rushing stream of kids racing to class. "Let's go get PE over with, and then we can relax for the weekend. I can't wait till tomorrow . . . it's going to be amazing. And E-Tube! Can you even believe Dad pulled that off?"

"Not really," I mutter as I follow in Becca's wake across campus.

After school, I race off campus as if a rocket is strapped to my rear. I do not want to talk to anyone about anything. If I can get home, I figure I still might be able to make the whole thing work, but if I talk to Fletcher or Becca or anyone, I have a feeling I'll spill my guts and ruin everything.

Unfortunately, Dad is home when I get there. He's swinging on the front porch again, which means he's depressed.

"Hey, Dad," I say as cheerily as possible.

He grunts and salutes me with a cup of coffee.

"Having a bad day?" I park next to him on the swing and move into the rhythm with him.

He sighs and drinks some coffee, which smells like it's been in the cup for a while. "Not really a bad day," he says. "I'm just taking stock of my life."

"Yeah, well, that's important," I say with very little enthusiasm. "By the way, you're still going to spend the weekend in Santa Barbara for the robotics conference, right?"

He yawns. "I guess. I'm not that excited about it, though. Maybe I should take Euphoria along as a sidekick."

"No!" I say too loudly. He stares at me, puzzled. "I mean, she probably wouldn't do very well on such a long trip. Delicate circuits and stuff."

"Yeah," he says, still studying my face as if he's checking for hidden information. "Anyway, I wouldn't want to leave you alone all weekend. She can keep you company."

Euphoria rolls out onto the porch. "Oh, Shelby, you're home." Her tone seems a bit frosty, but that could just be a change in humidity or temperature. I try not to read anything into it. "Were you mentioning my delicate circuits?"

"Uh . . . yeah. Anyway, Dad is going to that conference in Santa Barbara this weekend, you know, so it's just us girls."

Euphoria snorts. "Just us girls. Oh, Shelby, isn't your big Geek Prom event this weekend?" If I could've reached her, I'd have kicked Euphoria. Instead, I have to pretend that I haven't been dwelling on that very thought for the past month.

"Oh, you're right, it is. Tomorrow, in fact." I glare at her behind Dad's back. I don't know if she can see me, but I pretend she can.

Dad stretches, scratches his salt-and-pepper hair, and yawns again. "Geek Prom, huh? Your club's little slap in the face of the establishment? Sorry I won't be here to see that. Maybe I should stay home."

"Oh, no need for that Dad," I say as calmly as possible. Dad staying home would totally sink my plan, of course. "I'll be fine with Euphoria."

"How are you going to get there? Do you have a ride or something?"

"Uh, yeah." Well, that's not technically a lie. I *do* have a ride.

Dad kisses the top of my head in a very dadlike way. "I'm proud of you, honey. You're really standing by your friends even though you don't necessarily agree with what they're doing. That takes courage."

The bottom falls out of my stomach, and a looming gray cloud of guilt and dread churns up inconveniently. What can I say to that? *Well, Dad, as it turns out I'm a big fat liar and I'm double-crossing my friends, my boyfriend, and you.* In fact, I guess that makes me a triple-crosser.

That night, I have violent dreams involving earthquakes, police cars, and huge intelligent taffeta dresses that chase me through alleys and streets until I finally end up back at my house. In my dream, Dad is sitting on the porch swing, smoking a pipe, and then he turns into the caterpillar from *Alice in Wonderland* smoking a hookah. "Whooooo are yooooou?" drones my dad, the caterpillar, as he blows a ring of blue haze from his mouth.

"I'm not totally sure. I know who I was when I got up this morning, but I think I must have been changed several times since then. And now I'm just a dirty rotten triple-crosser."

"What do you mean by that?" the daderpillar says. "Explain yourself!"

"It's confusing trying to please everybody in a single day," I say, looking down at my prom gown, which has morphed into a sky-blue dress with a prim white apron. "I'm not doing a very good job."

"No, you're not. I think you should go to your room, lock yourself in, and fall down a rabbit hole so you don't ruin the lives of all those who trusted you." He takes one more huge puff of blue smoke, exhales, and says again, "Whooooo are yoooou?"

"I wish I knew," my dream-self answers as a huge swirling wind comes through, lifts me up, and flies me over my house, the town, the drive-in, and everything else I've ever known, leaving me sweating and awake in my bed, in the dark.

Euphoria, who always knows when I'm having a nightmare, has no sympathy. "Told you," she says mockingly. "No good will come of this."

"Shut up." I bury my head under my pillow, hoping to shut out any further fairy-tale characters who see fit to criticize my way of life.

Saturday morning. P-Day. I awaken before the sun comes up, my adrenaline pumping in overdrive. I hear Dad banging around in the kitchen, getting ready to leave for the airport, so I wander in, hoping against hope that he isn't smoking a hookah. He's not.

"Hey, it's the big day," he says as he pours coffee into two mugs and hands one to me. "Excited?"

"You could say that." Pulling my legs up under me on the kitchen chair, I huddle in my ratty blue bathrobe; I'm freezing, even though it's spring. Must be the icy coldness of guilt.

"Do you need some money?" He fishes his wallet out of his pocket and pulls out two twenties. "Just in case. I don't like to leave you with nothing."

I reluctantly take the money, fold it into little tents, and study it to take my mind off my stomach, which is roiling and churning like a hurricane surge. *It's not too late to confess*, Good Shelby, angelic in soft white linen, whispers in my ear, her halo shining gold. *This could stop right now*, she says. *You know it's wrong. Be brave. Do the right thing.* Evil Shelby, in her red corset and checked micromini, clubs her like a baby seal, boots her off my shoulder, and giggles. *Are you kidding?* she says, horns glowing red. *This is the perfect plan. You'd be an idiot to ditch it now, just when you're within sight of the end. That goody-goody is just jealous anyway; she never gets invited to anything.*

Just to prove that I do know right from wrong, I flick Evil Shelby off my shoulder, too. But I do follow her advice.

Dad's shuttle arrives within the hour, and I have the house to myself. To bolster my confidence, I put on soul-shaking loud, loud, loud rock to drown out my better judgment.

My cell vibrates; it's Becca. "Hey. So, are you coming over or what?"

"Or what." I am drying the fantastic polish job I've done on my nails, so the hair dryer drowns her out a bit. "What did you say?"

"I said, how are you planning to get to the drive-in?" Annoyance colors her voice.

"I have a ride, don't worry," I say breezily. "I'll be on time to meet the food people."

"Who do you have a ride with?"

Oops. Complication Number One: Where do I leave the car and Euphoria once I arrive at either event? The real prom, at a large generic hotel, is less difficult, but everybody's going to recognize the Volvo when I pull up at the drive-in. Drat. More complications. "Uh, I have a ride with one of the girls. You don't know her."

"I don't know her?" Becca shouts. "Are you nuts? What's really going on?"

Complication Number Two: Compounding lies on lies. At least things match that way. "It's a surprise. I got my license. Happy now? I was going to spring it on you tonight, but whatever. Thanks for ruining it." I try to sound as pouty as possible to pull off my newly minted fabrication.

"You got your license." She sounds like she doubts it, but could possibly believe it. "Well, that's great. Of course, you can't drive any of us, right?"

"Uh, no, not yet. State law. Trial period." I figure I should hang up before I tie myself in more linguistic knots. "So, I'll see you there, right? What time are you getting there?"

"Probably about four o'clock. The limo is picking us up at three, but we're going to drive around for an hour." The tone of doubt has faded; now she just sounds excited. "Oh, and Melvin says the E-Tube people are already setting up, and all the video screens are up, the light show is hooked up, everything's ready. It's going to be awesome."

"Yes, I'm sure it will be. Okay, gotta go." I hang up the phone and wiggle my fingers, hoping the polish is dry.

No sooner do I flip the phone shut than it buzzes again. "Hi, Fletcher." I've moved on to my toes, which are harder to do while talking on the phone, but I manage. "What's up?"

"What time am I picking you up tonight for dinner?"

Oops. Complication Number Three. "Dinner?"

"Uh, yeah. People always go out for dinner before prom. We talked about it, right? We're going with Carl and a few of the other student government kids at five."

Gotta get out of *that*. "Well, look. I really hadn't planned on dinner, to be honest. I . . . I didn't want to tell you, but I did say I'd go over and help Becca set up Geek Prom before I headed over to the dance with you. I hope you're not mad." Oooh! Sprinkle a little truth in with a lie, and suddenly, you have a soufflé of almost-believable fluffiness.

"Oh." He doesn't even hide the disappointment in his voice, which is, I guess, a compliment. "Well, I guess if that's what you want . . . we'll miss you. You'll meet me at the hotel? How will you get there?"

And back we go to the previous lie, which is strengthened the more I use it. "I got my driver's license. Aren't you proud of me? I aced the test, too. They said I got a perfect score." Wow. The more I lie, the easier it gets. Now I'm lying for no good reason. Next I'll be robbing convenience stores and stealing used lottery tickets.

Fletcher has decided not to be mad at me, I guess in order to preserve the harmony of the evening and increase his chances of making out (which were really good anyway. All this dangerous living makes me feel frisky). "You got your license, huh? That's great. I guess you'll be able to chauffeur me around town now." Awkward pause, and he waits for me to say something, which I don't. "Okay then. See you at the dance. Bye."

"See you there." I click the evil phone shut, throw it at my handbag, and hope it doesn't ring again.

Euphoria has been listening to my various verbal contortions and she is not happy.

"Shelby, you are digging yourself a mighty hole." She's whipping up a quiche for lunch/dinner, so I can eat early and not be too bloaty for my dress. Dresses. "When you lie to people who care about you, it always comes back to haunt you."

I dance around her, giddy in my new criminality. "That's true most of the time, Euphoria. But today, the world is mine. I cannot be defeated!" She groans.

I spend the rest of the morning watching old sci-fi shows on TV, eating bits of quiche, and ignoring Good Shelby, who keeps trying to annoy me. Bad Shelby has her stuffed into a white metal locker, and although she makes an awful noise as she bangs the door to get out, we are both totally able to pretend she's just a cranky washing machine with an imbalanced load.

The afternoon fades away, becoming golden and promising. Euphoria obediently allows me to dress her up in her Aunt Effie costume. She is a vision; if I saw her in the front seat of a car in the middle of the night, I'd think . . . well, I'd probably think I needed to be medicated, but if you don't look too hard, she's pretty lifelike.

"Oh, Aunt Effie," I croon as I carefully dab on my makeup, "you are so wonderful. Thanks for being my chaperone this evening!"

In my mirror, I see Euphoria/Effie shaking her metallic head. Her wig goes a little askew, making her look like a metal pedestal for a drunk Pekingese dog with the mange. "It's not too late to call this whole thing off," she says. "We can just stay home and watch a movie."

As I finish coating my eyelashes with mascara, I laugh. "This night is going to live forever in history. I will tell my children, they will tell their children, and their children will tell their children—"

"You won't be having children if you spend the first twenty years of your adult life in jail." Euphoria picks up a makeup sponge I've dropped on the floor and pitches it into the trash can. "But I'm through lecturing you—"

"Good!" I do a quick twirl on my chair, and show her my fantastic makeup job. "Do I look spectacular?"

"Yes," she says grudgingly.

I pick up the green Geek Prom dress and slink into it, sliding it up over my stocking-covered legs. I don't usually wear panty hose, but since I'm going to be active all night, I need something slick on my legs to help me slink like the snake that I am. I look good; in fact, it looks as if I've lost a bit of weight, and the dress over the sexy capris fits even better than it did when I bought it. "Now, help me with the blue one."

Euphoria wordlessly picks up the blue gown in her claw, drapes it over one arm, and presents it to me as if it's the funeral shroud of a fallen angel. "Should I help you into it?" she asks mournfully.

Nodding, I turn to slip my arms into the straps of the blue gown; Euphoria pulls it on, fastens the Velcro in the back, and voilà, I am transformed into a vision in classic taffeta. Turning in front of the mirror, it's almost impossible to see the lines of the green dress underneath, and although the blue looks a teeny bit bulky, it's not bad. Glad I dropped that weight. I take off the blue dress and fold it carefully.

Finishing touches: lip liner and lipstick in a deep pink shade, a little glitter spray for the shoulders, fluff of the hair and a spritz of hairspray, and then I grab my two pairs of shoes—one pair of blue satin heels, one pair of green Converse tennies.

It's nearly six, and it's time to get to Geek Prom. In my mind, I hear that trumpet-heavy music that's always in war movies, and I move in slow motion, going out to fulfill my destiny. "Come, Euphoria," I say, scanning the sunset horizon for possible obstacles to our mission. "It's time."

She sighs, and rolls toward the front door, clutching her hat and wig. "Why do I have to have hair?" she complains.

"Bald robots aren't believable. Let's go, Aunt Effie." Snatching the car keys from the hall table, I go outside, and Euphoria follows. I quickly lock the door, check for snoops, and dash to the car, open the passenger door, and shove back the front seat to give me better access.

"Watch my arms!" my robot squeals as I try to cram her quickly into the Volvo. "I'm not unbreakable, you know."

"I know, I know," I say, as I fluff her wig, reset her hat, and pull the little white net attached to the hat down past her eye lights. "There. Now you look totally comfortable."

She grunts in response. Well, nobody said she had to *like* being the accomplice of an evil genius.

I toss my blue dress, extra shoes, handbag, and a sweater into the back seat, scurry around, and slip into the cool interior. Hands on the wheel, I realize that this is a great moment: I am about to assert my independence, and simply grab life and swing it around my head like a dead cat. Or something.

"Here we go," I mutter as I back down the driveway. Euphoria pulls a harmonica out of her bag and starts playing that jail song everybody plays in the movies. "How can you play a harmonica? You don't breathe."

The tune stops. "Preprogrammed sound files. It's simulated." She goes back to pretending to suck and blow into her jailhouse harp. "Nobody knows the trouble I seen . . ." she sings.

I navigate the Volvo through the streets of my neighborhood, feeling for the first time like an adult. Driving alone! Well, almost alone. Alone in the sense that I'm the only living person in the car. I realize at that moment, though, that I don't know how to get to the drive-in. I've never driven there. "Euphoria, I need directions."

She stops singing long enough to shoot me an electronic raspberry, minus, of course, the spit.

"That's not very nice," I mutter. "C'mon. Just tell me where to go."

"That's very tempting, but I'd rather not." She plays the annoying harmonica tune again.

"Do you want us to end up in Tijuana or something? Tell me where to drive!"

She hums and whirs for a minute, then says, "Get on the I-5 North, get off on Hawthorne Street, go three blocks, right on Boyed Avenue, left on Busby, two blocks down and a dogleg on Lovett Road, two more blocks south past the Sasaki Business Park, do a U-turn at Darrin Street, and you're there."

"Are you serious? You expect me to remember that? And it sounds like you took me the long way around, too." I do manage to get on the freeway and head north. I'll figure the rest out as I go.

Driving on the freeway in California is a little like a ride at Disneyland, except that there are no machines or cheery operators to keep you from slamming into someone else. The lines are just about as long, what with traffic jams and all, but on the plus side there are no costumed mice trying to get in your face. It's just at the end of rush hour, so the traffic isn't horrible, but merging onto the freeway requires a lot of faith and constant mirror checks. A near miss with a huge steroidal pickup truck nearly costs me a bumper.

"You have to watch those merging lanes," Euphoria says matter-of-factly.

"Like you've ever driven," I mumble as I pass a wobbly, plywood-sided truck full of yard waste.

I manage to maneuver around the various speed demons, road-rageaholics, and bass-thumping stereo mad doggers and follow Euphoria's confusing but complete directions and steer the Volvo up the gravel-crunch path to the Springbrook Drive-in. I stop short of the ticket booth, which is tonight unmanned, but I realize I have just discovered Complication Number Four: It's very tough to drive out of a drive-in without being noticed.

"Dammit!" I mutter.

Euphoria perks right up. "Is there a problem?"

"Well, of course there's a problem. How can I secretly leave the Geek Prom if my vehicle is parked *inside* the Geek Prom?"

I probably imagine it, but Euphoria sounds almost gleeful at my impending doom. "That is a pickle, all right."

"Can you help me figure out what to do?" I whine.

"I'm fresh out of good ideas." She practically chortles with glee. Robots should never chortle.

Think, think, think, traitorous brain. You got me into this, you must get me out. Then, like a drink of cold water on a desert-dry day, the idea washes over me: Park somewhere else. Not that profound, I know, but it does the trick. I slowly reverse down the gravel drive and back onto the street, cruise about half a block away, park, and turn off the car. "Ha!" I chortle. (It's okay for me to chortle, because I've earned it.) As I lay out my blue outfit in preparation for my swift escape, Euphoria sighs and starts to play some dramatic movie theme music.

"What are you playing?" I smooth the wrinkles out of my skirt and check my eye makeup in the rearview mirror.

"Main theme from *Liar, Liar*," she says, then continues filling the Volvo with the strains of what I guess she feels is the tragic soundtrack to my misguided life.

"Thanks for the support!" I say, snapping at her as I slam the car door shut. She just waves from the passenger seat window.

In my heels, I trudge up the dusty gravel path, hoping my gorgeous green dress doesn't look gray by the time I get inside. I don't have to worry, though; once I get past the vacant ticket booth, the place is transformed into something other than the dusty shell of film glories past and the home of psychotic dancing popcorn. Inside, the huge movie screen is covered with slow-spiraling swirls of varicolored light; the walkway to the dance floor and food tables, lit tastefully with warm gold and pink lights, is covered with a red carpet that looks like it might actually be velvet. Huge speakers are set up in front next to the screen, and in a temporary booth erected over the former snack shack, a team of black-clothed techies works on getting the sound balance just right on a popular dance tune.

Most of the Queen Geeks are already here, as evidenced by the gaggle of girls twirling each other on the sprawling hardwood dance floor as the music plays. Becca sees me, and waves, her face dazzling with the happiness that comes with impending total success. "Shelby!" she shrieks as she runs to me, her cotton-candy pink dress flowing behind her. She's a vision in a poofy-skirted fifties throwback, her platinum hair (still in its new, slicked-back do) tinged just slightly with the same pink shade. As she gets closer, I notice her shoes: new pink and purple tennies spangled with pink and white rhinestones, and on the side, they read *Queen Geek*.

"Isn't this fantastic?" Becca, eyes shining, surveys her queen-dom. "Melvin really came through this time. Look, there's the E-Tube people!" She gestures toward a film crew set up to the side of the dance floor. Several huge cameras are mounted and ready to capture the action, and a couple of overly beautiful anchor types wait impatiently, getting powdered every couple of minutes or so by their makeup minions.

"It's really great. Congrats." I glance at the food table, and don't see any food. "Hasn't the caterer shown up yet?"

"They called. They're on the way but running late. I was hoping maybe you could watch for them, and then help them get set up?" She grins, fluffs my hair, and says, "You look so pretty. I almost wish Fletcher and Carl were here."

I don't reply to that. "I'll go out and watch for the caterer," I say, checking my watch. "What time are they supposed to be here?"

"They said seven. It's 6:45 now. Thanks for dealing with it. Gotta go check in with E-Tube!" She dashes off, a streak of flamingo bathed in amber.

Perfect. For once, things are going my way. Waiting for the caterers is a perfect excuse for hanging outside and jetting over to the regular prom. I saunter outside as casually as possible, then burst into a sprint when I hit the gravel drive. Euphoria is still parked in the passenger seat, in sleep mode. "Wake up!" I yell as I yank open the driver's door. "We're rolling!"

"Oh. So soon?" She simulates a yawn. "I thought you'd be at least an hour. Trying to break the sound barrier, are we?"

I start the car and pull away from the curb as quietly as possible; I don't even turn on my headlights. Euphoria begrudgingly gives me directions, and it takes us about fifteen minutes to zip onto the freeway and jet toward the Hyatt. Its glittering lights beckon me from the highway, and as I cruise down the exit ramp, I realize that I have to allow time to change into my blue dress.

"Hang on, Euphoria. We're taking this one on two wheels." Squealing my poor dad's Volvo into the bayfront Hyatt parking lot brings me to Complication Number Five: parking fees. I take one of those automatic tickets and the gate goes up, but I realize I'll have to pay to get out, which could be a challenge. I think I stashed the twenties my dad gave me in my teeny girl purse, but it may not be enough judging from the outrageous parking fees posted.

I park as far to the back as possible, and awkwardly pull on the blue dress. "How do I look?" I ask Euphoria.

"Like someone who's desperate. Have fun." She shuts herself off. Rude robot.

I clip-clip on my little blue heels toward the bayfront Hyatt's marble-trimmed entrance. As I approach, I see two of the school's security people, all dressed in evening wear, guarding the door like a couple of well-dressed pit bulls. Complication Number . . . ah, I might as well stop counting.

"Ticket?" one of them asks, extending a well-manicured hand. I look for a Taser, see nothing, and smile my most dazzling, persuasive smile.

"My boyfriend has them."

They look at each other. "Where's your boyfriend?"

"Uh . . . he's meeting me here."

One of them shrugs and begins to tell me I can't go in, when a voice from inside calls, "Shelby! Shelby!" Fletcher comes dashing out the door and grabs me around the waist, twirls me around, and sets me gently back to earth.

"I assume this is your boyfriend?" one of the security guys says, chuckling. Fletcher flashes my ticket, and the guard says, "Go on in."

"I'm so happy to see you!" Fletcher squeezes my waist, then pushes me back a bit and studies me. "Yes, I think it's true. You've never been more beautiful." He kisses my hand, making me blush profusely.

"Hi, Shelby." Carl looms above Fletcher, a sad giant in a too-tight tux. "How are you? You look great." God, he sounds just like Eeyore in the Winnie the Pooh cartoons. Eeyore in formal wear.

Fletcher walks me into the ballroom, followed by Carl and a half-dozen student government kids. "Look at the decorations!" He flicks his hand through some hanging green, purple, and gold metallic streamers, then points to the centerpiece of the whole event: a Mardi Gras float in the middle of the dance floor. "Isn't that cool?"

"It sure is." I check my watch as subtly as I can. 7:20. "So, good crowd?"

Fletcher scans the room; I can tell that he's a little bit disappointed that more kids aren't here, and I feel a stab of guilt. "I think it's great. The kids who did show up really are having a good time. But it would feel more like a real school event if there were more people here, I guess." He focuses on me again, all

smiles. "It means a lot to me that you wanted to be here, Shelby."
He pulls me closer, and my heart starts to pound with that crazy
hormone adrenaline rush I get whenever I can smell him. He gently takes my right hand, puts his other arm around my waist; I
gravitate toward him like a hopeless, mindless planet flying out of
orbit and into the sun. He nuzzles my neck as we sort-of dance,
and I sort-of forget that I'm supposed to be planning my escape.

"Hey," he whispers. "Remember the time at my house where
you kind of attacked me?"

I blush violently; thankfully, he probably can't see it since his
face is buried in my hair. "Um, yes. Yes, I believe I do remember that."

He chuckles, slow and husky, just a breath of suggestion
swirling like an intoxicating perfume at my ear. I feel my legs
going wobbly, but he catches me before I trip over myself and
fly headlong into the crab dip. "I never told you, but I was secretly hoping you'd win that fight."

I gulp with great difficulty. "Oh?" I whisper, choked up.

"I mean," he says a bit more loudly and seriously, "I'm glad
nothing happened, of course, and I know it's not really the right
thing, but . . . I just wanted you to know. It wasn't just you."

My dresses, both of them, might just spontaneously combust,
and my hair might catch fire. Must find some distraction . . . if I
don't, I'll never get out of here. Food! Glorious food! It's always
good for a munch and a misdirection. "Maybe we should get
something to eat. Oh, but you guys just ate dinner, huh? I'll just
go by myself, no problem."

"I'll go with you," Fletcher offers, grabbing my elbow and

walking me toward the elegant crystal punch fountain that pours sugary goodness into a reservoir of drink, which, at this point at least, has not been spiked. "What do you want?"

"Maybe just some punch." He ladles some into a little crystal cup and hands it to me. We turn and watch the other kids dancing, swirling awkwardly to avoid the big float in the center, which features a grinning oversized head and three gigantic feathered masks. I gesture toward it and ask, "Where did you get that?"

"We made it, if you can believe that." He snatches a mini-quiche from the table and downs it in one gulp. "I've been up for three nights in a row gluing feathers on that head. I've got feather burns." He tries to pop a quiche into my mouth. He even has sexy fingers! Not fair!

What I say is, "I'm not really hungry." The truth is, I have to get out of here before I change my mind and decide to marry him right there on the spot. What can I do to escape? Ah. Every woman's best defense. "I think I'll just go powder my nose."

"Why do girls even say that? Nobody even uses powder anymore," he points out as he dips another cup of punch from the bowl.

"Maybe I will." I give him a deep, satisfying kiss that is long enough to attract the attention of a vice principal. I head off to the bathroom, aka the parking lot, despite the intense ringing in my ears and the difficulty breathing, which could land me in the emergency room with an irregular heartbeat. At least I know I *have* a heart.

Dodging out a door marked "exit," I find myself next to a

very odiferous Dumpster that is full of the remains of someone else's great party. From the smell of it, the party was over quite a few days ago. I do have the presence of mind to jam a big piece of a discarded wood pallet inside the exit door to hold it open so I can return the same way I left. I hold my breath and step over the piles of trash, setting my beautiful satin heel down squarely in a tray of grease. Needless to say, I end up on my butt, one with the trash.

Great! I try to dab at the grease and gook as I stumble into the parking lot and walk unsteadily to my car, my refuge. "I guess I could explain to Fletcher that I wanted to do a costume change, like they do in Vegas shows," I rationalize to myself.

When I get into the car, I immediately start peeling off the offensive rags. "What is that smell?" Euphoria asks, sniffing resentfully.

"You don't even have a real nose, so just shut off your sensors," I snap. "I danced a little too close to a grease trap."

I throw the blue dress indignantly into the backseat, slapping Euphoria with one corner of the greasy hem, and wipe my hands on a few restaurant napkins that Dad left in the glove compartment. I adjust the green dress, switch out the shoes, and I'm ready to go. "Money, I need money," I mutter as I dig through the purse and produce a twenty.

At the parking kiosk, I check the time again: 7:35. The trash encounter cost me precious minutes. Some old guy is ahead of me in the line, and is apparently paying for his parking ticket with pennies. Pennies from the Civil War era.

Finally, we get out (after paying the outrageous amount of ten dollars to the vampire parking attendant). Maneuvering back onto my designated route, I start to feel a bit more calm. "I'm getting the hang of this," I mutter as I screech to a halt at a stoplight right before the freeway on-ramp.

"Fuzz at three o'clock," Euphoria mumbles.

"What's fuzz?" I check my lipstick in the rearview as Euphoria emits a series of high-pitched beeps. "Cut it out, that's annoying."

"Fuzz!" she hisses. "Authorities! Police! Coppers!"

I stare straight ahead, knuckles white on the steering wheel. Think mature thoughts. Taxes. Politics. Urinary tract infections. What do old people do in cars? Uh . . . not the radio, no, never. Adjust the mirror? No, should have already done that. I feel the cold, calculating eyes of the police officer boring into me, a laserlike beam of truth trying to melt my lies. Don't look. Don't look. But I can't help it. I look.

The cop is drinking coffee and talking on a cell phone.

The light changes and I realize something: I will never have a life in crime.

14

PROM QUEEN GEEKS

(and The Boys Who Love Them)

We make it back to Geek Prom by 7:50. I park near my previous spot, check as best I can in the dark for telltale Dumpster smears, and dash for the abandoned ticket booth.

When I walk in, things are in full swing. I mean, *full* swing. The place is crawling (or hopping) with kids in various forms of formal weirdness. One guy is sporting a kilt with a green brocade vest and cummerbund, his long, red hair plaited with leather strips down his back. A girl caught in one of the amber spotlights is wearing a satin sheath that's half black and half white—divided exactly down the middle and topped off with elbow-length fishnet gloves and black leather combat boots.

Music thumps from the speakers, so loud it hits my breastbone and echoes inside my ears, against my teeth. I'd guess there are maybe four hundred kids here, maybe more. I try to mingle, act as if I've been here the whole time, and sidle over to the snack area, acting as if I'm straightening napkins and plates and such.

Amber trots up to me, but at first I don't know it's her. She's in an aquamarine cocktail dress, knee-length, and her hair's swept up into this French-looking movie-star style. Her makeup is not the usual Goth/Cleopatra stuff; it's elegant and sophisticated, and she looks like she's about twenty-one. And on her feet she's wearing, what else? Her turquoise high-tops. She's a vision. Hanging on her arm is Jon, her partner-in-Goth, tonight all done up in black leather and what looks like aluminum foil.

"Hey." She gives me a squeeze and reaches for a crab puff. "Great food. Too bad you weren't here to help set it up."

"Yeah, sorry about that. I forgot something at home, then came right back. Bad timing. Anyway, you look amazing." I can't dwell on my failures at this point. I reach for some quiche-like tart thing and swallow it in one gulp. I realize I'm actually pretty hungry since I haven't really eaten anywhere. "And Jon? Nice foil."

"I'm trying to start a trend toward recycled fashion," he says, flipping the hair out of his eyes.

"The movie's going to start in a little while. Want to get a seat?" Amber asks. I check the rows of chairs set up under the screen, and notice that they're starting to fill up. "Sure. It's going to be a great movie, huh? Has Becca's dad said anything about it?"

Elisa pops up between us. "Just that it's scary, and that we'll all probably be wetting our pants before it's over." She reaches over with both hands and grabs a few snacks in each. Naveen is with her, and she also stuffs his outstretched hands full of snacks.

"You must keep up your strength," he says. "You scare easily." She rewards him with a kiss on the nose and a crab puff in his mouth.

The music abruptly cuts off and Becca's voice booms from the speakers. "Attention! Please take your seats for the world premiere of Melvin Gallagher's epic horror film, *The Drainpeople!*"

Kids scream, hoot, holler, and scramble for the rows of seats set up so they have perfect access to the jumbo screen and speakers. It's getting a bit chilly, so I see guys putting their coats (or fur jackets, or shredded denim, or long vampire capes) on their dates, and more than a few huddle together under one coat. Becca's dad hired private security to patrol the perimeter, and I notice a few of them are also acting as the moral police, too, separating kids who seem to be getting a little too warm. I guess Melvin doesn't want any babies named after him.

The lights dim, and an image resolves on the screen: a pair of wild eyes staring out from between two old, moldy plumbing pipes. Creepy electronic music fades in, and the wild eyes move, watching us as they peer from gaps in the plumbing.

There's enough light for me to see where I'm going, plus enough of a crowd still standing behind the seating area that I can mingle and pretend like I'm watching the movie. As I slowly drift toward the exit, Naveen and Elisa grab me by either arm.

"Hey, we know you're on your own tonight, so why don't you come sit with us?" Naveen says, wrapping a tuxedo jacket over my shoulders. "And you look cold. Let's find some hot chocolate and we'll all go have a good scream together."

"In fact," Elisa adds as they walk me toward the seating area, "we were just talking about how dedicated you are, and how much you deserve a fun night out, and all you've been doing is working. I know you missed most of the first part of this thing, so come on and enjoy yourself!"

Drat. I had almost made a clean escape. How to thwart the well-meaning sympathy of friends who think I'm desperately single? What else? "Uh . . . tell me where you're sitting. I need to use the bathroom."

"Oh," Elisa says, "we already have seats. I'll go with you. Naveen, can you get the drinks?"

"Of course," he answers, bending low and kissing her hand. She twitters and throws me a self-satisfied grin.

So now I'm on the hook for the bathroom visit. What do I do? Tell her I'm secretly a guy and need to use the *other* bathroom? What else could take me away for a moment . . . something important, something solitary . . . "Oh!" I stop short. "My phone's buzzing. It's probably my dad . . . he's out of town, so I really should take this. He's probably worried about me."

Elisa cocks her head to the side, puzzled. "I don't hear anything."

"Super-silent vibration setting. Only dogs and I can hear it. 'Scuse me." I duck past her, frantically fishing for my cell phone in the little bag, hoping I look important and hurried.

When I reach the actual exit, two shaved-head security

goons stand guard. "Are you leaving, miss?" one asks in a rumbly, Mount Rushmore kind of voice.

"Uh . . . I need to go to my car for a minute. My dad is on the phone and needs . . . a car thing."

Security Guard Two studies me suspiciously. "A car thing?"

"Look, don't you have a hand stamp or something, like Disneyland? I'll be right back, I promise."

"Sorry, miss. No reentry once you've exited the event." They both stand, arms crossed, little black communication buds in their ears, the Geek Gestapo.

"Fine." I brush past them, and say, sarcastically, "Have a nice night."

My blood pressure is skyrocketing due to the run-in with Dumb and Dumber, and I rush toward the Volvo, hoping my lungs hold out. They're not made for track-and-field events, after all.

Euphoria squeaks as I yank open the car door. "You startled me! I thought you'd given up on this back-and-forth ridiculousness." She bleeps and checks her time display. "You were actually in there for nearly forty-five minutes!"

"Great," I mutter, starting the engine. According to the dashboard display, it's 8:35. Pulling away from the curb, I imagine what Fletcher must be thinking: How can any girl spend *that* much time in the bathroom?

I get back to the hotel, take another parking ticket, listen to more of Euphoria's disapproval, find a spot even farther away than last time, and dash for the hotel's Dumpster, my home away from home. Luckily, the piece of wood is still jammed in the doorway, so I slip in unnoticed.

I dodge into the bathroom, hoping that I don't look as bad as I feel. Surprisingly, my hair is holding up pretty well, but my makeup needs a touch-up, which is not surprising considering I've done the equivalent of a semester's worth of gym class in one night. I spritz on more perfume, too, to camouflage any Dumpster residue, and go on the hunt for my date.

The ballroom is now crammed full of kids, although I don't think it's as full as Geek Prom, which makes me secretly happy. Bass-thumping music bounces off the Mardi Gras masks strung around the room, and I imagine them bouncing in time to the music, doing a bodiless boogie. I check my watch: almost nine. The movie will be over at about ten, so I figure I'm safe till about 9:45, then I have to get out of here. All the more reason to find Fletcher fast.

"Can I have your attention?" The music stops, and an officious female voice booms through the hall. "It's that time, everybody. Time to announce your choice for prom king and queen!" Somewhat enthusiastic applause works its way around the group. I have a feeling most people would rather keep dancing. "Could the nominees please come forward?" I try to find the source of the voice: It's Samantha Singer, student government puppet extraordinaire, and by her side, my neighbor, Briley.

Well, at least I've found Fletcher. He and Carl trot up onto the stage like fine show dogs, and stand with three other worthy contenders for the title of Most Popular Guy. Five equally fabulous girls line the other side of the stage, and all but one are blond. Is there some conspiracy going on here?

Under the scattering of multicolored diamond lights swirling like confetti from a huge disco ball in the ceiling, the crowd takes on a magical appearance of people watching a virtual parade. I guess that makes Fletcher a Macy's parade float. "And the moment you've all been waiting for!" Briley says breathlessly. "Your prom queen and her king are . . . Delilah Merryweather and Jeff Suaros!" Applause fills the ballroom, spiced with some hoots and hollers as Delilah and Jeff are crowned and take the dance floor in a show of graceful royalty. Fletcher dashes off the stage like his pants are on fire and makes a beeline for me.

"Where've you been?" He flicks at the sleeve of my green gown. "And what's this? Where's the blue dress?"

"Oh, this old thing?" I laugh as musically as I can. "Well, I had a mishap with the blue dress. There was this cleaning lady in the bathroom, and she had a vat full of bleach, and I just happened to slip in the heels, and then—" As I speak, Fletcher turns in response to a tap on his shoulder. Samantha is standing there, perfect in a sleek white gown that shows off her gorgeous tan.

"Hi there, Fletcher. Shelby." My name is more an afterthought, like something nasty that's left in your mouth after eating a rich dessert. "Fletcher, I was wondering: Could I impose on you and your . . . date . . . for a moment? I need someone to dance with to get a picture for yearbook, and Jeff is obviously busy." She gestures demurely to where Jeff is dancing politely with Delilah beneath their ponderous rhinestone crowns.

"Uh—" He looks to me to see if I approve or if I will send a heat-seeking missile his way. I smile my most compassionate, understanding smile, and nod. Relief floods his face, and he smiles back, takes Samantha's hand, and walks her to the dance floor, all the while watching me.

When his face is enveloped in fuzzy blond Samantha hair, I bolt for the back door. If I hurry, I can still get back before the movie's over.

"What time is it?" I pant as I yank open the car door one more time.

"Well, hello, stranger. At the tone, the time will be 10:13 exactly." Euphoria emits an obnoxious bleep that hurts my ears.

"Crap! I'm late!" I rev up the Volvo engine, dig through my purse for the remaining twenty dollars, and maneuver through the parking lot toward the little kiosk. Once again I am behind someone who cannot drive; the bumper stickers on the Toyota in front of me read, "Stop and Smell the Roses" and "One Day at a Time." Judging by how long it takes the person to get the money out, I'd say they are living the life their bumper wants them to have.

We finally get on the road, and I'm desperate—not only will Fletcher be wondering where the hell I went, but so will the Queen Geeks. "Euphoria, I'm gonna speed it up. I need to get back to the drive-in." I push my foot to the pedal, and feel the Volvo accelerate like a beast released from its cage. Okay, well, it's more like an old hound dog whose leash gets a little slack, but either way, we speed up.

"Shelby, I think this is a good time to tell you—"

"Not now, Euphoria! I'm trying to concentrate!" I peer at the freeway, trying to gauge the traffic ahead to see if I need an alternate route.

"But, Shelby, I really do think—"

"Can it! Can't you see I'm doing something important?" Irritating robot. I only brought her along so I wouldn't be totally alone, but I'm thinking now that alone would have been a good thing.

"But—"

"Don't make me pull this car over!" I yell. Just then the red-and-blue lights of a police car, accompanied by the heart-stopping shriek of a siren, causes me to launch into a panic attack.

I do, in fact, pull the car over. Like I have a choice.

Arrest and jail time seem imminent. I wonder if juvenile hall gets the Sci-Fi Channel? Or any channel, other than professional wrestling? "What am I going to do?" I whimper, turning in my seat to look at Euphoria for guidance.

She's turned herself off. No lights, no sounds, just a big lump of metal in a caftan and a pillbox hat. I'm sure *that* won't look suspicious.

I hear the crunch of boots on gravel, and will myself to disappear, but I don't. A tap on the window startles me, even though I expect it. Rolling down the window, I try my best to age quickly.

"Good evening, Officer," I say sweetly. "Nice night for a drive, huh?"

"License and registration." He clearly has no sense of humor. I make a show of digging in the glove compartment, rooting through papers and such, throwing things onto the floor of the car.

"I'm so sorry," I say pathetically, "but our car was just broken into yesterday, and I think they took all the paperwork, and they took my purse, which had my license in it. I'm waiting for a replacement right now." I keep riffling through the papers, trying to avoid eye contact. "I just got my license, too, that's the shame of it. Stolen barely a month after I get it. That's not right, huh? Criminals these days. They have no respect for anything."

"Miss, could you step out—" He stops cold, his focus on the passenger seat. "Uh . . . what is that?"

"Oh, that?" I gesture to Euphoria. "That's Aunt Effie. I'm transporting her to the hospital. She's had a stroke or something. See how she's unresponsive?"

"Hello," Euphoria bleeps, causing both myself and the cop to jump. "Nice to meet you, Officer Rodriguez."

The policeman looks confused for a minute, then realizes his name is stitched on his uniform. "Right. Could you please step out—"

My teacher once told me that teenagers' brains don't fully develop until their twenties or so, and the last thing to get fully baked is the common sense part of the brain. I do something at that moment that I can only explain as the result of undercooking.

I turn on the car, peel out onto the freeway, and speed away like somebody out of an action movie. The cop is so dazed that he just stands there for a minute, his ticket pad in hand. At least, I think that's what's going on. It's hard to tell from so far away.

"Yee-hah!" Euphoria screeches. "We're takin' these pineapples to Hawaii and no one is gonna stop us!"

"What does that mean?" I swerve in and out of lanes, dodge slow vehicles, pass fast vehicles. I glance every second or so into the rearview mirror to see if I'm being pursued, but I see nothing.

I rip along the route, now familiar, and finally park the car on a dark street a block from the drive-in. I cover the rear license plate with a tree branch snapped from a pine (subtle!), and use a paper napkin soaked with water to cover the front plate. "Thanks for covering for me," I mutter to Euphoria as I dash toward the fence of the drive-in. I can't get in the regular way (no hand stamp, remember?) so I will most likely have to go over the fence.

I can tell from the thump of music that the movie is over. I find a spot around the back of the perimeter where a few boxes are stacked, and so I climb up to check out the scene. No guards here . . . I guess nobody would be stupid enough to jump over the fence of a free event.

Wow! Hundreds of kids are dancing on the wooden floor, a light show plays madly across the screen in flashes of red, magenta, blue, gold; in general, everyone is having a fantastic time. I grab the wooden fence, breaking a couple of fingernails along the way, and heave myself up and over, where I unceremoniously land on a stack of empty cardboard boxes, rip my dress to the thigh, and break a heel.

I limp toward the festivities, realizing, of course, that everyone is going to know that this has not been a normal night for me. At least no one knows my plan.

The snack table, which is pretty picked over, beckons me. The caterers seem to have abandoned it. The only things left are disposable plates and cups; a few isolated, lonely munchies; and three gallon jugs of water, one of which I instantly grab and chug.

In a corner near the snack table, two shadows tangle: one is lumpy with an oversized foot, and the other has a rat's nest beehive hairdo. Just as I'm trying to figure out who it is, somebody charges over and knocks a near-empty table on end, scattering paper plates and cheese puffs.

"This is how you repay me for my kindness? You kiss the ashtray lady?" Thea screeches as she grabs one of the shadowy figures and hauls him into the light. Melvin stands sheepishly, shrugging his shoulders. Behind him, Maggie the Honeymoon Reject lady who runs the theater dabs at her lipstick and grins.

"Honey, don't get your panties in a bunch," Maggie croaks. "It is a drive-in, after all. Groping is always on the menu."

Thea narrows her eyes and focuses on Melvin. "I trusted you."

"Oh, honey, don't take it so hard," Melvin says, shaking his head. "It's just business."

Thea grabs one of the jugs of water from the table, dumps it all over Melvin's head, and says, "And so is this." She stomps off, leaving Melvin dripping and Maggie laughing hysterically.

"How'd you like the movie?" Becca asks from behind me. I whirl around mid-chug, and she's standing there, arms folded righteously across her chest.

"Uh," I say poetically as I wipe the water from my lips.

Now Amber sidles up to me. "What did you think of the graveyard scene?"

"Well, I thought it was very effective," I say, bluffing.

"Ah-ha! There was no graveyard scene!" Elisa stabs her finger into my chest.

Evie pops up next, looking hip in tight black pants and a beaded raspberry camisole. "We're about to switch on the virtual Geek Prom cams," she says. "We're really glad you made it in time to check that part out, at least."

The music fades out; the lights on the screen dim. Six giant-sized video screens come to life all around the dance floor, and one by one, static clears and faces appear. The kids on the dance floor jump, hoot, and send up a deafening cheer that could probably have been heard around the world even without satellite equipment.

From one of the screens, a dark-haired Asian girl in combat fatigues says, "Greetings from Tokyo! We're here to dance the night away with our Geek friends in the U.S.!" Music explodes from the screen, and a mass of bodies floods the Japanese dance floor. A red-haired girl with freckles and skin the color of milk comes to the front of the next screen, and in a thick Scottish accent, says "Hello from Glasgow! We're in the Highlands and ready to party!" Kids, mostly redheads, whirl into view. On screen three, a blonde who sounds a lot like Evie waves and says, "Hi, Evie! Jillian here, from Sydney! Greetings from Down Under!" More teenagers flood that screen, too; combined with our own group, it looks like thousands are dancing in infinite perspectives. It's like seeing a series of mirrors reflecting each others' images: From our own wooden dance floor to dance floors all around the world, to wherever else in the universe people might decide to dance in cool clothes and comfortable shoes, we're all one mighty Geek nation.

The fourth screen comes to life, and is swamped with kids sporting maple leaf gear from Canada; in the next, a crowd of kids from Brazil flashes, flows, and undulates in a safari-themed dance hall.

Then the sixth screen blinks on, but there's no group dancing on it. It's just a blank screen with a little office chair and I can hear what sounds like our own Geek Prom blaring behind it. "Where's that?"

Becca puts an arm around me and grins. "Wait for it."

A figure walks into the scene, and because the rest of the video feeds are so noisy, and because our music is also playing at ear-cracking decibels, the shadowy figure in the sixth video holds up something that looks like a cue card. HEY SHELBY, it reads. NICE DRESS. The person puts down the cue card and picks up another one. DRESSES.

I get a sinking feeling in the bottom of my stomach. The person on screen six, face still bathed in shadow, holds up another card. LOOK UP. So, I do.

In the makeshift sound and light booth, I see Fletcher waving his white cue cards, flapping them in the wind like bird wings. Becca and the other girls just laugh.

"What?" I groan, leaning against the snack table. "You didn't know about this all along, did you?"

"Sure we did," Amber says. "Euphoria spilled the beans."

I feel my cheeks burning. "She told you? When?"

Elisa grins. "It was about what . . . two weeks ago? It's been really fun watching you wrestle with your conscience. Just goes to show you . . . it's never a good idea to lie to your friends."

"It wasn't exactly a lie," I stammer, but a hand covers my mouth.

"You smell like rendered bacon fat," Fletcher says. He releases my mouth, turns me, and kisses me.

When I come up for air, I say, "That's my new signature scent. Do you like it?"

In answer, he scoops me up in his arms, carries me to the dance floor, and starts to twirl around with me until I feel dizzy. "Why did you feel like you had to make up this elaborate scheme?" he yells over the wall of sound.

"I didn't want to disappoint anybody," I yell back.

He sets me down, grins at me, and points to my friends, who are all standing off to the side beaming at me. "Does anyone look disappointed?"

And then I realize something: They all love me despite the idiot I am sometimes. The Queen Geeks love me, my boyfriend loves me, my family loves me. No matter what stupid stunts I pull, no matter how bad I smell, no matter what kind of trouble I'm in with the law, they're there for me.

"Aren't you mad that I basically ditched the prom?" I ask, turning my attention to him.

"Honestly, it wasn't that much fun. It was a lot more interesting watching you do contortions trying to run between events." He laughs again, his eyes twinkling. "And when the cop pulled you over? That was priceless. Lucky for you he was just a guy from the drama department who happens to shave. Didn't you even notice that the car wasn't a police cruiser?"

"Uh . . . sure I did." Well, at least I won't be going to jail. That's a plus.

A commotion at the entrance gets everyone's attention. To my great surprise and embarrassment, it's my dad with Euphoria, still in her Aunt Effie costume, in tow. He spots us, and strides over purposefully. "Dad!" I yell. "What are you doing here?"

"I never left," he snarls, hulking through the crowd like a man on a mission. "Where is that moronic celluloid ape?" Boy, when my dad decides to curse, look out.

"You mean Melvin?" Amber asks. "He's over there, still groping Miss Failed Plastic Surgery 1968."

Dad marches over to the dark corner where Melvin is, indeed, still disgustingly leeching the theater lady's face. He taps Becca's dad on the shoulder, and he turns him around. "Are you Melvin Gallagher?"

"Huh?" Melvin asks, dazed. "Uh, do I owe you money?"

Thea has seen the drama and has come running. "Rich," she says, breathless. "How did you—"

"My flight was delayed and delayed again, so I finally got sick of waiting and just came home in a cab. Euphoria called me after this . . . this . . ." He gestures disdainfully at Melvin. "This goon started to behave like a junior high school Casanova."

"Supersonic hearing, ma'am." Euphoria tugs at Melvin's shirtsleeve and pulls him away from Maggie Crazy-Pants. "It's a blessing and a curse."

"Euphoria told me where you were, and what was going on. And although I was really angry about my daughter stealing my car and lying to me multiple times and in multiple ways, I realized that the one thing that was really bothering me was the way Melvin was treating someone I care—someone I *love*."

"Oh, Rich." Thea, snuffling behind a tissue, shakes her head in disbelief.

"Anyway, since my car was gone, I borrowed a Harley from the neighbors, and here I am."

Melvin, who is still being tethered by Euphoria, says indignantly, "Well, that's great, but could you ask your garbage disposal to unhand me, please?" He glances over at Thea guiltily. "I mean, we're all adults here, right? What's the harm?"

A vein in Dad's neck is thumping and his jaw is clenched. "The harm is that you have tarnished the honor of a lady. Euphoria?"

My robot shoves Melvin, plastered foot and all, toward Dad. "Thank you, Euphoria," Dad says, ultra polite. Then he pulls his arm back and throws a punch at Melvin that seems destined to fracture what wasn't already broken by the cow mosaic. Melvin, taken by surprise, spins once, then falls, facedown, into the drive-in gravel.

"Oh, Rich," Thea cries as she squeals and hugs my dad. "I'm so sorry. I don't know what I was thinking. Can you ever forgive me?"

He hugs her, and I feel a warm glow watching my dad. He looks, honestly, happy. And Thea looks happy, not that fake happy that she's been painting on her face the whole time Melvin has been here. Genuinely, normally, happy.

I glance at Becca to see how she's taking it. She shrugs. "Hey, as I've said before, he chose the fine art over me. I am totally okay with this." Melvin moans, and two security goons help him scrape his wounded limbs (and ego) from the stones. "Dad," Becca says as they help him out, "just send cash next time, okay?"

As things blend back into normal conversation (as in no fistfights, no crazy declarations, and no light shows), Becca steps away and leans against a table; she gazes up at the stars, then out at her creation, this Geek Prom that she willed into existence. For a moment, I feel bad that she doesn't have anyone to share it with. I lean into Fletcher a little bit closer.

A long shadow falls over Becca's profile; it's Carl. I see him face her, but this time, he's standing taller, even for him. They argue, and things look pretty nasty, like the mall incident all over again. But then he takes a step toward her, firmly tilts her chin toward him, and kisses her with the authority of a real, live boyfriend.

"You're awfully stubborn," he says.

"I am," she agrees quietly. "But isn't that why you love me?"

He shakes his head, picks her up off the ground, and, holding her like a baby in his arms, he gives her a long, lingering kiss that seems to melt all the fight out of her. When she comes up for air, she just says, "Wow. Where did that come from?"

Carl grins. "I got tired of feeling sorry for myself and decided to do what you always do—go out and get what I really want."

Becca laughs softly, throws her arms around his neck and gazes into his eyes, all the anger and resentment miraculously gone. Then *she* kisses *him*.

"Well," Fletcher says, contented, "I guess that worked out."

The whole group, Amber, Jon, Elisa, Naveen, Evie, Thea and Dad, Euphoria, and of course Becca (who is now curiously standing really close to Carl, who looks curiously happy), all come slowly toward me. Not in a scary way like in the Michael Jackson "Thriller" video, but in the nice, happy, friendly way that makes you feel good to be alive.

With the glory of geek all around us, we dance.

Check out the rest of the Queen Geek series!

The going gets tough for the Queen Geeks when one of them falls in love, breaking the first rule of the Queen Geeks—never let guys get in the way.

978-0-425-21717-7

"Give the nerd in you a chance to get up and shout!"
—*Girls' Life Magazine*

978-0-425-21164-9